A Private Prosecution

by Eileen Dewhurst

A PRIVATE PROSECUTION
PLAYING SAFE
THERE WAS A LITTLE GIRL
THE HOUSE THAT JACK BUILT
WHOEVER I AM
TRIO IN THREE FLATS
DRINK THIS
CURTAIN FALL
AFTER THE BALL
DEATH CAME SMILING

A Private Prosecution

EILEEN DEWHURST

PUBLISHED FOR THE CRIME CLUB BY
DOUBLEDAY & COMPANY, INC.
GARDEN CITY, NEW YORK
1987

All of the characters in this book
are fictitious, and any resemblance
to actual persons, living or dead,
is purely coincidental.

Library of Congress Cataloging-in-Publication Data

Dewhurst, Eileen.
A private prosecution.

I. Title.
PR6054.E95P7   1987   823'.914   86-32867
ISBN 0-385-24146-1

To John Gittins, gratefully

A Private Prosecution

CHAPTER 1

The telephone bell shrilled into Detective Chief Superintendent Kendrick's dream, played a part in it, shattered it, and continued to ring. Foggily apprehensive, he reached for the receiver with the instinctive minimal gesture he had long ago perfected.

"Kendrick."

"Sergeant Matthews of the Uniformed Branch here, sir. We've found another girl."

The fog cleared, the apprehension in a second had turned to rage.

"Where, for God's sake?"

"Near the sea, sir. Half-way up East Cliff just inside that bit of wood. Out of sight of the road, which is a help."

"Signature?"

"The body's signed."

"I'll be with you in a quarter of an hour. You've gone through the usual procedures?"

"We've radioed in, sir. Photographer and the rest of them are on their way. There's a phone-box here so I thought I'd get in touch with you direct. I knew you'd want—"

"Thank you, Sergeant. Get back now to your constable."

"Yes, sir. May I suggest you wrap up, sir? It's cold."

The curtain he ripped back revealed a still, grey world, the damp condensing in the air and gleaming on the thinning leaves, rolling in tiny droplets down the dark gloss of the rhododendrons beside his window. When he got outside he had just enough feeling spared from his anger to be surprised it wasn't actually raining. He hadn't thought it was cold as he shut his front door, but the short walk to the garage told him Matthews had given good advice.

It was barely six-thirty and there wasn't much traffic. The world looked like an old film, black and grey and white. The bright orange-red of Matthews's rain jacket was a violation of the monochrome scheme, unless it was just that it focused his senses on what they were up against —although, with this killer, blood was the least of it.

"Just in here, sir." Matthews had been sitting in the car, looking as if casually through his mirror. Not that there was anyone to observe him; there was only the grey sea with the steep gradient of the cliff road turning it into a long thin triangle, the grey sky scarcely distinguishable. Gulls were crying, sparrows were perched on the spiky stalks of dead plants surrounding the group of seats placed for summer lookout. There were two unmarked cars parked just beyond the police car Sergeant Matthews had scrambled out of.

"Constable Harris and I were patrolling, sir. We stopped and Harris went in among the trees." Sergeant Matthews coughed into his blotched red hand, as if in acknowledgement that the constable partook of one universal human weakness. With the furious reluctance which was becoming so familiar, Kendrick followed him up the slight grassy slope.

"Good morning, sir." Constable Harris was stoutly standing, in passable imitation of a police cordon, at the beginning of the trees among which Kendrick could see the photographer looking for an angle and the Scene of Crimes Officer bending over. Sergeant Matthews stopped beside the constable and Kendrick went on alone into the area which one man's activity had ensured was temporarily reserved for very senior police officers and specialists.

"Ground churned up, sir." The SOCO stood upright. "No usable prints as far as I can see, although having seen the shoes you can recognize hers. One on her foot, one off. Over here."

The sight of a female shoe lost in a struggle for survival always in some obscure way hurt Kendrick, symbolizing the helplessness of the girl or woman who had worn it. This shoe was no more than a couple of patent leather straps and a long thin heel. Penny-size indentations in the disturbed area of ground showed him the attempts of its owner to get free.

The photographer was packing up, smiling grimly at Kendrick as he swung past him. Swearing under his breath, tugging at a tuft of his curly hair in the impotence of his anger, carefully Kendrick approached the body. As with the three earlier deaths, the throat had been constricted manually, the bare breasts had been cancelled (the word had come to him the first time and he hadn't found a more appropriate one) by a superficial yet clearly defined cross centred on the breastbone, scored perhaps (they still didn't know) by the tip of a knife.

The signature. The unique mark of what was growing into a series of crimes, the one thing which so far they had managed to keep hidden from press and public. Staring down, Kendrick thought she was probably in her late teens, and had been pretty. Abundant dark hair fanned out on the muddied grass.

The doctor and Forensic's back-up were approaching. Kendrick raised his voice. "For heaven's sake get a screen round her!"

Reporters with sharp eyes and noses, tensed as he had begun to tense in anticipation of the next Monster attack (one of them had coined the title, which had taken on), could be cruising about, although it was his personal sense of outrage which he heard keenest in his voice.

There was no need for him to stay now, and he wouldn't. He heard the police surgeon pronounce that the girl had been dead for at least five hours, then made his way back to his car. The uniformed sergeant and constable were confronting a dozen or so pedestrians who were trying to peer among the trees but scarcely presenting any threat that they might leave the pavement. Restrained by fear of the unimaginable, thought Kendrick, as much as by the two representatives of the law. A comparatively large crowd, though, to be rendered suspicious by no more than one obvious police car drawn up among a few unmarked vehicles. But the inhabitants of Seaminster were growing angry and alert.

He was uncommonly tall, and under his gaze the two women nearest to him fell back, in one case onto the toes of the man close behind, setting up a chain reaction of slight disturbance. On another day, in another context, this might have struck him as funny. The faces of the sergeant and constable continued sternly grave.

"I should go home, or wherever you were going," Kendrick told the people. "There's nothing for you to see here."

"Is it that Monster again?" He hated the excitement in the eyes of the man who had spoken, unmixed with pity.

"If anything has happened which deserves your attention, you'll hear of it."

"I saw you on television," said a woman at the back, blond hair exploding from under a brown plush hat like a mushroom. "He's the top one," she offered, tapping the woman in front of her on the shoulder.

"What are you doing about it?" asked the youngest man in the group.

"All we can," retorted Kendrick. "You can help us now by being on your way."

There were a few seconds in which he thought the authority of his presence wasn't going to be enough, but they drifted off. He could hear hooters and saw that the damp was manifesting into a fret. No buildings just here to break it up, no houses to be systematically visited for the recurrent series of questions. "Did you by any chance see . . . hear . . ." Nothing but strings of mist among the trees, across the faint horizon, twining and unravelling . . . He must get back to his temporary Seaminster office and relocate the nucleus of the organism which was his police force shifting this way and that about the town, stretching, contracting, concentrating, feeling its way in the dark. . . .

"Carry on, Sergeant. Most people will stop when they see the cars. They're getting jittery. Look as casual as you can but move them on, at least until the body's gone." And the signature. "I'm going to the office."

"Yes, sir. That was the day shift on their way to the hotels. There'll likely be more of them."

Intelligent observation, good for Sergeant Matthews. And after the next bunch of day-shift workers, there would be passers-by. This was the most public place the Monster had chosen; it would be hard to keep the thing quiet until they were ready to release their censored bulletins. As if in illustration of his thoughts, another police car drew in.

With a brief acknowledgement of its occupants, Kendrick got into his own car and drove off. He tried to imagine himself accelerating away from unwelcome reflections, but they went with him. Four murders of young women in five weeks within the confines of one seaside town, and perhaps one murder nearer, now, to the moment when his chief constable might feel obliged to call in the Met. As head of Divisional CID and a resident of Seaminster he'd been very much the man for the job, but he couldn't go on assuming his suitability if the murders piled up and he continued unable to come up with anything whatsoever. . . . He didn't want breakfast, the thought of the hot smelly canteen turned his stomach, but he would send for coffee. The local station was doing its best to make him feel at home. . . . The first three victims had been local girls, born and bred in Seaminster. One still at school, two in their first jobs. The fourth? If things went on, one day he might know the distorted face above which he would be trying not to weep. The holiday season was over, but before the day was out he would have heard from a few more anxious hoteliers. Which was absolutely the least of it . . .

He should have Forensic's preliminary report within the hour. With the girl's identity, if they were lucky—the other times there'd been a handbag about, unrifled. And then the journey to a certain house or bungalow or flat. "If I might just come inside for a moment . . ." He could fairly depute the chief inspector but he wouldn't, again he would go himself.

It was so terrible it almost made him glad he and Miriam were no longer together. Their separation meant she and Jenny were safely away from the town where the three of them had been so happy. When he thought of Jenny in relation to what was happening in Seaminster his anger swelled until it threatened to affect his driving and he had to switch his thoughts to let it subside. Perhaps it was harder because there was no one to talk to about it apart from his colleagues, no one on whom to rant and rave some of his outrage away.

Except, of course, Humphrey. On whom he would call that evening. A small cool oasis at the end of the desert day ahead.

At eight-thirty they broke into the local radio programme with a short announcement, and Humphrey Barnes heard it. It was hardly possible for his pale pessimistic face to assume a more lugubrious expression, but he shook his head and sighed deeply, getting up from the round Regency table which bore the remains of his breakfast and walking slowly across to the window, where he stood watching the sea through the diamond-shaped leaded lights. Seven years ago, when his house had been advertised for sale, it had been described by an estate agent as "bijou" and Humphrey had approached it with deep reserve. But his first glance at its exterior had been enough to reassure him that it lay well the acceptable side of kitsch, was in fact a minor miracle awaiting him in its snug spot between two yellow-brick Edwardian mansions, bearing no relation to them or to any other property in the row which faced the sea just beyond the fashionable summit of the East Cliff. It hadn't, of course, helped him to get over Emily's death, but it had been the best sort of fresh start. . . .

"If you want to know the time, friends, it's coming up to eight thirty-nine."

And the postman was coming past the window, pausing at his door, meeting Mrs. McNicholl coming the other way to judge from the two voices—one male and calm, the other female and impassioned.

Humphrey's high brow wrinkled slightly at the thought that Mrs. McNicholl might have heard by some other means the news which had just been broadcast, and be eagerly set to impart it to him. On the other hand, he had not yet known his domestic treasure to hold forth on any subject, however trivial, at less than full emotional intensity, so the tone in which she was addressing the postman might not be of significance.

Reassurance came as she opened his front door onto the tail of her discourse. ". . . So I said to him I'll thank you sir to keep your opinions to yourself these for Mr. Barnes are they I'll take them in shall I good morning. Good morning, Mr. Barnes." The pause was all the more dramatic after the unbroken mounting excitement. "Here's your *post!*"

"Good morning, Mrs. McNicholl. Thank you. So you're here to set me to rights again."

He had a feeling he had used this form of words as greeting to Mrs. McNicholl not once but many times, but unfortunately the feeling never came over him until after he had uttered them. It would have been helpful, as well as rather pleasant, if Mrs. McNicholl had been the sort of woman to notice his pedantic repetition and joke him out of it. But one couldn't have everything.

"Set to rights, did you say, Mr. Barnes? I'm blessed if you'll ever need any setting to rights." He'd heard this before, too. "I never did work for a more tidy gentleman. I stake my soul on it!"

Mrs. McNicholl was bustling through to the back of the house, depositing her coat on the hall rack as she went by. (Fortunately she could move and talk at the same time.) She was an amiable woman, and he didn't think it was anything in her tone of voice which made him suddenly feel that it was perhaps inappropriate, in so disorderly and casual a world, that his own life should be so well and—now he thought of it—so formally organized. Not that he had ever tried to make it that way, and he had been entranced when Emily had entered it with her erratic brilliance, keeping him waiting all over Seaminster, disrupting his routine. Then, when he had married her, hopelessly undomestic, forgetting to leave her studio in time to get dinner ready, running out of things like bread and butter, apologizing enchantingly even though he had never shown her the least anger. Then driving in her little car to her death, with him beside her getting no more than a smashed-up leg . . .

He must still veer away from this piece of memory, remind himself instead of the extraordinary and wonderful fact that Emily, in the midst of so many young adorers, had chosen to marry *him*. In a way, now, firmly relinked to the self he had been before he met her, he almost felt she was something he had dreamed. . . .

Eight-fifty and time to be setting out for the office. Back at the window he decided it was a day to go by car rather than walk. And anyway he had two appointments outside town. The one with the publisher in Midchester might well result in an important specialised order. . . . Hadn't Mrs. McNicholl mentioned the post? Yes, here on the table.

Humphrey carried the letters into his sitting-room at the back of the house, in order to pick up the paperknife from his desk so that he could slit the envelopes neatly. To stick in his thumb and tear them open would, he reluctantly recognized, be one small act of rebellion against his consistent orderliness, but he couldn't bring himself to do it. One of the very few things which had stirred a slight irritation with Emily had been the way she devastated envelopes.

Bank statement, much as he had expected it. A letter from Emily's brother's wife confirming his annual visit to them in Edinburgh—perhaps this time he'd get round to asking them if he could perhaps change it from November to a more kindly time of year. Except, of course (this thought always came to qualify his feeling that he'd rather visit them in summer), that his garden would be better left in November than, say, June, apart from the pile-up of leaves he always came back to. . . .

A note from his sister in Cornwall, hoping he was going down there for Christmas. She must have forgotten it was his year for staying in Seaminster and eating a late Christmas lunch with their brother and family. . . . No, she hadn't forgotten, she was inviting Derek and Marjorie and the children, too, suggesting they make a week of it. The mere idea made him feel tired, and anyway he did rather think he or Derek ought to be on hand so far as the business was concerned. He didn't think he minded the prospect of Christmas on his own.

An invitation from George and Fabia Douglas to their Silver Wedding party. Humphrey frowned again. If only he hadn't met Fabia just when he had, in Fine Foods while she was making final arrangements for the catering at the party supper. There had been no need for her to feel guilty because he hadn't been invited, it was George's brother Frederick and family who were his friends and George and Fabia really not much more than acquaintances following business contacts. But Fabia had there and then insisted he come, she couldn't for the life of her think why they hadn't asked him in the first place, and she would send him an invitation that very day. "So there, Humphrey!"

And so here was the invitation. *George and Fabia Douglas. At Home. Buffet. Dancing. Fancy Dress.* He wondered if they had had to buy another card, or had had one left over. He wouldn't go, of course, although he hadn't made a thing of it in the shop. He'd plead another engagement which he'd overlooked at the time, and when he eventually saw Fabia again she would have forgotten all about it and be on to something else.

To George and Fabia, a son. To Frederick and Marie, a son and a daughter . . . Eleanor would be at the party, of course, as George and Fabia's niece. But if he went simply because it always vaguely pleased him to see Eleanor, that would be absurd; so far as Eleanor was concerned his middle-aged presence would signify merely one more family friend to have to be polite to. It was ridiculous for him to have begun to feel, since he had lately taken to accepting Frederick and Marie's standing invitation to call in on his way home for a drink, that he and Eleanor were becoming friends in their own right.

The schoolboy sons were of an age and Humphrey had sometimes idly imagined there having been a switch at birth. George and Fabia's son Jonathan—Fabia had referred to "poor Jonathan" in Fine Foods, to Humphrey's annoyance—bookish, awkward, given to flashes of clever talk, seemed out of place amid the extroversion of his immediate family, more in tune with Frederick and Marie's self-deprecating reserve. But David, of course, Eleanor's handsome and well-adjusted brother, would fit both halves of the Douglases with equal ease. David and Jonathan. Well, the boys were friends as well as cousins. Attraction of opposites, that would have to be.

He looked again at the invitation. A party was bad enough, with its attendant inevitable embarrassments, but a *fancy-dress* party!

After parking his car in the small private park attached to his office building, Humphrey crossed the road to the pillar-box opposite to post his acceptance.

"I really think, Eleanor," said Fabia Douglas, stretching her legs out to the simulated blaze, "that you should take the car if you so much as go out of the gate once it's dark. This is a terrible business." She sighed and shuddered. Then brightened. "Fine Foods can manage all the party exotics, you'll be pleased to hear."

"That's splendid, Auntie. And I'm twenty-five, by the way. Those poor girls were all in their teens. Today's as well, according to the radio."

"That's coincidence," said Fabia decidedly. "Fifteen, twenty-five, thirty-five for that matter—these days girls all look the same."

"I will be careful, of course, Auntie. Have we all decided on our costumes?"

"I don't know about the boys. Uncle George is going as the saint. I drew the line at playing the dragon, and it wouldn't do for Jonathan either, so George has asked that small boy who was so good as the cat in last year's school pantomime. He's probably grown bigger than any of us by now, but George has promised him a professional costume whatever his size, and of course an evening full of eating if the dragon head will allow it."

"If you're not to be the dragon then, Auntie . . . ?"

"The Queen of Hearts in *Alice.* After Tenniel. I'm using one of those old tinted Victorian Alice card-game cards as a model. Red-dyed and white cotton stretched over cardboard. It's almost finished."

"You are clever, Auntie." Eleanor strolled over to the window. "The mist's cleared. Probably because there's a wind getting up, the treetops are agitating." Her brother and cousin came in sight on the curve of the drive, appearing to be of a height because of David carrying himself so well and Jonathan stooping. David was a bit ahead, throwing back a remark, laughing, moving lightly and with grace. Jonathan lumbered as well as stooping, looking like a boffin or an absent-minded professor before he had even left school. If he was intelligent enough to have got himself into Mensa he ought to have the sense to make the best of his physical self; he wasn't devastating like David but he wasn't bad-looking. If she hadn't known him so well, she would have accounted it arrogance.

"Hi, Auntie!" David was into the room and across it, flinging a kiss at Fabia's cheek.

"Hello, Eleanor." Jonathan was a few steps inside, standing still and smiling at his cousin in pleased surprise.

"Our current exhibition is my partner's inspiration, so I left her to it and came to see if brother David was with you. We haven't had any clients to speak of, anyway. Perhaps today's local news."

"Dreadful, isn't it?" said David.

Fabia put her hand on his where it lay on the arm of her chair. "What are you going to wear for the party, David?"

"A surprise," said David gravely. "I'm not going to tell anyone until I burst upon you all. Except Jon, of course. I'll need his help."

"That's nice," said Fabia, after a pause during which her face registered the impression that she wasn't sure what it was. "Nice to have one surprise. Jonathan hasn't decided yet, have you, darling? Darling! Jonathan!"

Jonathan, they suddenly noticed, had sat down on the chair nearest the door and was reading a book he had apparently taken from the case open at his feet.

"Sorry, Ma." He looked up, blinking.

"For goodness' sake, Jonathan," said Fabia sharply. "Can't you keep your nose out of a book for five minutes?"

"We have to go," said Eleanor miserably.

"All the more reason why Jonathan should remain of the party," retorted Fabia, unappeased. Jonathan had let the book fall back into the case and got to his feet. "You look awful, even paler than usual and those bags under your eyes. It isn't natural, to be reading all the time."

"He was out last night, Auntie," murmured David, grinning at Jonathan.

"Yes, at evening class. Work again! As if he hasn't enough to do at school at the moment."

"He's got a rather extraordinary brain," contributed Eleanor, who believed in the total good nature of her cousin and hated to see him chastised.

"I am here," protested Jonathan mildly, "so there's no need to talk about me as if I wasn't. I've got a headache. I didn't sleep last night."

"All the more reason to keep the books closed for a bit," said Fabia.

"Oh, I know he's got an extraordinary brain. I'm proud of it. What are you going to wear for the party, darling?"

"He's going as a pirate chief," said David, gurgling with laughter. "You know, he'll look jolly good."

"Ye-e-es. Yes!" Fabia, appraising her son, decided to be delighted as well as surprised.

"I thought, Why not?" said Jonathan.

"Why not?" said Eleanor. "But you'll have to hold yourself straight if you want to do justice to the costume. Not like a backroom boy." She thought she saw a flicker of unhappiness across Jonathan's face, and immediately and sharply regretted having added her quota to what she suspected was a fairly steady stream of parental exhortation to social improvement. "No, I think you'll look really debonair. That scarf thing they have round their heads is always frightfully becoming." She moved away from the window. "We really must go, Auntie. I've got our next exhibition to work on at home, and I've got to feed David—Mummy and Daddy are going out."

"I'm starving," said David, taking her hand and making a gesture of pulling her towards the door.

"I've sent Humphrey Barnes an invitation, by the way," said Fabia, an indulgent smile on her handsome face. "I met him while I was in Fine Foods the day before yesterday, and I told him he must come."

"He said he would?" asked Eleanor.

"Of course he will! He's lonely, I'm sure. It must be six or seven years now since he lost his wife, and one never hears his name associated with anyone. Man or woman if it comes to that."

"He's a solitary, I think," said Eleanor, seeing David wink at Jonathan as she tucked his hand under her arm. "He's nice enough. I like him."

As she opened the front door she was pleased to hear Aunt Fabia's voice addressing Jonathan as if he were one of her committee colleagues rather than an unsatisfactory son.

CHAPTER 2

They left the disco in a foursome, three of them giggling together like the old friends they were, the fourth silent, watchful, his fitful smile ambiguous but his hold firm on Doreen's arm. As the shops turned to houses and the houses and street lights spaced out, Doreen's laughter grew nervously shrill, and by the time they reached the corner where her friends' way home diverged from her own she was as silent as the stranger close at her side.

"You all right, then, Doreen?" Len kicked at a pebble, looking down as he spoke, aware of Barbara tugging at his arm.

"Of course she's all right," said the boy holding on to her, the first time he'd spoken since they'd come outside.

"Of course I'm all right." Doreen spoke more stoutly than she felt, but he seemed decent enough, clean and nothing extreme and buying her a Coke without her having to say she was thirsty. She thought he'd shouted that his name was Kevin, but she wasn't sure about that. He'd asked her if he could see her home. She was only bothered because it seemed so strange to be standing on that corner with Len and Barbara but without Ray. If Ray had been beside her instead of this Kevin or whatever his name was, she would be pulling at his arm the way Barbara was pulling at Len's, wanting to get away on her own with him, and they would have hung around only as long as it took to say good night and agree the next meeting. And she supposed she was bothered a bit, too, because of all the awful things which were happening in Seaminster. Things you couldn't forget because of the posters everywhere. *An urgent message to women. Do not walk alone after dark.*

Well, she wouldn't be alone, would she, when Len and Barbara had disappeared round the corner. She would be with Kevin or whatever his name was as far as Mrs. Crale's front door, and if she had any trouble shutting it on him she only had to call for Mrs. Crale. Then up in Mrs. Crale's first-floor back she would feel really safe again, behind her own front door with its Yale lock. It was only because of their trust in Mrs. Crale and the obvious security of her house that Mum and Dad had let her leave home and go and live on her own in the middle of Seaminster when she landed her job in the Rates Office. . . . There'd been nothing in Kevin's behaviour to make her think she'd have any trouble with him when they were on their own. All he'd done was to ask her for a dance and then buy her that Coke and then stay around for a couple more dances and just sitting while the sound beat through them, then say he'd like to see her home. Quite flattering, really. It wouldn't do Ray any harm to hear that the first time she'd gone to a disco without him she'd had a partner all evening and then an escort home. At the same time, of course, she had no sort of idea of making any more of it than that. She would say good night as they reached Mrs. Crale's door. Nothing to do with her reaction to him—she hadn't really had one, favourable or otherwise, because of being Ray's girl—she just didn't want to give him any impression she might be available. She didn't believe in two-timing, and neither did Ray (not so far as she was concerned, at any rate, and she had to believe he had the same standards for himself). Even so, it had been hard to feel as pleased as she had made herself out to be when he'd got promotion and started to work now and then away from home. Thank goodness he'd be back tomorrow night. If Kevin or whatever his name was wasn't prepared to leave her at the street door she'd say something about Ray. Anyway, there was no point in hurting Kevin's feelings. . . .

"Right you are, then." Len had found another pebble, annoying her because she knew his downward glance meant he was ashamed of himself for giving in to the pressure of Barbara's hand on his arm, for not insisting they all walk to Mrs. Crale's door. Ray wasn't like that. He did a thing with conviction or he left it alone.

"Good night, then," said Doreen decisively. "I'll ring you, Barbara."

"Yeah, OK. When's Ray—I mean, you're busy tomorrow, aren't you?"

"Yes, I'm busy tomorrow." Barbara was annoying her, too, behaving as if Doreen could possibly want to hide the central fact of her life from a stranger. Well, she knew Barbara wasn't above a bit of fun when Len wasn't around. "Cheerio!"

She and Kevin or whatever his name was started to move off first, and as the other sets of footsteps died away he squeezed her arm more tightly against his side. Even without the extra pressure she found the contact, now they were alone, disagreeably significant, and tried to free herself.

Unsuccessfully.

"You live alone?" asked Kevin.

"No!" She heard the exclamation mark in her voice, and was annoyed yet again by her overreaction. "I live in digs," she added more calmly. Dad had told her never to admit to a stranger that she had a flat, and in view of the posters, at least, she thought this made sense. She tried to make herself relax, taking a deep breath of the mild air and looking up at the stars which had appeared since the early-evening rain.

"You can have visitors, though?" The pressure at her side was unrelenting, and she was trying not to realize that they had slowed their pace.

"Not at night."

It wasn't true that Mrs. Crale had laid down any rules, although Ray had never stayed all night. If he ever asked if he could stay she would probably let him, but so far they had always acted as if Mrs. Crale was expecting to hear him leave. . . . She felt her body reacting to the thought of Ray staying all night and her resentment grew at the heavy hand on her arm. Also a sense of what she reluctantly recognized as fear. Again, and more forcefully, she tried to free herself.

"Don't start playing hard to get with me, baby!"

It was so rapid, she was hardly aware of the transition from the sodium-lit pavement to the near-blackness of the entry, the painful constriction of her back against the damp bumpy wall. Each morning she stepped light-heartedly into this dark hole, but then it was splashed with light and thronged with people she had come to know. There were no people now, only Kevin with his breath on her face, his body ramming her harder and harder against the wall.

"Come on, sweetheart, don't be shy. If you can't have visitors this isn't such a bad place. Just you relax."

She had enough feeling left over from her shock and her fear to realise and be amazed that he seemed to believe he was proposing a treat for two, that if she just let herself go she might actually enjoy being pressed up against a wall in a public entry like the lowest, commonest . . . The Monster killed women by strangling them. Kevin's hands were at her breast, fumbling her coat, her blouse, travelling downwards. . . . Anger took over from the fear.

"Get away from me! I'll see myself home!" What she was saying was idiotic, but the gush of anger gave her strength and she lunged forward, throwing him off balance. He fell heavily against the other wall, dropping to his knees.

"Are you all right?"

Even more idiotically she was standing waiting while he dragged himself to his feet. But she was sure now that she had nothing to fear from him.

He glared, wiping his hand across his mouth, and she saw blood beading from the gritty graze across the back of it. The knees of his pale trousers were filthy and one was torn.

"Bitch!" he pronounced, unfairly, and turned and ran limping the way they had come.

Doreen stood shaking, automatically fastening buttons and making sure her bag was still on her shoulder, then herself turned out of the entry and started walking quickly the rest of her way home.

She heard her sudden hysterical laugh without having known it was coming, but she wasn't amused. She was angry with herself for not insisting Len and Barbara stay with her—they'd have stayed if she'd really asked them—or ringing for a taxi. She'd been asking for trouble and she'd been lucky to get off so lightly. The absurd thing was that she hadn't even wanted Kevin or whatever his name was to walk home with her. Or only her vanity had. She wouldn't tell Ray; he'd only call her a fool and perhaps begin to think she was one. She'd ring Barbara from work first thing in the morning and ask her and Len not to say anything to Ray either.

She was more than half-way home and there was only the bit of wood before the houses came on both sides of the road and more lamps. The wood was lovely in the mornings with the sun on it, and lovely tonight, too, where the one lamp shone among the branches, not a twig moving in the quiet air.

She heard her voice again, a long a-a-h of shock as a woman stepped out from behind a tree right in front of her, a tall woman in a long heavy coat, wearing a deep-brimmed hat. A funny old-fashioned figure, like the nanny she'd seen in a film the other night on television.

One hand seized her arm. "There's been an accident," said the woman, "just in there." She had a curious, strangulated kind of voice, to which Doreen had to listen hard to realize what she was saying. The dark brim of the hat cast a shadow over the upper part of her face, and a heavy scarf muffled her mouth and chin.

"There's a phone-box round the corner," said Doreen. "If you'd like me to run and—"

"A tree's fallen across my friend's leg." It was as if the woman hadn't heard Doreen's suggestion. "She's trapped. Two of us I think could get it off. Will you help me?"

Doreen was going to say yes, of course she'd try, had started to say it, but the woman had already turned the pressure of her hand into a viselike grip which was pulling her in among the trees. Almost at once she stumbled, and with an exclamation of impatience the woman bent and scooped her to her feet, making Doreen aware of a strength which reopened the way to the fear from which she had so recently been delivered. Panting, trying to articulate words, she was dragged along, desperately rationalizing—the woman knew that her friend needed urgent help, a few minutes might mean the difference between life and death. . . .

The difference between life and death.

Doreen didn't want to go with the woman, she had definitely decided against it, but against her will she was still running, she was fighting vainly to root her feet to the uneven ground, free herself from the powerful hand.

As abruptly as she had begun to move, the woman stopped, bringing up the other hand to cut off the screams which, now she was no longer running, were gushing loudly out of Doreen's mouth.

"It's all right," said the woman. They had reached a gap among the trees, and by the light of stars Doreen could see between the hat and the muffler a pale strip set with two faint gleams. "We're here."

"Where's your friend?" asked Doreen, the hand having been removed and a shaft of optimism lighting her terror. The last thing the woman would want would be for her friend to be further scared by the screams of an hysterical girl.

"It's all right," repeated the woman. Doreen was aware, behind the jerking muffler, of heavier and heavier breathing, beginning to carry a rasping note which sounded almost loud in the stillness around them.

The hands had made another gesture, and she was sitting on the ground, leaning against a tree with the woman kneeling in front of her, the hands at her waist but travelling up and fastening, meeting, round her throat. Doreen's eyeballs rolled up and she saw the stars above the clearing, the cold lights which her now-silent prayers were unable to reach. She would die, when she had never so much wanted to live, she would die against the awful, the growing, the world-excluding sound of that heavy, rasping breath. She knew the secret of the Monster but she would never be able to tell. . . . The end was beginning, already the stars were fading, her own breath was a gasp, her hands and legs were ceasing to thresh, she was going, losing. . . .

The sound of the breathing had been growing faint, slipping away from her as her senses ceased to work, her sight, her touch, her hearing, but now she was aware of it again, wheezing, rasping. And of the stars, sharply shining. She knew she was moving her legs, painfully working her throat. . . .

The hands were no longer at her throat. She tried to lift herself away from the tree, but one of the hands, or perhaps it was part of the enormous body, was still holding her down. She was aware of movement below her chin, of sudden cool air on her chest. The breathing, now, was more like a snuffling. She felt a wet drop between her breasts, cold, so cold it hurt her and she tried to call out. She made no sound but the effort seared her throat, her breasts, wrenched agonizingly at a nipple, the breathing seemed to be part of the pain, she wasn't sure whose breath it was, but on a choking snort it abruptly ceased, and there was a heavy thudding sound beside her which shook the ground.

She didn't know how long she waited for the next sensation, the next stab of pain, how long it was before she realized there was no more pressure, no new pain, that it was over. Even then, aeons went by before she was able to lean away from the tree and support herself while she drew her blouse and coat round her, over the strange, smarting breasts she was almost afraid of as she gingerly buttoned them out of sight. Then, as carefully, she tested her legs. One was restricted, but as she leaned effortfully forward she saw by the starlight that the woman's heavy body had fallen across it. It took more time again to draw on the courage to risk disturbing the blessedly inert mass, but when eventually she tried to slide her foot free it came easily enough and the mass subsided without changing shape. The small circle of darkness nearby was the hat, and as she dragged herself to her feet Doreen's one inadvertent glance showed her what could have been a grey head on its side and large dark shoes jutting from the spreading edge of the long coat. There was still no sound or movement, and she would leave it that way, she would start to run while she could towards the almost unimaginable safety of Mrs. Crale's house. The woman on the ground would either recover and get up and go or she would not. . . .

Doreen was standing up now, leaning against the tree again, evidently having picked up her bag unless it had never left her shoulder, getting the strength together to move away at a run. Her eyes flickered unintendedly down again. The mass hadn't moved, but wasn't the nearer shoe narrowing its distance from her own foot?

On a soundless shriek Doreen plunged away from the clearing, silently sobbing her way between the trees, driven by the energy of her fear. Much later she realized she could have run blind among the trees all night, but whether by luck or instinct she blundered in minutes onto the road.

If there had been anyone in sight she would have run up to them, trying to sob out her story. But the road was deserted all the way to the corner round which was Mrs. Crale's door, and by the time she reached it she was recovered enough to have realized that if she told anyone but Ray she would undoubtedly be returned to her parents' house. The prospect of losing her flat and her Yale key was not to be contemplated. And there was no special merit in reporting what had happened, because nothing had happened in the end (except, she knew, to her breast, and when she had reluctantly assessed that, she could keep it to herself and Ray). There was a chance, of course, that the woman might be in a state to respond to treatment, but even Doreen's tender conscience was proof against any sense of obligation to see that this chance was taken. No, she would keep her mouth shut, and recover in the peace and safety of her own home. Ring up the office and report a sore throat, no doubts that it would be genuine.

She shouldn't be courting more horrors by lingering on another corner, even one so well lit. But there was a chance Mrs. Crale might hear her key in the street door and come out to greet her, even though she kept early nights and would be in bed. So if she wanted to keep her secret she must at least pull her physical self together. Forcing her thoughts back to the small realities of her everyday life, Doreen realized she didn't want Mrs. Crale putting a dishevelled appearance down to questionable behaviour in the absence of Ray; she had Mrs. Crale's affectionate trust and she wanted to keep it. Hastily she smoothed her hair and buttoned the collar up round her throat, which was painful outside as well. As she turned the corner she brushed her coat to dislodge any evidence of her violent contact with the woodland floor. Fortunately the material was smooth and nothing seemed to have stuck. She took a long time over the little iron gate, which sometimes creaked, and longer than she intended opening the street door, her hand trembled so. But inside all was silent, the dim night bulb illumined the inside of the lock as in her hand it slid soundlessly back, then the short flight of stairs as she delicately climbed them, her own bright new cooperative brass lock.

When her front door was closed behind her Doreen ran into her bedroom and tore off her coat. Then found herself tearing off blouse, bra, skirt, slip, shoes, tights, briefs. The knock and Mrs. Crale's voice came just as she was free.

"You all right, ducky? You're a bit late. Don't worry, you didn't wake me, I've a touch of indigestion."

It was a glass door but she went close up to it because of not being sure about her voice. "I'm fine, Mrs. Crale." The voice came out as a stage whisper. "Except I've got a bit of a sore throat. I'm not opening the door because I've just undressed."

As Mrs. Crale would be able in a shadowy way to see. She could see the outline of Mrs. Crale's small plump body swathed in its heavy dressing-gown.

"That's all right, ducky. Have a gargle, now."

"Yes, Mrs. Crale. Thank you. Good night."

"I can hear your throat. Good night, Doreen."

Her hand at her aching neck but her arm held self-consciously clear of her breast, Doreen tiptoed slowly into her tiny bathroom, staring for a moment at her silhouette in the long mirror before reluctantly raising her other hand to jerk the cord of the light.

In the sudden brilliance she went on staring, taking in her still untidy hair and unfamiliarly mottled face before slowly letting her hand fall from her throat.

Her throat was mottled, too, with bruises, which seemed to brighten as she watched them. After a few seconds her eyes moved downwards and stayed riveted. Across her breasts, waveringly but unmistakably, here faint, there suddenly thick with blood, bisecting one nipple and bypassing the other, a cross had been cut into her flesh.

CHAPTER 3

"You haven't just put on fancy dress," said the pretty girl admiringly. "You've taken a time machine from the age where you really live."

"How extremely kind of you to say so," murmured Humphrey, feeling anything but complimented by confirmation of what his bedroom mirror had suggested. Hang it, he didn't want to be an anachronism, nor did he feel like one.

"Those splendid side-whiskers. How long did it take to grow them? It's crazy, but I just never sort of imagined they would grow at that angle out of modern men's faces."

"But you've just told me I'm not a modern man." Humphrey gazed, he hoped not too wistfully, into the pointed face under the bright yellow buttercup hat, realizing how much he wished he and Emily had had a daughter.

"Oh . . ." She giggled, enjoyably embarrassed. "And I didn't grow them, I'm afraid, I stuck them on. I'm glad they look so authentic."

"Absolutely . . . Oh hello, darling. I'm sorry . . . Excuse me."

"Of course."

The buttercup, claimed by a spaceman already looking perspiringly regretful of having chosen so substantial a costume, wafted away, leaving Humphrey standing in the pleasant gloom at the edge of the tented dance floor to continue his ocular search for Eleanor. At least the music and dancing were of his own era—he had been afraid George and Fabia might feel this to be too old-fashioned so far as the younger people were concerned.

He might not, of course, recognize Eleanor. He had not immediately recognized her father, browned up and beturbaned as a pantomime Ali Baba, or her mother, the fine straight hair he always thought of as childlike transformed into the elaborate height of a Gainsborough lady. She leaned up to kiss his cheek.

"You knew me at once," he commented gloomily.

"Of course, Humphrey, Victorian whiskers don't obscure the features. How well they suit you! I know they're not real because I caught sight of you in Beaumont Street yesterday without them, but they so well could be."

"I didn't see you in Beaumont Street, Marie, so I can believe your new hairstyle to be home grown. Magnificent it is, too."

"Humphrey! Of course it isn't home grown. I didn't even make it. I hired it as it is." In fulfilment possibly, it struck him, of a lifetime's longing to have a good head of hair. It would be interesting to study all the guests in relation to their choice of costume and see how much wish-fulfilment there was about. Subconscious, a lot of it would be. There were quite a few new things he didn't much like, but he'd never thought he would prefer to have lived in the nineteenth century. . . .

". . . isn't it, Humphrey?"

Frederick was addressing him. The music was crescendoing to a temporary stop and he nodded and smiled, hoping this would prove adequate response. Nodding in turn, apparently satisfied, Frederick turned away to survey the infinite sweep of floor which was what optical illusion made of the George Douglases' back lawn. A bank of flowers, cinerarias predominating, marked the platform on which pianist, saxophone, and drums were taking a bow.

"Isn't it nice?" Marie squeezed his arm. He noticed she had covered her mole with a black spot.

"I'd been afraid it would be a discotheque." Another pedantic thing about him, he resignedly reflected, was the way he found it impossible to use the shortened forms of words—even words for which he had no respect.

"It will be, eventually. To suit Jonathan's friends, if not Jonathan. I suspect Fabia was thinking about David. Luckily for us it won't be until pretty late on."

Yes, he was of Marie's generation rather than her daughter's. . . . It would be comparatively easy for him to find Eleanor if he asked her mother what she was wearing. More fun, though, to run her to earth without clues. "You really do look handsome, Marie."

"Thank you, Humphrey. I was fifty last week and can do with that kind of comment." At least Eleanor's mother had five years on him. "You look handsome, too. Aren't you going to dance?"

"If you'll dance with me."

"I thought you'd never ask. Frederick, I'm dancing with Humphrey."

They were half-way round the floor before he remembered, with a stab of excitement, that he had been a good dancer. Extraordinary to have forgotten. But the inordinate pleasure with which he'd learned from Fabia that it was to be ballroom dancing had probably been a subconscious remembering. He'd also forgotten what an agreeable sensation dancing was. Marie was as lithe and light as her appearance promised, but he'd found in the past that the only women he didn't turn into good dancers were the exceptionally heavy and the rhythm-free. Emily had been the best dancer he had ever encountered. Forgetting, he supposed, had been an act of self-defence.

"Lovely, Humphrey, lovely. I want to say 'More, more!' like a little girl. The slow foxtrot is so tricky; did you notice how few of the young ones have the subtleties? Never mind, let's be glad they want to do it at all. I did so enjoy that!"

"So did I, Marie." As they joined the temporary exodus from the floor he suppressed his impulse to tell her it was his first dance as a widower, and that he was glad she had been his partner. They stood together in companionable silence while his eyes resumed their search for Eleanor.

"Hello, gorgeous."

The strikingly pretty girl who was lolling in front of him was looking over his shoulder, and he turned to see who had claimed her languorous attention.

There was no one there, there was no possibility of anyone being there, he was standing almost against the canvas. The girl was addressing him.

Humphrey's instinct, after an absurd flash of imagining himself with permanent whiskers, was to apologize to Marie that her partner should be the kind of man to attract such an approach. But to his surprise Marie was laughing in an approving sort of way, telling him he was a lucky man and moving off on the arm of Lawrence of Arabia.

"Hello," said the girl again.

"Hello," responded Humphrey warily. While having to acknowledge her obvious charms, he knew she was not the type to have attracted him even when he was very young; she had too full a mouth, rosily rounded a cheek, untidy a cloud of hair, bold a look.

"I'll be devastated," said the girl in a low, seductive voice, "if you don't dance with me." There was something dancing already in her eyes which made Humphrey hope she might be teasing him. He would prefer teasing to the straightforward vamp of her first approach.

"Let's dance, by all means."

"Thank you," she breathed.

On the dance floor, to his intense embarrassment, the girl immediately pressed her cheek against his. She was tall for a woman, just below his five feet eleven, and it was all too easy for her. "Nice," she murmured. It was naturally at this moment that Jane Austen's Emma (or Elizabeth Bennet, or Anne Elliot), dancing close by, was whirled by her partner to face him and reveal herself as Eleanor. The agreeable impact of the ringleted frame to her face and the delicate white gown gathered under the breast was dissipated by the shame of his own position. He had a second surprise when she smiled as gaily as her mother had done. Well, it was no doubt amusing to see him so ludicrously out of character.

He wasn't even having the incidental pleasure of enjoying the dancing. His partner was unexpectedly heavy and awkward, unamenable to his firm yet unobtrusive attempt to lead. His leg twinged as he forced her round, reminding him, with a stab now of shock, that this was the first time he had danced since it had been broken. He wished fiercely that it would really hurt him, but it was a relief when his partner murmured into his ear that she would like to sit down.

"Certainly." Humphrey took the first opportunity to steer them to a table well away from the dance floor. "Would you like a drink?"

"I'd love one, gorgeous. Do you think you could find me a glass of white wine?"

"Certainly," repeated Humphrey, more miserably.

"Don't be long," pleaded the pouting lips, but he took his time at the bar, returning with two glasses of white wine and the half hope that his companion would have realised she was wasting her time and transferred her attentions.

To his amazement Eleanor had joined her at the table. The two women were leaning forward whispering together, but as he appeared they both drew back.

"Hello, Humphrey," said Eleanor.

"Hello, Eleanor. May I get you a drink?" He looked from one smiling face to the other. "I see you know . . . I'm sorry." His eyes stayed reluctantly on the face of the younger woman. "I'm afraid I don't know your name."

"For a man dancing with a girl whose name he doesn't know," observed Eleanor, "you were doing rather well, Humphrey. No, I won't have a drink at the moment, thanks."

His embarrassment now was being diluted by another sensation, less superficial. Disappointment? He had scarcely expected Eleanor to speak as she had just spoken.

"You appear to know her," he responded stiffly. "Perhaps you will make good my solecism."

"Oh, you are so marvellously stuffy, Humphrey." Eleanor reached for his arm in an impulsive gesture rather like her mother's. "This is Davina."

"Thank you, Eleanor." He gave a stiff little bow. He knew he was sulking, and the whiskers were the wrong shape to hide the woodenness of his face. But he couldn't help it. He would hardly have thought the girl to be Eleanor's type, either. And surely she must be several years younger. But perhaps there were ties of blood. Eleanor would have to make the best of unacceptable behaviour in a member of her family. To have made him, Humphrey, appear to be the one whose behaviour left something to be desired could be accounted an act of loyalty.

Able at last to stretch his mouth in the direction of a smile, he asked Eleanor if Davina was her cousin.

As both girls burst out laughing, the situation began to feel surreal. "I'm glad it's all so amusing," he said, and knew Eleanor read a danger signal in his eyes. She stopped laughing abruptly, wiping hers with a wisp of handkerchief.

"Oh, Humphrey, I can't keep it up any more." She turned to the younger woman, whose eyes were still fixed provocatively on Humphrey's face. "I'm sorry, David, I shouldn't have joined you, I should have given you a longer run for your money."

"That's all right, I've lots and lots of potential victims. Sorry, Mr. Barnes."

It was a strange process, to have the face under his eyes change through no agency of its own, merely because he was looking at it in a different way. David Douglas's features appeared one by one behind the make-up. Then, in David's contribution to the metamorphosis, his characteristic grin.

"I hope you'll forgive us, Humphrey," said Eleanor.

"As long as there really are lots and lots of other victims." He was still put out, but by his own humourless overreaction to their joke. "Not that you'll be able to find a more satisfactory one than I've been." He didn't think he really was without humour. But tonight, from the start, he had somehow been on the defensive.

"Oh, Humphrey, you are generous. I'll snatch the photograph down the moment they pin it up."

"The photograph . . . *Eleanor!*" He had been aware, ever since he had entered the marquee, of flash bulbs indiscriminately popping. So frequently and simultaneously that after the first few minutes he had ceased to wonder what they were recording.

"I'm sorry, Humphrey. I'll give it straight to you, I promise."

At last he wrenched himself free of his discomfiture. "I'd like a record of this evening, certainly, but not especially that one. Would you consider dancing with me? And David will want to get on." He turned to the boy. "You're tremendous, David, and you must be having an awful lot of fun."

"Oh, I am. Thanks for being such a sport."

This was undue praise, but he welcomed it as indication that his stuffiness would not be the brother and sister's prime memory of their charade. He and Eleanor walked the few steps necessary to reach the dance floor and turned into the conventional embrace. His pleasure at the discovery that she was a good dancer was only slightly marred by his puritan disappointment that his leg was no longer hurting him.

"Where did you learn?"

"I had to learn for a school play. It came easily, and I suppose it's like riding and skating. You don't really forget."

"You haven't. You went away to school, didn't you?"

He had a vague memory, which as he spoke came into sharper focus, of his wife and a shy schoolgirl getting out of the train together when he was meeting Emily once from London.

"Yes. Funny for the daughter to go away and the son not. But St. Saviour's is such a marvellous school for boys. My father and my uncle were there too."

"St. Saviour's has been a good school for a hundred years."

"Did you go there, Humphrey?"

"No. I was sent away." He remembered the arguments on the subject between his father and his mother, his silent anguish that his mother wouldn't prevail. "The three of us were. Father thought it would be good for us. I'd much rather have stayed at home and gone to St. Saviour's."

Eleanor was leaning back, studying his face. "Yes, I don't suppose you're exactly the sort to have got on well at boarding-school. I can tell, though, you went away at some stage. It's pretty obvious you haven't spent all your life in Seaminster."

The oblique compliment eliminated at a stroke his lingering self-displeasure. "I went to Oxford, and then to London to be articled to an accountant. I came back here eventually to join the family firm. As its accountant, but I find I've become something of a printer as well. I like Seaminster, actually." Not just because of its associations with the two women he had loved, his mother and his wife. He really liked the place.

"I do, too, I suppose. I certainly like being my own boss—well, half of it. Do you think this costume was a good idea?"

The straightforward inquiry in her face might have accompanied a query as to what time it was. He said, as expressionlessly, "I do, it suits you admirably."

"I'm glad you think so, Humphrey. Let's manoeuvre into range of a camera."

Although bulbs were still popping freely, the dance was ending as Eleanor was at last able to stretch out a hand and secure a photographer. When the picture had been taken she asked Humphrey to excuse her.

"There are so many people I feel I've got to make a bit of a fuss of for Uncle and Auntie's sake. I'd like to get them over as early as possible so that I can please myself later." Stopping suddenly and reddening, she stamped her foot. "Oh, Humphrey, I am a fool, *please* don't think I was putting you in that category. If I was, I wouldn't have said it. Please ask me to dance again later on."

"Don't upset yourself, Eleanor. I'm far too conceited to see myself in any category." Nevertheless, what she had said, however genuine her attempt to make amends, had negated her earlier compliment. He found himself almost eager for her to leave him. "Off you go now and attend to your duties. I ought to look for Fabia." A dancer skirting the floor caught him a stinging blow on the ankle of his good leg.

"See you later, then," said Eleanor, smiling at him in her readiness, he thought, to accept his response at face value.

He must have managed to keep the pain out of his face. As she turned away he limped over to an empty table near the canvas and sat down to rub his ankle and watch her disappear across the marquee. He leaned away from the table and put out a hand. "Sit down a moment and have a drink with me."

It wasn't Fabia, it was her son Jonathan, who would do very well for the time being, resplendent in a pirate's costume which ill accorded with his—to Humphrey's sympathetic eye—obvious attempts to make himself unobtrusive. Jonathan frowned and stiffened, then smiled in relief as he turned and saw Humphrey.

"Go and fetch yourself something," urged Humphrey, touched by the boy's reaction. "Plus a glass of white wine for me. Then come and sit down."

"I will, yes!"

Jonathan was back very quickly, with the wine and some orange juice. "I'm glad you're here. We can sit and talk or not, as we feel, and you won't keep on telling me to go and dance."

"I won't, no, but I think it's rather a shame you don't want to. Don't you like girls?"

"I don't dislike them. It's just . . ." Jonathan shrugged.

"It's just that you'd rather be sitting in front of your computer?"

"I suppose so. Or reading. I can't dance, anyway. Not this way. And the other's noisy and a waste of time."

"Don't you ever feel like taking time off from work?" asked Humphrey curiously.

"Sometimes I do, of course. And I quite like just looking at people. Watching what they choose to do, and wondering why. *People,*" emphasized Jonathan, turning his head quickly away from the dance floor as his mother swept past in the arms of Charlie Chaplin. "Not girls, or boys, or young, or old, particularly. People. If I could just watch without being watched, I'd be fine."

"No you wouldn't," said Humphrey. He, too, had once thought in that way. "Not in the long run. But you'll find that out for yourself. I agree you shouldn't be nudged into it. Well, you can't be."

"You tell Mother," commented Jonathan gloomily. "I don't know why she and Dad had to go in for something like this anyway." He swept an arm round the marquee, narrowly missing Humphrey's glass. "Uncle Frederick and Auntie Marie had their Silver Wedding last year, and Uncle Frederick took Auntie Marie away for the weekend. You'd think Mum and Dad would have enjoyed that better than this. I bet it would have been cheaper, too."

"I expect they were thinking of you."

"Oh yes. But they should know by now not to. Not in this sort of way."

"Did your mother suggest the pirate outfit?"

The boy reddened. "No, actually . . . I— A friend offered to lend it to me, and I couldn't be bothered to think anything up for myself, so I took it."

"You should have done what David's done. You'd have had some fun then; you couldn't have helped it. He gave me a terrible time."

Humphrey winked at David as David winked at him, gliding by cheek to cheek with the Prince Regent.

"He's awfully good, isn't he," said Jonathan. "I wonder how it is that men make such good women, but never the other way round?"

"I don't know, I'd have to think about it, but you're quite right. Have you and David decided what you're going to do with yourselves eventually?"

"I'm going to Cambridge if I can get in. To read medicine. I'd like to read law as well, but you can't do both."

"Not at the same time, no. What about David?"

"David's bright," said Jonathan, "but I don't think he's all that ambitious. He always says he wants to do something which will give him lots of free time to play rugger and golf and tennis and whatever. But I expect he'll train as an accountant; he's specially good at maths."

"Having met Davina, I thought he might be interested in the stage."

"He says you only get free time then when you can't get work."

Jonathan looked at his watch. "I think supper's due. In the dining-room. It's a jolly good spread. Shall we get in early?"

"Men don't go in to supper together." The seductive drawl came from behind Humphrey, then the hand on his shoulder, kneading it. "Besides, there's the supper dance first. Jonathan?"

"Can't you find someone more interesting?" asked Jonathan, but half rising.

"You know you'll be put out if we don't manage to dance." Davina made a Marilyn Monroe–like moue with her lips. "So you'd better come now. I can't promise anything later on."

"Oh, all right. See you later, Mr. Barnes."

It was entertaining in two entirely different ways to watch the cousins dancing. Above, all was languorous *legato,* Jonathan entering into the charade, his expression as engrossed as David's, his large hand spread over David's blue chiffon back. Below was a series of *staccato* failures in co-ordination between the pirate boots and the dainty high-heeled sandals. Jonathan, Humphrey suspected, was one of the unrhythmic ones. David he couldn't fairly judge, having seen and experienced his dancing only in the wrong role. The photographer caught them as the music ceased and they staggered to a stop.

"Supper, Humphrey? Do you think you might like to see if Mrs. Talbot would care to go through? She's looking a bit lonely, isn't she?"

"Yes, Fabia."

Edna Talbot was a widow, attractive and sophisticated and probably about forty. Her husband had left her a great deal of money, and her active life about Seaminster was all honorary. It was virtually impossible to bump into her without being asked to sit on one of her committees. Humphrey, to his recurrent chagrin, was slightly afraid of her. Nevertheless, obeying his hostess, he could tell he was succeeding in diverting Mrs. Talbot through the length of her supper, and beyond into the renewed dancing. He supposed it must be his dress and whiskers. So reluctant did she seem to turn her attention elsewhere, in the end he delivered her into the arms of St. George on the honest pretext that his hostess appeared to be free and he must secure a dance with her. Relieved, he watched St. George dancing off into the crowd with a firm hold on the medieval lady in the high pointed hat (Humphrey had told her absent-mindedly that she should be leaning out of a magic casement), accompanied where practicable by a lithe and gleaming green dragon.

"Hello, Humphrey," said Fabia, out of the dazzlingly accurate animation of Tenniel's Queen of Hearts. "Are you enjoying yourself?"

"Very much, thank you, Fabia. Even more so if you will dance with me."

"Of course, flatterer."

To his slight surprise she was a good dancer, light and confident-footed.

"I'm glad it's this sort of dancing."

"So am I, really. We're switching about midnight to the disco, to suit the young people. Although heaven knows they get more than enough consideration these days."

"It certainly seems to be the age of youth." Humphrey was speaking automatically, craning round the large red frame surmounting Fabia's head to notice Eleanor still in the arms of the Roman emperor with whom she had had supper, and was surprised to realise he had given voice to an aphorism.

"It certainly does!" Fabia might not have appreciated the form of what he had said, but she had seized on its content. It was quite restful just to relax and half listen for the remainder of the dance, while she held forth on the thoughtlessness and selfishness of the majority of young people. They danced so well together he was almost sorry when the band stopped playing, although to his gloomy satisfaction his bad leg by now was really springeing.

". . . it was David, really, who talked me into the disco," Fabia was saying, her normally severe features softer than their wont. "Thank you very much, Humphrey, you dance beautifully." Another dutiful guest was bowing beside them. "Oh thank you, yes, that would be nice. . . ."

Alone again, Humphrey stood watching the dancers. David, to his amusement, went by in the arms of a young man who was obviously getting interested in Davina. Eleanor was still with the Roman emperor and being held, he fancied, a little closer. St. George, the dragon respectfully hovering, was talking to Ali Baba near the entrance to the marquee, and even as he grew wary he was conscious that the widow Talbot was standing alone and surveying the room as he was, a few tables distant. Without looking directly at her, he knew her eyes had swivelled to take him in and that she was smiling and starting to move towards him. Not hurrying, but steadily, Humphrey turned and left the marquee and went on walking until he was inside the downstairs cloakroom, which had become for the night the prerogative of gentlemen. An elderly gentleman was at that moment donning his coat.

"You're off?" asked Humphrey enviously.

"Don't see why not. That noisy business will be starting soon. It's half past eleven and one's done one's duty."

"I suppose so," said Humphrey, brightening. He picked up his own coat and accompanied the elderly gentleman back to the hall, where he cast a cursory glance round in search of any Douglases. There were none in sight. Nor, as yet, Mrs. Talbot. Holding the front door open for his senior, Humphrey followed him out of the house.

CHAPTER 4

This time the call came from the station and when Kendrick was already awake, up and breakfasting. It hadn't been Matthews and Harris who had made the discovery, but half of another sergeant and constable patrol obeying nature (as the desk sergeant put it).

It was always a long moment in which he took in these succeeding revelations. Long enough, this time, for him to see his happy-faced kitchen clock pointing to just before eight, and to reflect that the weather at least was different from the last time—bright and windy, the tossing trees sharply outlined against a hard blue sky.

". . . wouldn't say just what it was, sir, but I gather there's something different."

So not just the weather. The sudden access of outrage brought with it a sense of shame that it had been delayed, that he had begun by taking the desk sergeant's call almost for granted. As a theoretical optimist he reproved himself. But he was a realist in practice.

"Give me the geography, Sergeant, and I'll go straight there."

"It's that old garden in Birch Road, sir, where they've been going to build a bungalow for so long. The stone wall's all but pulled down in one place and anyway there's no gate. Couples go in—"

"I know it, Sergeant, thank you. I'll come on to the office afterwards."

Birch Road. Not so far, again, from Humphrey, whose little house probably formed a right angle between the two latest murder sites. The road he took to reach the East Cliff when he was visiting Humphrey from home. He'd been aware for some time of the wall crumbling far too steadily for it to be a natural process, and he'd been going to depute someone who had some comparatively spare time to look into it. Those old blocks of sandstone would transform a new rockery at a stroke; he'd thought it each time he'd driven by. No merit in letting his conscience rampage because he hadn't got round to having the gaps plugged. If it hadn't been there it would have been somewhere else.

He was as angry now as he had ever been, with an extra queasy sense of apprehension. *Something different.* Please God different didn't mean even worse.

It was worse already that it should be such a brilliant morning, and he was absurdly glad to feel the cut of the wind through his body as he strode out for his car. His anger, now, was beginning to spread and to take in himself and his staff, that they were letting this dreadful thing go on happening, failing in their prime duty to protect the young and the innocent. But where there was no one left to tell a tale, describe a size, a shape, a voice, a way of walking—what was there beyond vigilance, questioning, exhortation? He drove past one of his posters as he turned into Birch Road, urging anyone who might be able to help to come forward, warning the young women of Seaminster to take care. His anger was spreading even to the victims, that they hadn't heeded him. *Do not walk alone after dark.* The message was clear enough.

The police car was beside the gap in the wall fronting the road. He recognized the photographer's car beyond it, the Scene of Crimes Officer's. The local detective chief inspector and a sergeant were drawing up, the doctor on their tail. In the back of the CID car were a couple more uniformed men to protect the site (of special scientific interest, thought Kendrick bleakly). He plunged out of his car as a uniformed constable opened the door.

"Glad to see you, sir."

Kendrick hadn't encountered the constable before, but he'd come to recognize the expression and manner common to all who welcomed his arrival on this particular scene, and saw that the man was registering something extra. Shock, he would have said, if it hadn't sounded crazy. And the sort of shock where people say "I'm shocked." Usually women, and older ones at that.

"Something different?" he asked sharply.

Colour flooded the anxious pale face. "Yes, sir. That is—we think so. We haven't touched—anything."

He deputed the uniforms to fill the empty gateposts, then set off across bumpy terrain which still showed, if by no more than an ungrassed cindery line, the ample ground plan of the Victorian house which had stood there before what were now saplings of silver birch had seeded themselves within its boundaries.

When he reached the group of men near the intact side wall in among the overgrown vestiges of a shrubbery, he found that the photographer had done his work and the screen was being assembled. He was aware of an extra reaction here, too, and the queasiness twisted his guts. He joined the Scene of Crimes Officer and the doctor beyond the screen, and looked down.

The body was dappled by bright sky and evergreen shadows, but he noticed at once the straggling uncertainty of the signature. A cross, clearly, but not on the confident lines cut into the earlier victims. Above it a choker (inwardly he groaned) of fat blue beads was still round the throat, pressed here and there into the flesh. The face was heavily made up, the hair . . . Dear God, was scalping the new, the different, ingredient? For a unique moment he thought he would have to turn his back and vomit as the SOCO bent towards that partially detached hair, but as the man straightened up with the dark mass in his hands, the head on the ground still had a normal hairline, fair and high. At the same time Kendrick's eyes were returning to the wavering cross and the breast—a breast so immature even the nipples scarcely extended. A *child,* he thundered in his head, then bent closer.

The Monster, even as he was signing his latest victim, must have half known, the truth of things must have trembled from his subconscious to his hand, weakening and distorting his purpose.

"Sweet Jesus," said the SOCO, turning large-eyed to Kendrick. "It's a boy."

At least he wasn't entirely unexpected on this latest doorstep. At half past nine Mrs. Marie Douglas telephoned to report the nightlong absence of her son, and how he had looked when she and her family had last seen him.

"He could have been a girl, Superintendent." The voice was soft and calm, but he thought she was having difficulty with her breathing. "The way he moved and spoke as well, he's had years of experience in school plays at St. Saviour's. He's probably still playing his part somewhere but we're beginning to worry. . . ."

Kendrick called for copies of the murder photos, the addresses of David Douglas's form master and the St. Saviour's master responsible for drama, and sent his Sergeant Grant round to see them. The sergeant dumbly nodding in his doorway was no more than confirmation of the fear set up in him by Mrs. Douglas's call.

It was the father who wrenched open the front door, taking in the presence of WPC Thomson before asking them both to come inside. His wife was in the hall, a small pretty woman like her voice on the telephone. Kendrick put his hand on her shoulder and pressed it in silence while WPC Thomson slipped unobtrusively to stand behind her.

The long silent pressure took things a stage farther, but only to the point where he must speak.

"It grieves me to tell you that your son is dead."

This was the fifth time he had said those words, though now one of them was different. Long before the Monster first struck he had learned that it was best to deliver such information straight. WPC Thomson caught Mrs. Douglas as she swayed, her husband added his support, and she stumbled between them into a room off the hall. Kendrick was following when a slight sound above him made him turn back.

Standing on the stairs which descended wide, straight, and shallow to the hall was a tall, frail-looking young woman with a pale thin face, gazing through him like a sleepwalker. She had untidy dark hair, making him relive the worst moment of the morning.

"I heard you," she said, not moving, and Kendrick sprang the steps necessary to reach her and repeat his pressure on a woman's shoulder.

"Miss Douglas?"

"I'm Eleanor Douglas, yes. I heard—what you said."

Her voice gave him the impression it was hurting her to speak. There was a tic at work beside one of her pained steady eyes.

"Come downstairs, and I'll talk to you and your mother and father together."

She said, on a flutter of breath, "There's no doubt?"

"No doubt, I'm afraid. I'm so very sorry. Come now."

He put his hand on her shoulder again as she descended past him, and kept it there on the sedate walk down the rest of the flight, across the hall, and into the bright room, but she walked independent of it.

The mother was sitting on the edge of a chair, a glass in her hand. In the doorway the daughter broke into a run, taking Kendrick by surprise, throwing herself into her father's arms. When she, too, was sitting down he told them what he must, then expressed his alarm at the father's sudden pallor.

"I'm all right." Douglas had given brandy to the two women but taken none for himself. Kendrick motioned the WPC to pour a third measure.

"It was a fancy-dress party. . . ." The man sounded as though he had had a stroke, and with its fine features the face would look delicate at the best of times, but Kendrick could now see there was blood in the veins.

"We know. We know why your son was—dressed up."

Marie Douglas murmured, "It was a very effective disguise." *Oh yes.* It was too soon for her to realise the whole of what she was saying. He could only just hear her and went to stand by her chair. "You're certain it's David. . . ."

"I'm afraid so. A master from St. Saviour's—"

"A-a-ah." The acquiescent sigh made him swallow savagely.

"He took his own clothes," said the daughter, scarcely more audible. "He promised to change into them if he came home alone."

"What time did you leave the party, sir?"

"About half past midnight." The man was rigid in his chair.

"You spoke to your son before you left?"

"Yes," said Frederick Douglas. He coughed, as if trying to clear an impediment.

"I didn't," whispered the mother.

"He said he might come home with Eleanor," continued the father expressionlessly, "but that he might not. We were to—expect him when we saw him. It was obvious he was having a good time, and I didn't make any comment." His face went down into his hands.

"And you, Miss Douglas?" asked Kendrick.

"I saw David several times, always enjoying himself." The daughter closed her eyes, then shot them open to gaze up at Kendrick. "I wasn't in the marquee the whole time. I was in the drawing-room talking at some point—it's all run together rather. . . . About two o'clock I decided to accept a lift home. I started to look for David then—I hadn't seen him for a while—but I couldn't find him. My aunt and uncle, Jonathan my cousin—they hadn't seen him for a while either, and we realized he must have gone. I was surprised, because of how he'd been enjoying himself so much taking people in." Her eyes closed again. "His own clothes were still in the cloakroom, where he'd left them when he arrived—the cloakroom was for men only last night. David wanted to use the ladies' upstairs and we wouldn't let him. Then he insisted on Daddy escorting him to the men's. Well, he couldn't have gone in on his own, looking how he did. . . ."

The groan wrenched from her as she slumped across the chair arm had WPC Thomson scurrying across the room and crouching down. The mother continued to sit very neatly on the edge of her chair, the father to stare down at his twining hands.

"Were you surprised he'd left without telling you?"

"Not really. David's always been very independent, and very sensible. You didn't worry about David. Oh, Mummy . . ."

Kendrick waited while Eleanor Douglas stumbled across the room to embrace her passive mother.

"You worried, though, when you saw that his own clothes were still in the cloakroom at your uncle's house?"

"I think—even then—I felt more surprised than worried." She was back in her seat, motionless and calm. "David usually had a reason for doing things. I assumed he'd gone off with someone or some people." Her eyes swooped up to Kendrick's. "You'll realise—he took his own clothes because of—these murders. In case he—went home alone."

"I realise that, yes. It was very sensible. You went home without your brother, then."

"Eventually, yes. And of course I went straight to his bedroom, but he wasn't there and his bed hadn't been disturbed. My parents sleep with their bedroom door open and I crept in and could tell they were both asleep. No point, I thought . . ." She wrung her pale hands, making Kendrick think of a pre-Raphaelite maiden.

"So you went to bed yourself?"

"Yes. Not that I slept much. I was sort of listening even while I was dozing. I got up a few times to have a look in David's room, although I was pretty sure I'd hear him when he came in. I kept reminding myself about all the friends he has, and even that he might have gone back to Auntie's, but by the early morning I was worried. I rang Aunt Fabia about half past seven. She hadn't seen David, nor had Uncle, nor Jonathan. I waited a bit then and made some tea, then rang the friends David used to see most of. No one knew anything. Then I made some more tea and took it up to Mummy and Daddy. That must have been about half past eight. I remember I was trying to tell myself I was angry with David for being so thoughtless and letting us worry. I went in to Mummy and Daddy in that sort of mood, or trying to be. . . ." She shuddered, holding her body in her arms. "It kept us all going for a while, and then Mummy rang the police."

"Thank you," said Kendrick. "That's very helpful." He put his hand on her shoulder again. Somehow he felt more inadequate with this stricken family than with any of the others. "Is there anything else any of you feel you'd like to tell me?"

"There's perhaps one thing." The mother had been too controlled for Kendrick's liking, and he was pleased to see that tears had begun to pour down her face. "Just before we left we noticed David dancing with a boy who really seemed to think he was dancing with an attractive girl. Not that you'll be interested in that, with it being the Monster . . ." Her tears hardly affected her voice.

"We're interested in everything," said Kendrick. He turned to the daughter. "Did you see this, Miss Douglas?"

"Yes." He thought she was reluctant. "David did dance for most of the later part of the evening with a boy who obviously hadn't seen through his spoof. When the disco took over it was dark and dazzle of course and one couldn't really see. But I did notice them on and off. As Mummy said, though, it can't be of any importance—"

"D'you know the boy's name?"

"I'm afraid I don't." She paused. "Jonathan will know. Aunt Fabia asked him and David for the names of twenty or so of their schoolfriends. To make the party more fun for them . . ."

"Thank you," said Kendrick. "We'll probably need to talk to you later—I'll hope to talk to you myself—but this is enough for now, unless there's anything you want to ask me."

"I don't want to know anything," said Eleanor Douglas. "Except that I'd like to be able to think he didn't suffer."

"I'm certain it would have been over very quickly. There was no sexual interference."

"Perhaps in the circumstances that's not surprising." The girl's soft voice was suddenly harsh.

"There never has been," said Kendrick gently. "But I take your point." He started to move towards the door. "I regret more than I can say having to bring you news like this." He paused. "And having to ask if one of you will identify David's body. A formality," he added quickly. "We know . . . I'll take you myself, now." He had been going to say that he would send someone, but their brave faces silently begged him for the best he could do for them.

"I'll come, of course," said the father.

"Thank you, sir."

"What happens now?"

He had to look from one woman to the other before he was sure the whispered words had come from the daughter.

"The post-mortem," he said, reflecting that this had recently become his least favourite phrase. "A routine in cases of—violent death. Then the inquest will open—probably on Tuesday—and will be adjourned for police inquiries. At the inquest the coroner will release—David—and the funeral can take place any time afterwards. The inquest will resume within a week or two, I should say, because of it being clear how and by whose hand David died."

The mother moaned softly, and he suggested leaving WPC Thomson behind, at least while Frederick Douglas was at the mortuary. But Mrs. Douglas said it wasn't necessary, in fact that she would prefer to be on her own.

"Fabia could be glad of her," she said, very quiet and calm still and, thought Kendrick, even smaller and slighter than on his arrival. "She's —she was—very fond of David."

"She can come with me, madam."

The father managed nobly, but Kendrick had the car stopped on the way back, so that Frederick Douglas could weep. He waited patiently, glad to see it. He felt so wretched when he was eventually driven away it was scarcely a relief.

And there were still the George Douglases. As the imposing house came in sight round the curve of its drive he thought with longing of Humphrey's tranquil sitting-room, the particular soft chime of the clock in his hall. Then he remembered that Humphrey was a friend of the Douglases. So the visit he would inevitably pay that evening would mean at best an attempt to console, at worst another revelation. In either event, a withholding of the whole truth . . .

The car drew up at the front door, Kendrick reproving himself for his selfishness. It would be best for Humphrey, at least, if the revelation came from him. Which would be more likely if he went at lunch-time.

On the step was a large man with a large round face in sharp contrasts of red and white—no fraternal resemblance. So someone had telephoned. The daughter Eleanor, he thought.

"Is this true?" asked George Douglas sternly, as Kendrick and the WPC got out of the car. "I could hardly hear what Eleanor said."

"It is true, yes. I'm very sorry. I'm Detective Chief Superintendent Kendrick, and this is WPC Thomson." In the hall he asked, "None of you saw David leave last night?"

"No. We all remember we didn't because Eleanor was looking for him about two o'clock, when she was thinking of going home, and couldn't find him."

"He left his own clothes, I believe."

"In here." George Douglas opened a door where they were standing. The cloakroom was large, matching the house and its owner. It contained an outer room with hanging space, a shelf and a mirror, an inner room with lavatory and wash basin. The hanging space was cluttered with the usual family array of drab and practical outer garments, among which the white pierrot hat with its black fur trimming and blood-red pompon stood out bizarrely.

"Someone forgot part of his costume," said George Douglas absently. "Here, Superintendent."

Neat on one hook were a pair of jeans, a check shirt, and an anorak. On the floor directly beneath, a pair of running shoes with socks folded inside.

"David was unusually tidy for a boy."

This voice held the ominous forced animation which Kendrick had known to precede hysteria. Swinging round, he saw in the doorway a tall handsome woman, her elegance enhanced by a pile-up of red hair which in most other women would have looked old-fashioned. He thought it was probably uncharacteristic that a couple of strands had escaped their coiffure and were trailing down. The make-up was so total, and so good, it was impossible to see the fluctuations of natural colouring.

"Mrs. Douglas. I'm Detective Chief Superintendent Kendrick, and this is WPC—"

"It's not true, Inspector. It couldn't be."

She hadn't been hearing him. WPC Thomson murmured the word "Superintendent."

"I'm afraid it is. I'm so very sorry. Your niece telephoned? She told you?"

"Eleanor said some very dreadful things. She didn't sound well and I thought perhaps . . . Inspector? Oh please . . ."

"All right now. Come and sit down."

Again WPC Thomson assisted a husband to half carry a wife across a hall. Kendrick experienced a *frisson* as he noticed the boy on this other, more elaborate, staircase.

"Tell me it isn't true," said the boy, completing his descent and twitching his shoulder to free it of Kendrick's hand. His face was very pale and his large pale blue eyes looked through Kendrick, who remembered something Humphrey had once said. *David and Jonathan, friends as well as cousins.*

"Jonathan?" he inquired.

The boy nodded. Kendrick saw him as an unusual mixture of the gauche and the mature. "It is true," he said. "I'm very sorry."

"I told him to change," said Jonathan, "before he left for home. If only he had."

"If only he had," echoed Kendrick. "You saw him, then, before he left?"

"Not before he left, no. I said that when he arrived, when he was hanging his things up. I was sort of joking, but of course I meant it. Everyone said the same thing to him, he was so good. That's why he brought his own clothes."

"If you didn't see him before he left, Jonathan, you won't know if he left alone?" If David had left with someone who hadn't been let into the joke . . . Kendrick was briefly dizzy, wondering if it was possible that the Monster had been one of the George Douglases' guests. "I don't know." Kendrick noticed that the boy's steady eyes scarcely blinked, and was reminded of the Frederick Douglases' daughter. "But he must have done, mustn't he? Otherwise . . ." George Douglas was looking impatient in his drawing-room doorway, and Kendrick started to walk towards him. The boy went on talking as he followed. "I suppose it was about half past twelve when we happened to meet and both decided we were hungry again and went into the kitchen and mopped a few things up. David said he was coming up for air and I think he'd given Bunny the slip. That was the last time I spoke to him. He was dancing pretty well all evening and I hardly danced at all. I hardly went back into the marquee after supper, and then I just sat and watched. I saw David a few times, but I can't remember if I saw him again after we'd been into the kitchen. . . ."

Jonathan Douglas sat down suddenly and pushed his head between his knees.

"So neither of you saw David leaving?" Kendrick repeated, turning from the son without comment as WPC Thomson ran across to him.

"No, Inspector." Fabia Douglas attempted to tuck one of the loose strands of hair into the elaborate arrangement of the rest of it, but it was refused admittance and drifted back down her cheek. "Eleanor was looking for him, and between us we carried out quite a thorough search. Sometimes these young people, you know, get into the most unlikely places. . . ." He thought her shudder was involuntary. "He'd obviously left."

"You were worried?"

"Not exactly worried, but we weren't very happy to see his own clothes still in the cloakroom—that was what made us go on looking for him, we couldn't believe he'd be so silly as to go off as he was. In the end we decided he must have had a lift home or gone with some other people, and just forgotten about the clothes. He'd certainly want to put off changing for as long as he could, he was having such fun. . . . Oh God, George . . ."

"It's all right, darling." The husband and the WPC just averted a collision. "David is a great favourite of his aunt's, Superintendent."

There was no possible response to this observation. Kendrick turned to the boy.

"Your cousin—" as soon as he had said the word he hoped the
Douglases would not realize that it was no longer ambiguous—"told me
David was having a long dance session fairly late on with someone you
know, and you yourself mentioned the name Bunny."

He heard the catch of breath. "Oh yes. Bunny Holden. That was
going on the last time I was in the marquee. Bunny was making rather a
fool of himself. I wondered if David would let him take him home. But
he can't have done, or this wouldn't have happened." Kendrick thought
the composure was only just intact. "Anyway, I remember thinking it
could only be a matter of time before Bunny caught on. Everyone
seemed to know eventually that Davina was David."

"Thank you, Jonathan." Kendrick turned to the father. "I noted
coming just now from your brother's, sir, that David would have had
quite a short walk home."

"That's right, Superintendent. A quarter of an hour or so."

"And that he would pass the old garden off Birch Road."

"But he didn't," choked Mrs. Fabia Douglas.

At least he had upset the aunt rather than the mother. "I expect you
slept late this morning?" he asked eventually.

"Certainly not!" Fabia Douglas was braced in an instant by indignation. Kendrick noticed she had managed to trap one of the strands of
hair back into the arrangement. "In fact we had breakfast earlier than
usual, with Eleanor telephoning. I had to wake Jonathan, but there was
no lying in."

"No one would think you'd just had a large party," said Kendrick,
looking admiringly round the room and signalling departure to WPC
Thomson. The room was immaculate. Also rather ornately appointed,
and less attractive to him than the paler colours and fewer, plainer
pieces of the Frederick Douglases' living-room.

"Most of the tidying up was done before we went to bed," said Fabia
Douglas, suddenly forlorn. "I wish I had more to do now. George, do
you think we might go to Freddie and Marie?"

"I think so, sweet."

Watching the mutual gentleness of two decisive people, Kendrick
decided he was looking at the portrait of a happy marriage. He started
towards the door.

"Thank you for your help. We'll see ourselves out."

"I'll see you out!"

But George Douglas held his wife back in her chair with an affectionate gesture before himself walking with Kendrick and WPC Thomson to the front door. On the hall table was a tumbled stack of photographs. "Taken at the party," said Douglas. He picked them up gingerly and held them out to Kendrick. "People placed orders, but that's all gone by the board now. Take them, please."

"Thank you," said Kendrick, as WPC Thomson took the photographs from George Douglas's extended arms. "I'll be glad to have them."

"It's the only place for them. Identification?" whispered Douglas as he opened the door. "To spare Frederick?"

"Your brother has already furnished proof of identity," said Kendrick formally. "But thank you." He had found the Frederick Douglases the more attractive branch of the family, but both were decent. In the car he ran through the photographs. David Douglas featured in just about every other one. Only one of his partners looked unembarrassed, and that one looked blissfully happy. Bunny Holden? Jonathan Douglas would have told him, but he could find out for himself and anyway, he thought he already knew.

CHAPTER 5

"Maurice, what a nice surprise! You're just in time to help me try a new sherry." Humphrey blinked at the brightness of the coast beyond his open door, which made of the tall figure in front of him a silhouette, only just recognisable. "Come in, come in. This must be the first time the tide of crime has held back for you to come and have a drink with me before lunch on Sunday. There's plenty for lunch, too, if there's any chance of you—"

"The tide of crime isn't held back," said Kendrick, following Humphrey into his lookout dining-room. "It's engulfing the town, drowning it in sorrow."

"Yes. Oh yes. I shouldn't have been facetious, in view of . . ." Nevertheless, Humphrey was taken aback by his friend's vehemence. And by the look of him, his wind-blown brown curls an inappropriate frame to a face so heavy with anger.

Kendrick could feel his brows lowering over his eyes. This wasn't the guise in which he had intended to present himself to Humphrey, but his mood was insisting on turning everything casual and comfortable into fuel for his rage. All at once he was agog to change the polite inquiry in Humphrey's face into shock and sadness.

"We found another Monster victim this morning," said Kendrick, watching closely.

"Oh no!" Going through the motions so far, of course.

"Not quite like the others. This one was a boy. Dressed as a girl."

"Where . . . ?" Humphrey's lips were suddenly white and stiff. Kendrick hadn't expected anything so dramatic. That Humphrey would think at once of the belle of last night's ball.

"Oh, Hump, I'm sorry to have to tell you." He was already ashamed of himself. "It was the son of your friend Frederick Douglas. You were at the party last night, you'll know how he looked. I came because I wanted to be the one to break the news." His anger, insofar as it had unreasonably touched Humphrey, had melted away. "Sit down. And if you haven't started on the sherry, I'd advise whisky or brandy. I'll pour it for you."

"A little—whisky." Humphrey slumped into the wing chair by the fireplace. The word "Eleanor" occurred to him.

"I've seen the sister." Kendrick wondered why Humphrey had said "Eleanor." "And the parents." He put the glass into Humphrey's hand and watched in silence while he drank. There was no point in looking for colour to return to the pale visage, but at least the lips were redefined. "The other Douglases, too."

"Yes, of course," said Humphrey dreamily. He had the absurd feeling that if he could go back to the moment of letting Maurice into his house he could prevent this terrible thing from happening. He was seeing the faces of the Douglases as he had seen them last night, then trying not to imagine how they must look now. Look now . . . David . . . Stray phrases floated in, as painful as the faces. Marie saying "Isn't it nice?" *Marie. A marvellous day.* Fabia so proud and pleased. Eleanor . . . Maurice was asking him if he was all right.

"Yes, I'm all right. Just feeling—they shouldn't have been allowed to be so happy last night, it should have cast a shadow. Coming events . . . Oh, Maurice, forgive me, I'm shocked, I think. Thinking and talking nonsense. Good, I see you've taken whisky, too. Awful for you. I'm sorry."

"Being angry keeps me in adrenaline." Kendrick tried to smile and succeeded in stretching one side of his mouth. "It is awful, though, going to see families."

"Perhaps the worst part," said Humphrey automatically, imagining that to see the victim must be the most terrible part of all. *The victim. David.* Last night he had been David Douglas, enjoying himself, hardly having begun his life. This morning he was a victim. His last role.

"What time . . . ?"

"Somewhere between one and three."

"Was he . . . would it have been quick?"

"Minutes, no more." Minutes Kendrick always feared must be as distorted and swollen as the victim's face, but Humphrey would be spared that comparison. Not David's father, though.

As if reading his mind, Humphrey asked, wincing, "Did Frederick have to identify him?"

"Yes. I always wish there was some other way. George Douglas offered, which was decent, but the father had already done it."

"Frederick wouldn't hesitate." Thank goodness he was functioning normally again. He felt there had never been a time when he hadn't known this monstrous thing. Monstrous. "You're sure it was the Monster?"

"There was the usual signature." In their discussions about the earlier murders, Humphrey had never asked what the signature was, and Kendrick would not have told him. "Which we hope is still a secret inside the Force."

"But . . . Maurice . . ." Humphrey's sense of disbelief wasn't entirely for the idea that sorrow could so outrageously swallow joy. It was partly based in practicalities. "David wouldn't have gone home on his own looking like *that.* He'd brought his own clothes with him, for heaven's sake, in case he stayed on beyond his parents and Eleanor,

which was more than likely—" what time had Eleanor gone home?—
"and didn't get a lift back. I can't believe he'd have been so *stupid.*"
"Neither can anyone else. The trouble is, no one saw him go. All we
know is that at about two o'clock, when Eleanor Douglas was ready to
go home and looked round for him, he wasn't there and his clothes
were. Aunt and uncle and cousin all joined in the search because they
couldn't believe he'd have gone off dressed as he was, but it was obvious
he had. And he must either have left alone or found himself alone on
the way home, unless . . ."

"Unless the Monster was one of Fabia's guests." (Who had gone
home with Eleanor?)

"Yes."

The two men stared at one another across Humphrey's elegant Adam
grate. This was not the first time their trains of thought had run parallel.

"Tell me—if you can, Maurice—did it look as though the Monster
thought he had another girl? I mean . . ."

"There were signs that he realized after he'd killed David that he'd
made a mistake. I think we can take it that the Monster believed he'd
got hold of another attractive girl."

"David did look attractive. He took me in. We danced together—"
there was a pang (no doubt the first of many) as he remembered David's
warm cheek against his—"and I only found out because in the end he
and Eleanor told me. If the Monster had been one of the guests he could
very easily have been taken in. Except for one thing, I would have
thought."

"What's that, Hump?" Kendrick realized he had subconsciously seen
Humphrey's presence at the Douglas party as his first possible source of
help in this whole ghastly series. He got up and poured them both
further whiskies.

"Well, as the evening went on more and more people got to know
about David simply because he always eventually confessed the truth
before starting on someone else. And of course people would tell other
people—I overheard several. David's was definitely the fancy dress with
the biggest impact. I would have thought that by the end of the evening
there wouldn't be many, if any, people who didn't know who Davina
really was."

"Yes, I see."

"I suppose—there could just be another possibility."

"Tell me!"

"I don't—didn't—know David very well, but he was obviously delighted with the success of his disguise, and I suppose it could just be that it went to his head to the extent that he didn't change into his own clothes because of feeling reluctant to abandon his splendid joke." He was speaking diffidently because David was dead, and it could just be said that he was speaking ill of him, or at least a bit critically. Silly and illogical, but folk taboos were supposed to have deep roots in human nature. "I think he could even just have decided to walk home alone and vulnerable as the ultimate test of his success."

"Yes . . . That's very interesting, Hump." What had Eleanor Douglas said? *David usually had a reason for doing things.* Worth seeing if the members of David's family were prepared to consider Humphrey's idea, or dismissed it out of hand. "I think I knew I was glad you were at the party, and that you'd have at least one good idea as well as being my ideal witness." This time his smile just made it. "I'm afraid you've already answered my most madly optimistic question, though, by implication. But I have to ask you, as we'll have to ask every other guest: Did you see David leave?"

Reluctantly Humphrey shook his head. "I left early, you might know. If I could have helped you over this, Maurice, I'd have stayed all night. All I can personally tell you is that just before I left—about half past eleven, I suppose it was—I saw David dancing with a young chap who was obviously very much *épris.* The only man I saw actually being more forward than David himself."

"I think that must be the boy Jonathan and Eleanor Douglas mentioned. Is this him?"

Kendrick whipped out the clearest of the three relevant photographs, getting up and putting it into Humphrey's hand.

"That's him, yes." Humphrey didn't hesitate. "I don't know his name."

"I do."

"I just saw them, and I remember it went through my mind that David might have trouble if he let the illusion persist. Perhaps he did."

"In which case the Monster could be a teenager. Possible, I suppose. Tuck your son up at bedtime, call him down to breakfast in the morning, and sleep soundly yourself all night. A bit risky this time, though—all too easy for one to check."

"So that will be your next move."

"The next specific move. The central area of questioning will be shifted—has been shifted—from the area of the last death last week. Last week! I'm so angry, Hump, I'm so angry."

"I'm angry, too." He realized he was. "The families—how did they take it?"

"Pretty well. They're a tough breed, aren't they. The sister was like a sleepwalker. Then suddenly and briefly broke up."

"Eleanor?"

"She was recovered by the time I left. The mother wept, very quietly, after I'd started to get worried about her unnatural self-control. Look, Hump, I think when I arrived you were starting to say something about lunch. I'll stay, if we can get on with it now, and quickly."

Kendrick was touched to see a wan light in the sad face.

"We'll have it right away. Just some pâté and cheese and some nice new biscuits I've found. Oh dear, though, do we really want it?"

"Yes," said Kendrick firmly. He followed Humphrey to the door of the room, then overtook him and led the way to the kitchen.

"You are neat, Hump."

"So are you," retorted Humphrey quickly. "Remember, I've seen your kitchen in the throes of a dinner-party."

"I think men are, or they aren't." Kendrick generalized the issue, after casting a quick glance at Humphrey's face and seeing the brief suffusion of colour. He was aware that people ignorant of Humphrey's history had been known to refer to him as the bachelor par excellence. And that Humphrey had sometimes heard them. "You and I, I think, are simply rather well organized. To be orderly is to be far more relaxed than people give credit for. The chief character in Solzhenitsyn's *First Circle*—I can't remember his name—says at some point that he's orderly because he's lazy—it's so much *easier.*"

"You're right, Maurice!" But Humphrey's smile was aborted before it was fairly begun, and he sat down suddenly at the kitchen table and stayed there while Kendrick marshalled the things his host had earlier brought out of cupboards and fridge. Nor did he protest when Kendrick roughly laid the kitchen table.

"Tell me about the Douglases," said Kendrick as he, too, sat down. "You know them pretty well, don't you?"

"I know the Frederick Douglases fairly well, but I haven't seen all that much of them. My own fault, we are friends, yes, but I'm so inclined to think how nice, so-and-so's there for me to get in touch with, and then I don't. Although lately we seem to have got together more. . . . It began with business ages ago—they're civil engineers and we did printing work for them, still do. It's not much more than business with the George Douglases still. They only asked me to the party because I was in Fine Foods when Fabia was ordering her party food."

"Can you tell me anything at all about David?"

"I wish I could. It's always seemed to me that David was just about the ideal son—healthy—" both men stared at one another, then dropped their eyes—"good-looking, easy-mannered, bright. But I don't know him at all."

"The daughter?" asked Kendrick, hiding his quickening interest by helping himself to cheese.

"Eleanor seemed to grow up all of a sudden," said Humphrey. "But that was some time ago." He looked depressed, and sounded it, Kendrick thought. "She makes me wish I had a daughter." Kendrick had the impression Humphrey was trying to explain something. To himself, maybe. "I was going to say you're lucky, Maurice, but in the circumstances . . ."

"I see Jenny as often as I like. What sort of a young woman is Eleanor Douglas?"

"A rather special one. You've seen how she looks—"

"Not how she usually looks," interposed Kendrick gently.

"Ah no." Kendrick witnessed his second involuntary shudder of the morning, and saw Humphrey's hands jerk apart on the table-top. "I'm inclined to believe," continued Humphrey resolutely, "that she's as good as she's beautiful." His rare smile appeared, as always surprising Kendrick with its charm. It disappeared abruptly, having served its purpose of diffusing the absolutes in his description of Eleanor Douglas. *Beautiful?* Kendrick asked himself, and answered: yes, in an un-obvious, nineteenth-century sort of way.

"Strong character, I could imagine."

"Oh yes. Eleanor studied art history in London and she and her friend Marian West Foster opened a gallery in Seaminster a couple of years ago which is actually paying."

"Called?"

"Douglas West. In Clive Street, just—"

"I've seen it. Intriguing windows. Did she get on well with her brother?"

"She seemed to. She's—was—always inclined to spoil him, which he liked, of course."

"Did David get on with his parents, too?"

"So far as I could see, Maurice. David was a model son and brother, I should say."

"He and his cousin were friends? David and Jonathan appropriately named?"

"It always seemed like it. It didn't appear to me that they had a great deal in common—Jonathan's very bookish and no good at games—and I remember either Fabia or Marie once saying that in school they went their own ways, but at home I believe they sought each other out quite regularly. David seemed to be the one more inclined to make the moves —Jonathan's very self-sufficient. He's even a member of Mensa."

"More academic than David, then."

"More academic than David wants—wanted—to be. Jonathan told me, only last night, he thought David wasn't very ambitious, just wanted to do something where he could manage to wangle himself a lot of spare time for games and so on. Jonathan mentioned accountancy, which never seemed to leave *me* a particular amount of spare time. . . . Now I think of it," said Humphrey, and Kendrick had the idea he had made a discovery which intrigued him, "it's hard to say anything about David beyond generalities. Although he was so open, he didn't some- how give himself away, if you can see what I mean."

"I think so. You're a most reliable and sober witness, Hump. All appears and apparentlys. Would you say the Douglas brothers seem close?"

"In a way. They work well together—Frederick's the engineer, George the business man—and they seem to be fond of one another. Socially I think they have their separate circles. The differences between them are compounded, I should say, by their wives. Marie's lower key, like Frederick. Have you seen enough of them yet to know what I'm trying to say?"

"Yes." Kendrick thought merely of the two living-rooms. "I always feel Jonathan's something of a cuckoo in that nest." Kendrick's head shot up from his plate, and he and Humphrey locked eyes again. "I keep having to remind myself he belongs with the Georges and not the Fredericks," said Kendrick. "Exactly. Only it took me years to put it into words. The same thing doesn't quite apply to David the other way on. He'd be—would have been—equally at home, I should say, in either family. A son like David would have delighted Fabia's heart."

"She's less than pleased with the one she's got?"

"I wouldn't say that, Maurice. In a way she's frightfully proud of him, but his strengths are strengths she doesn't quite understand. She tends to keep up a sort of routine chastisement, but I suspect Jonathan doesn't take too much notice. And one has to admit that so far he's socially less than satisfactory to a woman like Fabia."

Both men briefly grinned. Kendrick, who did a bit of drawing and painting, for an instant saw Humphrey's mouth as the one arresting horizontal in the prevailing downstrokes of his appearance—long nose, long teeth, long fingers. Even his fine dark hair fell straight from the crown.

"You're doing awfully well, Hump, for one who professes to be a lazy friend. I think you know them all quite well."

"Lately, perhaps . . ."

Kendrick forbore to ask what lately had brought the Douglas family into clearer focus, convinced that the answer, however interesting to him personally, would not have assisted his investigation. He got to his feet. "Thanks, Hump, more than I can say. You've told me things about those two families I don't think I could ever have discovered in the ordinary way. Not that I think this case is anything but straightforward. The only mystery seems to be why on earth an intelligent boy like David Douglas should have courted danger in the way he seems to have done. I'm inclined to think from what you've told me that if he did set off for home on his own he *was* in fact courting it. And if he set off in company . . ."

The front doorbell pealed into the uncomfortable silence. Kendrick had been half expecting it, and followed Humphrey out into the hall.

"Good afternoon, sir. We're police officers and we'd be glad if you would be good enough to answer a few routine questions with regard to a fancy-dress party we understand you attended last night. I'm Detective-Inspector— Good afternoon, sir, I'm sorry, sir." The mackintoshed man doing the talking withdrew his foot from Humphrey's threshold.

"That's all right, Inspector. I've asked Mr. Barnes the necessary questions. If you'll wait in your car for a moment I'd like a word with you."

"Of course, sir."

The inspector and sergeant retreated, and Humphrey closed the front door.

"Nearly two hundred guests, Fabia so proudly told me. You're not actually taking statements from them all?"

"Not statements, thank heaven. Just, at this stage, listening to their observations with reference to David Douglas and his unique activities. There probably won't be a grain of gold among the dross, although it really doesn't seem to me to be *too* much to hope that one person saw the manner of David's departure."

"From the house, you mean," said Humphrey in a stifled voice.

"Yes . . . Oh, Hump . . ."

"I'm glad you got here before those other two."

"I was determined to. . . . I'll go and call now on the young man you and Jonathan saw dancing with David. Not a word about that, or about the photograph I showed you."

"Of course not. One grain of gold, perhaps . . . But you're treating it as a Monster murder." Humphrey reopened his front door. The brightness, now, had lost its colour and sparkle and grown hard and grey. The wind was colder and stronger, and Kendrick's curls took off the second his head left the sanctuary of the doorframe.

"Without a doubt. But remember we don't know if the Monster way-laid David or accompanied him. And even with the orthodox Monster murders we've had to try and find out how and why and at what time the victim was in the spot where she died. Without success, need I say. And if David's inamorato set off with him from his uncle's house and is innocent, he might realize with hindsight that he saw the Monster."

"I was forgetting about that aspect of things. There were no—clues of any kind? But I suppose I shouldn't—"

"No more than there were on any of the other occasions. Which is to say, bloody nothing."

His anger was up again, as if by stepping out onto the pavement he had lost the immunity of Humphrey's oasis.

"It's dreadful, Maurice. I'm going to have to go and sit down and take it in."

"If I were you I should try and resist doing that. Pity it's Sunday. What were you going to do this afternoon?"

"Read and garden and maybe do some work."

"I wish I could keep you to them, but I've stayed too long as it is."

"Come round again tonight?"

"It'll be late."

"Doesn't matter."

"All right. I'll have eaten. Would you think of getting in touch with the Frederick Douglases?"

"Oh no!" Kendrick fancied he could detect wistfulness as well as disapproval. "I don't know them as well as that. I'll get a letter written. It'll be difficult. . . . You're going to lose your hair, Maurice, off you go."

The inspector had parked just behind him. When he'd seen Humphrey's front door close, Kendrick tapped on the window of the car, putting his head in as it was hastily wound down.

"Nothing significant about my presence with Mr. Humphrey Barnes. He's a friend of mine and an articulate observer. Put down beside his name that he was aware in the later evening that David Douglas was dancing with a young man probably called Bunny Holden. He didn't see David Douglas beyond half past eleven, as that's when he left the party himself. I presume there's the name Holden on your list?"

The inspector glanced down. "No, sir, I'm sorry, sir. Must be on Inspector Crowther's. He's taking care of the bulk of the guest list. This is our first call so far as that list's concerned. We've been covering the houses near the murder spot."

"So what about the neighbours?" Kendrick swallowed his impatience.

"Nothing, sir, I'm afraid. The people living alongside and opposite the old garden have all been questioned and no one was any help at all."

"I didn't really expect it. The houses are all so well set back and hidden by old trees." His disappointment was offset by the prospect of the Holden boy. Who was almost bound to be the young man Humphrey had recognised in the photograph. The first semblance of a lead since the first murder, however unlikely. "Thank you, Inspector. Carry on."

When he had shut the front door on Kendrick, Humphrey resisted the temptation to go and sit down and stare into space, returning to the kitchen to remove the remains of lunch. He then went to the sitting-room and Emily's Sheraton writing-table, where before Maurice's visit he had intended to compose a letter of thanks that afternoon to Fabia. This, now, would remain unwritten, but he must wrestle with a letter to Marie. Images of her recently smiling face had to be pushed aside as he struggled against his verbal tendency to be mock-serious over trivial things—now he wanted to give words their due weight it seemed to him that he had devalued them. It was half an hour before he was half satisfied with what he had managed to write.

By now the dove-grey world had turned slate-coloured and the gusts were carrying stinging diagonals of rain, but after dropping the letter into his local box Humphrey forced his way the length of the cliff road and downhill into the centre of the bay, the impetus of his sorrow and fury sending him half-way up the West Cliff before the rain became blinding. Nevertheless, and already soaked, he made a detour on his way home which took him past the Frederick Douglases' house.

CHAPTER 6

By the time he was back at the Seaminster station, Kendrick's desire to talk to the Holden boy had become a burning impatience. He went straight to the Incident Room.

"Any sign of an interim report from the guest-list team?"

"Something's coming through now, sir."

The response was a chorus, accompanied by slight moves to attention around the room as Kendrick's arrival was noted. His effect on an

Incident Room might have amused him, if he hadn't always been angry, worried, or tired when he entered it.

Most of the report was already on tape. Silently Kendrick joined the listeners for the rest of it. There were a couple of mentions of David Douglas having been last seen dancing with a Bunny Holden, none of a visit to a Holden family. At the end of the report Kendrick asked the travelling inspector if he'd reached them.

"Yes, sir. But we didn't call. By the time we got there we had so many independent references to young Holden and the Douglas boy we thought you might prefer to be the one—"

"I appreciate your thought processes, Inspector Crowther. I do prefer it." He was surprised at the strength of his satisfaction that he was to be able to take the Holdens unawares. "I've just come on the scene and I'll hear you through on tape. But if you could sum up for me."

"Of course, sir. Over half the party guests we've been able to question so far told us their last sighting of the victim was dancing with the Holden boy. I gather it was quite a talking point. Nothing much to see on the dance floor once the disco took over, but all those who noticed the pair of them say the way they sat it out was pretty steamy. . . ." The voice paused to cough; the inspector had possibly embarrassed himself. "Also, sir, I gather there was quite some amusement that young Holden was too—er—absorbed to realise what just about everyone else by that stage had realised—that he was making up to a lad. So far as the victim's departure from the party's concerned, sir, no one so far appears to have seen him leave, or show signs of leaving. But we're barely half-way through. It was a large party. We have to be glad at least that it's Sunday and no one's at school, although with not being able to question the younger ones without their parents around, it's all on the slow side."

"I appreciate that." Kendrick hoped his fretful reaction hadn't made his tone belie his words. "Nothing else that's struck you, Inspector?"

"Not yet, sir. I'm sorry."

"Thank you. I'm going to see the Holdens now."

Without waiting to hear the tape through, Kendrick strode along to the large bare room which had been temporarily assigned to him and his Sergeant Grant, to bring the sergeant up to date and appoint him his driver.

The sudden keenness of eye in the broad, expressive face matched Kendrick's own new sense of alert.

"Is it too far-fetched to consider, sir," asked Sergeant Grant as he eased out onto the pleasant lime-tree-lined road where the Seaminster Constabulary was housed in a Victorian mansion, "that the Monster just might have been at the party?"

"The idea occurred to me, Peter." As it had occurred to one of the guests. Kendrick all at once appreciated how disagreeable an idea it must be for Humphrey. "And then I thought that, if he was, and killed a fellow guest, he would be throwing away his trump card—the fact that we have absolutely nothing to distinguish him from any other man in Britain."

"With respect, though, sir, he could be moving away from common sense, his madness could be spreading to other areas."

And overconfidence could be one sign of madness. Was something going to break at last? He said cautiously, "It could be, Peter."

The woman who opened the front door of the Holdens' shrubberied Edwardian house was the type, instantly recognisable to Kendrick, before whom his heart always sank when he was making an investigation, the type which was invariably aware of itself and the impact it was making and to whose ego, if he wanted to get anywhere, he had to defer.

"Mrs. Holden?"

"Yes." She dimpled the confession at them. She had probably been rather pretty, reflected Kendrick wearily, but whatever beauty there had been was now in ruins, the deterioration pointed up by the long, youthful brown hair, streaked with grey where it fell across one eye. The elaborate make-up of the other eye made Kendrick somehow more aware of the fact that the slippers Mrs. Holden was wearing were badly broken down. "What can I do for you?" Her assessment of their maleness, and subsequent approval of himself, was easily apparent to Kendrick, but he was not in the mood to find it even slightly gratifying.

"We're police officers," he said, offering his ID. She gave it a cursory glance, the interest in her face intensifying, no trace of reserve. "I'm Detective Chief Superintendent Kendrick of Divisional CID and this is Detective-Sergeant Grant. We should like—"

"Police officers! I can't think there's any way *I* can assist police officers." Kendrick credited her with inducing her sudden blush. "But please come in. Of course it's my husband you want to see. He's in the garden, I'll just go and—"

"Your son was at a fancy-dress dance last night." Kendrick's interruption was more forceful than he could have wished, but in the past weeks his patience had been tried. "I should like to have a few words with him in connection with it."

"The Douglases?" She looked blank. And, suddenly, not very intelligent. "Why on earth should you want to talk to Bunny about the Douglases' party?" It seemed, to Kendrick's satisfaction, clear that she knew nothing of David Douglas's death, although there had probably been more than one news bulletin carrying the information. Information, too, about the Monster and his error; he hadn't seen any reason to suppress it.

"If your son is in, madam, I should be grateful if you could tell him I'm here."

"Ah yes, of course. Your business is with Bunny. I'm so sorry, Superintendent, I ought to watch my television detectives more carefully." Kendrick and Sergeant Grant had to spend a few minutes responding to her exaggerated retraction of interest. "He is in," said Mrs. Holden eventually. "Go into the sitting-room and I'll call him."

The room she indicated was furnished with taste and some things which looked valuable, but it was shabby and unpolished and the ashes in the grate had probably accumulated over several days. The first responses to Mrs. Holden's raised voice were distant and non-committal, and they heard feet ascending and descending stairs before she returned with a young man whom she pushed fussily in front of her into the room. The young man of the photograph.

"Here you are, Superintendent. Now, I'll leave you to it, which is the correct thing, I believe?"

"Actually, madam—" Sergeant Grant broke off, as a large man with a calm, half-smiling face appeared in the doorway. Kendrick felt better the second he saw him.

"What is happening?" asked Holden senior politely.

Kendrick reintroduced himself, and told the father he wanted to ask the son (who had wriggled free of his mother's exhibitionist embrace and was standing mistrustfully near the wall) a few questions in connection with the Douglas Silver Wedding party.

Sergeant Grant moved slightly towards the boy, asked him how old he was.

"Seventeen."

The heaviness of Bunny Holden's features was emphasised by his sulky expression, but he had a good-shaped head and wide-spaced eyes. Also an air of sophistication which Kendrick's experience read as a veneer and which was aided by a precocious physical development: height, width, shadow of beard and moustache. No stripling youth, this. Would have had the strength . . .

"In that case, sir," said Sergeant Grant to the father, "there is no legal requirement for you or your wife to remain while we talk to your son. But if you prefer to, of course, and your son has no objection—"

"Oh my boy!" said Mrs. Holden dramatically, unable, thought Kendrick unkindly, to induce a pallor to go with the sudden hand on heart.

"Just a few questions," he reassured. "We're talking to everyone who was at the party."

"But why—"

"I think, Eve," said the husband gently, putting his arm round his wife's waist, "that it's probably best if I stay. All right, Bunny?" There was no sign of agreement from the boy, but neither was there any sign of dissent. After looking at him steadily for a few moments, the father turned back to the mother. "It's obviously only a routine matter, dear, and I'll tell you all about it."

There was a short pause of some anxiety to Kendrick, and then Mrs. Holden, draggingly and with a little moue of dissatisfaction, went to the door and let herself out, closing it noisily behind her.

"Please go ahead, Superintendent," said the father, seating himself in the most distant chair.

"Thank you, sir." Kendrick turned to the boy. "Bunny Holden?" He had slightly emphasised the first name.

"Bruce, actually." Under Kendrick's gaze he came forward to stand in front of the two policemen.

"You were at the George Douglases' Silver Wedding party last night?"

"Yes. What of it?" The bad temper of disagreeable recollection flared unrestrainedly in the face.

Kendrick ignored both words and tone. The father said "Bunny," in a level tone which managed to contain a warning.

"You spent some time dancing with their nephew David Douglas in the guise of a girl?"

The scowl intensified, the lip curled. The chosen means of conveying anger, thought Kendrick. The brick red flooding the face was the involuntary means of indicating shame and embarrassment. He must not imagine, at this stage, that it indicated more.

"The shit!" Kendrick's back was to the father, but he heard him move sharply in his chair. "He led me on for half the evening. DD was always full of himself, but this perverted joke of his really went to his head. Got arrested for soliciting, has he?"

"No," said Sergeant Grant. "Did you take him home?"

"No, but I wonder he didn't let me. He took me into an empty room and when I was going to . . . that is . . . he took the wig off and laughed. Laughed . . . I could have killed him." Kendrick noticed a wet gleam on the temple. He heard the father catch his breath and was cravenly glad he couldn't see him. "I don't have to tell you all this." Bruce Holden had come back to the present. "There's no law against—"

"You're quite sure you didn't take David Douglas home, Bruce, believing him to be a girl?"

"I tell you I didn't. I know whether I did or I didn't; you don't have to ask a question like that twice. Why are you asking it, anyway? It's no business of anyone else's. I've a right . . ."

To make a fool of myself in my own way. Kendrick finished the sentence in his head.

"I'm sorry, Bruce." The boy looked so unyouthful, he had almost called him sir. "David Douglas was found dead this morning, in that old garden off Birch Road, which he would pass on his way home. We're asking everyone who was at the party if they can throw any light on his movements towards the end of the evening, and we gather he spent most of the latter part of it exclusively in your company. So we hoped you might be able to help us."

"Better sit down," suggested Sergeant Grant, moving quickly forward to support the swaying, white-faced figure. The father was there almost as fast, still calm, it seemed to Kendrick, but sitting down this time close to his son on the faded chintz sofa. In his face as he turned it to the boy was, so far as there was anything, a puzzled sorrow.

"Help you with your inquiries," gasped Bruce Holden. "I know what that means." He seemed unaware of the close presence of his father. "But I can't help you, I've told you all I know. He pulled his wig off in that room where he took me and then laughed. Dead, though . . ."

"You also told us you could have killed him," pointed out Sergeant Grant.

"D'you think I'd have said that if I had done?" Kendrick had his first impulse of sympathy towards the boy as he heard these words and looked into the straight-eyed gaze which accompanied them. The straightness of truth, or of desperation? The first, surely. Momentarily he had forgotten the cross on David's breast. But the boy would have to be investigated on that possibility, too, if nothing else came out of the interviews of the other party guests. Which if he was innocent would be another monstrous act.

"What did you do, Bruce, when David—laughed?"

"I ran out of the room and out of the house and drove home."

"In your own car?"

"Yes." Each response was a muted challenge.

"What time was it, do you remember, when you drove home?"

"I didn't look at my watch, actually." He was out of shock.

"Naturally enough," Kendrick conceded. "Even so, you'll have some idea."

"Quarter to one, one, I don't know."

"And David was still in the room when you ran out."

"*Yes.* I've told you. I didn't see—I never saw him again."

"Did you tell anyone what happened in that room, Bruce? Did anyone know about it or see it?"

"Of course I didn't tell anyone. And I'd closed the door and the curtains were drawn. No one could have seen. I tell you, when I'd . . . when he'd . . . I just ran out to the car and got in and drove home."

"Without thanking your hosts, or saying goodbye to anyone?"

The boy's eyes now were searching the confines of the room. "I was so mad I couldn't have spoken to anyone, I just had to get away. I was going to write to Mrs. Douglas today to thank her. Thank her!" Suddenly the eyes focused on Kendrick's. "*You* wouldn't have told anyone. *You'd* have wanted to get away."

"I suppose so, if things happened to me like that." His second involuntary impulse of sympathy awakened in Kendrick a sudden intense revulsion for what he was doing, which sharpened as he looked at the controlled tension in the father's face.

"Did you or your wife hear Bruce come home, sir?"

"I heard the car and the garage door, Superintendent, but without really waking up. I didn't put the light on and I couldn't begin to tell you what time it was."

"Your wife?"

"She appeared to be asleep." There was a fractional pause. "You'll have to ask her."

"Of course," said Kendrick reluctantly.

"Why don't you ask other people whether they saw David?" asked Bruce angrily, wrestling to Kendrick's dismay with the onset of tears. "Ask Mrs. Douglas when he left. She'll tell you I wasn't around."

"We're asking everyone, Bruce, as I said. No doubt someone will have seen him. Thank you for answering my questions. Thank you, sir. . . ." With so many people still to be questioned it was too early to have the boy's car taken away. If David Douglas's fingerprints were anywhere in it, they'd really have something to go on. And if they weren't, that wouldn't mean they could forget about young Holden. Birch Road was within strolling distance and the night had been fine. . . . And Inspector Crowther was probably being given, at that precise moment, chapter and verse about the departure of David Douglas from the party.

"Superintendent! Oh, Superintendent!"

Mrs. Holden was irrupting into the room, aware, even through what seemed to be genuine excitement, of the effect she was creating. The husband was off the sofa and at her side almost before Kendrick saw him moving.

"Yes, Mrs. Holden?"

"Oh, Superintendent, I've just been listening to the radio—well, I wasn't listening, not at first, but it was on, you know—and I heard—I heard on the news that David Douglas has been found murdered. I thought perhaps you mightn't know and that I ought to tell you." No, she wasn't very intelligent. Kendrick had a sudden terrible desire to laugh. "And how extraordinary that you should have come here to talk about that party. The fatal party they'll call it now, won't they? Apparently David was dressed up as a girl. For the fancy dress, you know. Bunny went as Pierrot. The Monster must have thought he really was a girl. David, I mean. Oh, I didn't tell you, did I, it was another Monster murder. The police can tell, can't they, because of some special mark. . . ."

She was so wound up she went on gabbling for a few seconds after her son had cried out, then shrank back into her husband's arm, terrified by the atmosphere in the room, thought Kendrick, rather than by any sudden understanding.

Bruce Holden was on his feet, almost lunging at Kendrick, shouting his outrage. "Monster murder! You didn't tell me, you just asked me those questions. I didn't strangle him!"

"Steady, son," advised Sergeant Grant, interposing himself. "And we didn't tell you David Douglas was strangled."

"The Monster always strangles!" The boy whirled round to the door. "They think I did it, Mum," he shouted. "And all the other murders."

"Oh God, oh my boy . . ." She was white this time. Between them, the father and Sergeant Grant helped her to the sofa.

"We don't think anything of the kind, Bruce." Kendrick had to shout, too, above the uproar. "We know only that you spent the last hour or so of the party in the company of David, believing him to be a girl. You've told us you left the party alone, and we hope we shall soon have independent evidence that you did." He must hope it. Dear God, he must. Sergeant Grant, who had a pleasant habit of stepping in just when required, eventually elicited from Mrs. Holden the fact that she must have slept through her son's return from the party, as she had no recollection of hearing it.

"Thank you, madam, we'll be on our way now." Kendrick was disgusted, having to walk out on the chaos his visit had created. And to recognise his disappointment that he wasn't yet in a position to ask the boy and his father to go with him to the station.

When he and the sergeant were back there, after a silent journey, he took his own car and drove to the sea and sat with his window down, welcoming the rain on his face. He had to let a certain self-distaste evaporate, if it would, before he could return to the fray with the essential belief in it.

He glanced at his watch. Four o'clock. Sunday. Miriam, once, would have been at home at this time, on this day, in his house, and in the mood which was on him now he would have driven the short distance and gone indoors for the few moments it took to lay his head against her heart. . . .

Back at the station, only partially restored, Kendrick forced himself to get abreast of all the other continuing avenues of inquiry, even undertaking personally the unavoidable interviewing of two people, an old woman and a young man, who had come to confess to David's murder. Fortunately both put themselves quickly out of contention.

Which meant that not all that much time had passed, and Inspector Crowther and his team still hadn't finished. After hearing from the chief inspector that the inquest on David Douglas was fixed for Tuesday morning, and a third radio conversation with Inspector Crowther, Kendrick scooped up Sergeant Grant and was driven to the people on the last page of Fabia Douglas's list.

He'd been back only a few moments when Inspector Crowther came into the Incident Room.

"Good evening, sir. With your help, that's the lot." The inspector slapped his copy of the list onto a table. "No joy, I'm afraid, sir."

"Nothing, Inspector? Not one person having seen David Douglas leave the party, or announce his intention of leaving?"

"Not one, sir."

"No one saw the Holden boy go?"

"No one, sir. People either didn't see anything, generally because they'd gone home earlier themselves, or they saw the two boys—Douglas and Holden—and then didn't see them. You, sir?"

"The same." Kendrick was still holding his own copy of the list, noticing that his hands were trembling slightly. "I'll go and see Mrs. George Douglas. Give her another chance to tell me she forgot to put someone's name down. If she doesn't take it, I'm afraid we'll have to bring young Holden in for a statement. On his movements so far as the other murders are concerned, too. And his car. But that will be all for tonight. Thank you, Inspector."

The door was opened by George Douglas, his red face, bull neck, and broad shoulders in heavy tweed jacket striking Kendrick all the more powerfully for their contrast with the appearance of the brother.

"Ah, Superintendent. You wish to see us." The moist eyes registered with Kendrick before the pomposity of tone.

Douglas shut the door and led the way across the hall without further word, standing aside silently for Kendrick to enter the drawing-room.

Fabia Douglas was sitting by the merrily flickering artificial coals of a
fire whose three burning bars had made the room stifling. It seemed to
Kendrick as if days rather than hours had passed since he had first seen
her—perhaps because, although her coiffure was now immaculate, her
face and her bearing had changed under the absorption of the tragedy
which at the time of his earlier visit had struck but not penetrated. She
looked older, even the high cheekbones less prominent, the shoulders
rounded, the features slightly blurred.

"Forgive me for disturbing you, Mrs. Douglas." Kendrick advanced
a little way across the strongly patterned carpet. "I just came to ask you
to have one more look, if you will, at the list of party guests you gave
us. I want to be certain no one was left off."

"Of course no one was left off." It was a shadow of her earlier indig-
nations. "Here's Inspector er . . ." she said crossly as Jonathan Douglas appeared at Kendrick's side. "Go and sit down, dear." She had not
appeared to take her eyes off Kendrick. "You had a photostat copy of
my own list, Inspector."

"I appreciate that, Mrs. Douglas. But—no one ringing up at the last
moment, saying they had a cousin unexpectedly staying, and would you
mind . . . ? No gatecrashers?"

"No gatecrashers, certainly not!"

"There were those two French boys, Mother," said Jonathan Douglas
from the upright chair where he had obediently gone. His voice was
quiet and flat. "You remember, they were staying with the Kings and
Tim King was going to bring them with him and then Tim had flu and
you suggested the boys came on their own."

"Oh well, yes," conceded Fabia Douglas, trying, thought Kendrick,
to subdue the irritation in her face as she turned it from her son to
himself. "There were those two boys, yes. But they were hardly *guests.*"

"I think they were going back to France this morning," continued
Jonathan in the same expressionless way. "Crossing in their car."

"I'll have Tim King's address," said Kendrick. "Is there anyone else
you might not have thought of writing down?" he asked the mother. He
realised he had a migraine coming on.

"There is not," said Fabia Douglas.

"I'll get you that address," said Jonathan.

"Thank you," said Kendrick. "And I'd like to use your telephone."

"Certainly no one else," repeated Mrs. Douglas, as Jonathan got up and led Kendrick out to the hall, where he supplied him with an address book open at the appropriate page, indicated the telephone, and retreated. Kendrick sat down on the uncomfortable little decorative chair attached to the low table holding the telephone and rang the Incident Room to ask for a call to be made on the Kings.

"Now, sir?"

"Of course now." Kendrick lifted his head and saw that the small window beside him was a rich midnight blue. Cradling the receiver he wrenched his sleeve back to look at his watch. Ten o'clock. It must have been dark for hours; he hadn't noticed. "It's not so very late, Sergeant. This could be important." He couldn't imagine that it was, but it could be. "When you've found out where those two boys were headed, set things in motion to catch up with them. Radio pictures of the Douglas boy and Bruce Holden. All right?"

"Yes, sir."

Kendrick put the receiver back and sat hesitating, monitoring his head. When he had established the regularity of the hammerstrokes, he dialled again.

"Hump?"

"Maurice! How are you getting on?"

"Unhappily. I'm sorry you haven't heard from me before."

"You've eaten?"

"Enough," Kendrick lied. He hadn't noticed that, either. "Look, Hump, I'm still working and I'm getting a migraine. Can we make it tomorrow? Without fail and earlier than this." What he had to set up in the morning would be completed by the evening.

"Yes, of course." Listening as hard as his head allowed him, Kendrick couldn't hear disappointment. "May I have a meal ready?"

"I'd love you to. But something which won't spoil. I'll try to make it eight, but I can't be certain."

"Of course not. Come when you can."

"That pierrot hat," he said casually as he was leaving. "Do you know who it belongs to?"

"Bunny Holden," said Jonathan. To Kendrick's inordinate relief, the tone was as casual as his own. "Well, it must have been. He was the only pierrot."

"Superintendent," said George Douglas, contriving to make Kendrick's rank sound absurdly inflated. "My wife and Jonathan say that

this boy Bunny Holden was dancing with David late in the evening.
. . ." The eyes gleamed and blinked. "We've wondered . . . We
thought he might just have seen David leave. My wife wanted to telephone."

And perhaps get Mrs. Holden. "We've already asked Bunny," said
Kendrick lightly, suppressing a shudder, marvelling not for the first
time at the naïvety of the general public. "David was still at the party
when he left."

"The pierrot hat was in the *small study,*" said Fabia Douglas, whip-
ping up a grievance, it seemed to Kendrick, in an effort to whip up some
strength. "Almost every room in the house open and welcome to our
guests, but that wasn't enough for some of them."

"Bunny's all right," muttered Jonathan. "He probably just went in
for a breather."

"Or for some other purpose," said Mrs. Douglas, still severe. Still not
thinking of her nephew, to Kendrick's continued relief, in connection
with any erotic behaviour on the part of Bruce Holden. "Jonathan can
take the hat to school tomorrow and give it back to this boy."

Who wouldn't be there.

"I'll be on my way, then," said Kendrick.

He was scarcely home when his migraine burst into full riotous life.
His preference was for continued abstinence, but experience had taught
him what that could mean for the morning. The next day had to start
early and significantly, so he propped himself up in bed and forced
down some dry toast and a glass of milk.

CHAPTER 7

Humphrey was glad to see the light of Monday. It removed, if temporarily, the dual temptations to brood and to call on the Frederick
Douglases, while bringing nearer the time when he might properly un-

dertake the latter activity. Best of all, it was a Monday on which he had the distraction of a meeting in London.

Curtailing rather more speedily than usual his post-breakfast conversation with Mrs. McNicholl (her side of it pursued him as far as the rented garage next-door-but-one which could be accounted the single possible disadvantage to his property), Humphrey drove into town, put his car in the office park, and dealt with his mail until his brother arrived. He'd told Derek on the telephone, of course, about what had happened after the George Douglases' party, and the morning papers were full of it, but the outrage was new enough to form the chief topic of their few moments together. He couldn't blame Derek for being unable to share his personal distress, but Humphrey set off for the station freshly depressed, full of an unfamiliar and chilling sense of the vulnerability of the agreeable life it all at once struck him he had heedlessly taken for granted. If a schoolboy could be choked to death on his way home from a party, all dreadfulness was possible. It wasn't that he hadn't already known this, of course, but knowing and feeling were different things and he had steadily schooled himself not to feel since he had climbed up and away from Emily's death. Now David's seemed to be linking him with that other frightful aftermath, bridging the years of increasing peace and comfort, handing him a key and forcing him to unlock a host of old, small, hurtful memories.

In some absurd way, though, the renewed suffering made him feel less outrageously separated from Marie and Frederick. And Eleanor. And it was less painful in fact to recall how *he* had felt and what *he* had done than to imagine their flayed feelings and somnambulistic movements. For them, there was a terrible extra element; the laws of nature rather than a pair of hands had killed Emily and she hadn't had time to be afraid. And he had been able to decree the demise of that little car, whereas David's killer was still inviolate.

"I could kill him," muttered Humphrey to his unwelcome reflection in a shop window, annoyed by the calm of his face. As a boy he had attacked a man who was beating a horse, and had had to be dragged away. While vaguely proud of the memory, he had always been slightly apprehensive as to what his action might have signified. Without interrupting his steady strides, he held one of his long white hands out in front of him, imagining it futilely avenging, then aware of the sun on it. At the same time he realised that the wind which had raged through

Sunday had vanished without trace and that the pale sun shone from a high pale sky, casting the rich yellow light which is the paradox and the particularity of autumn. Against his will Humphrey responded, pleased with his alliterative description of the season, slightly soothed inside as well as out by the lingering warmth, noting the absolute stillness of the regularly spaced cherry trees which lined the hill up to the station, their remaining leaves as vivid as their spring blossoms.

Seaminster was a rail terminus and although, as always, he was early, the train was waiting. Looking the length of the carriage before he sat down, Humphrey wondered if Seaminster–London commuters were always so unhappy-faced, or whether the hovering blackness of his own mood was part of a descent of communal darkness. He wondered if Eleanor would have gone to her gallery that morning.

An excellent photograph of David in school uniform on the front page of *The Times,* and his pang renewed his anger. No one had helped David in that garden in the night, but too late a nation was aghast.

It is understood the body bore the mutilation which has characterised the killings carried out by the so-called Monster. . . .

So Maurice was keeping his secret. But . . . *mutilation.* A word which echoed through the imagination, paralysing it in the face of the unthinkable. The face . . . It couldn't have been on the face, or all the next of kin would have suffered an additional ordeal over which they could hardly all have kept silent. The sheet need be turned back no further.

Humphrey, roughly, turned to an inside page. A warning on the economic state of the country from an Opposition Front Bench spokesman. A demonstration in the gallery of the House of Lords . . . He would go to David's funeral and so, of course, would Maurice. To watch people. He would watch people, too, although if the same outsider had attended even two of the earlier funerals, he would have been caught by now, and David, this morning, would have been at school. If the Monster was an outsider . . . He had instincts about people, it had been Maurice who had once remarked on it. Because Humphrey had been less than enthusiastic about a detective-sergeant Maurice had thought was promising and who had turned out to be not a white hope but a rotten apple.

Any man's death diminishes me, because I am involved in Mankind. That wasn't in *The Times,* it was in the recesses of his head. The woman he could see making a bed in a first-floor room as the train on its way into London slowed down between the bulbous backs of Victorian houses, that woman was diminished by David's death, just as he was. Disappearing beyond recall, David had become mysterious by taking his mystery with him, the mystery which is all of us when we can no longer be called upon to open up, explain, share. Not that David when he was alive . . .

The crossword would be a more reliable distraction. Humphrey filled in clues until the train, having gathered speed again, slowed finally for its entry into its other terminus. It had left Seaminster on the end of the morning rush hour and was full rather than packed, but as he stepped out he was immediately a man in a crowd. Looking long-sighted over the hurrying backs in front of him, as he always did, he saw one which made him attempt, without much success, to quicken his already rapid strides. A collision with a British Rail trolley laden with luggage and out of its driver's control slowed him to the extent of losing sight of the hastening figure so far ahead of him, and his native pessimism, when he finally emerged through the ticket barrier onto the concourse, made him give no more than a hopeless glance round.

But at once he saw her again, separated from him now by comparatively empty ground. Eleanor, poised at the entrance to a narrow passage between left-luggage lockers, wearing the familiar casual tweed coat which with the cloudy dark hair had alerted him to her, her pale face in profile as she stood intent, a flat, brown-paper parcel clutched to her chest.

Humphrey set off, as eagerly as his cast of mind allowed him, across the space between them, slowing in the first instance only because it suddenly occurred to him that he should consider in advance what best to say to her, and how. Then slowing again, even as his steps quickened, because of something in her manner as she stood, her breathing agitated (he could see whatever she was carrying rising and falling between her hands), her head back now so that she was staring towards the Victorian ironwork of the station roof.

As Eleanor brought her head down and began to turn towards the concourse, Humphrey found himself moving speedily and laterally into the shelter of a revolving frame stuffed with paperback books, from which he could see and not, unless he was singularly unfortunate, be seen.

His instinctive sprint had in fact brought him close enough to be able to read the features of Eleanor's face and to confirm his impression of the size and shape of the parcel she was, he felt, almost passionately guarding. Pallor and strain, of course, to rend his heart, but to be put away for feeling sad about later, because of the expression which was superimposed upon them as very slowly Eleanor turned a circle, eyes darting, to resume the position in which he had first seen her.

Fear. Furtiveness.

Later, he knew, he would attempt to persuade himself that he had been mistaken, that Eleanor, in whatever situation she might find herself, could never look as he was seeing her look now. . . .

Loitering with intent. Acting in a suspicious manner.

The phrases floated in unbidden, and despite his indignation continued to repeat themselves in his head.

Eleanor was about to do something she didn't want anyone to see.

Humphrey all but turned away, in deference to her glaringly obvious wishes, then glued his eyes once more miserably upon her.

Almost at once she disappeared into the slit between the pewter-coloured blocks of lockers. He was lucky that there were some travel posters pasted across the end of one of the blocks facing the concourse, and he transferred himself to them at normal walking pace, rewarded on his arrival to discover some information about the train service between London and Seaminster. It was almost easy, from this position, to edge towards the corner of the block and let one eye overrun it.

Eleanor was about half-way along on the far side so that to watch her he scarcely needed to desert his shelter. She had her parcel now under her arm as at eye level she swung open the door of one of the smaller lockers. Humphrey dodged away as again she comprehensively surveyed her surroundings, then he returned to his post as she held out her package at arm's length, retaining it a few seconds before sliding it into the locker, inserting into the open door the money she had ready, closing the door, and twisting out the fat red key, which she put quickly into her handbag. Light was dim at the level where Eleanor was operating, but Humphrey was certain that, in the moment when she had held the parcel away from her, her face had lost its expressionless rigidity and twisted into a grimace. Pain? Revulsion? He had no way of knowing.

"Humphrey!"

Fear was leaping in her eyes, too obvious for him to deny it in retrospect, even though it was so quickly suppressed.

"Eleanor, dear." He put his hand on her arm, which was trembling. "I'm so dreadfully, dreadfully—"

"Did you catch the nine thirty-two?" asked Eleanor hurriedly. Her usual tranquil gaze was gone, replaced by rapid glances which slid aside.

"Yes, I—"

"So did I. I've just been to the ladies'. The train's been in ages. What have *you* been doing?"

"You might guess," he said, and thought she shrank back. "I'm too early for my appointment, as usual, and I saw these reduced books. Irresistible."

"Of course. Oh, Humphrey . . ."

She was reassured that he hadn't seen her down that narrow corridor, and her attention was back on her grief.

"Eleanor," he said, as if they were just meeting and the two sets of falsehoods had never been uttered. "I'm so very sorry. For you and for your mother and father. It's—unbelievable."

Before Maurice's visit he had thought of his next meeting with Eleanor, of how they would fence agreeably together about Fabia's party. He had hoped to find out how much she had enjoyed it. But it was a party which would never, now, be discussed, dissected, thanked for, assessed—except as the cause of David's death.

"It is unbelievable. But I can't imagine a time when it hadn't happened. It's like being suddenly born into a terrible new world. And still having memories of the old one."

He had merely suspected her originality of mind, and her words suffused him with a sense of potential riches which slid under his wretchedness and threatened to make him happy. (Although, as Emily had once said to him in a moment of petulance, his face hardly showed what he was feeling so he didn't have to worry about keeping it under control.) Thinking of Emily made him realise how well Eleanor had described his own reaction to bereavement.

"Oh my dear. I was in that world when Emily died. But I never found words for it. You won't stay there, but for a time, you know, you'll want to."

"Thank you, Humphrey." Her eyes, characteristically steady once more, gazed into his. He realised he still had his hand on her arm, and removed it. "But David was murdered."

It could be she was testing her ability to use the word without breaking down. If so, she had just passed the test, but at the cost of her pallor turning ashen and a sudden difficulty in breathing.

Humphrey this time took her firmly under the elbow, and felt her weight. "Shall we go and sit down somewhere and have some coffee? I think it would be a good idea if you're not in a hurry. Are you? But I don't suppose you'd have come up to town today if you hadn't had to—"

Her eyes were swivelling away again. "I've got to see a man about a picture. No precise time factor. Yes, I'd like to have coffee, Humphrey. But what about you?"

"I told you, I'm much too early as usual." He was, but he would have to make a telephone call if Eleanor didn't bring their meeting to a close within half an hour or so, something he himself had no intention of doing. He started steering her across the concourse. "Not here, I think."

In the taxi she seemed to relax, back into her sorrow. He had to fight his instinct to counter it with brittle, inconsequential talk, and reproved himself for his clown's tendencies. Apart from monosyllables Eleanor spoke only once on the short journey, but it was to say, "I'm glad it was *you* I met, Humphrey." In his head he found himself adding, "If I had to meet somebody." Then, to his annoyance, mentally answering her. *You wouldn't be glad if you knew I'd seen you . . .*

Eleanor giggled, rather than laughed, when she saw where the taxi was drawing up. "Is this necessary?"

"Absolutely," he said firmly. Then, with gambling boldness, "David would approve."

"Yes, oh yes . . ." She giggled again, more ominously. Perhaps he had made a mistake.

"Take it easy," he whispered, holding her firmly up the steps to the Ritz. When they had been shown to a table in a corner of the lounge and had settled themselves, he turned to look at her and saw she was sunk in a deep and distant calm.

It seemed as good a time as any to ask her some questions, if only those which anyone would ask.

"How is your mother?" he gently inquired.

"She's wonderful," said Eleanor, on a deep strangled sob. His hand moved without his volition across the table-top towards her, and he was devastated that she eased hers from beneath it. "Don't be too kind," she whispered. "Not in public. I don't want to break down in public."

"You won't." He knew she wouldn't, however near she came to it. He was going not merely on the strength he had always suspected, but on the power of the dissemblance she had shown that morning. . . . He was reproving himself, again, for his sensation of objective excitement. The sensation which followed the discovery of a mystery, wanting to penetrate it. It had helped Maurice before now, but not this time. Dear Lord, not this time.

"You mustn't stay away too long. Marie will need you. You won't go back to the gallery for a while?"

"Oh yes. But Marian's there and I shall keep going home. I'll be all right, Humphrey, but I'm afraid of it breaking Mummy and Daddy. It's against nature, isn't it, for the parent to lose the child."

"Yes." The coffee and its paraphernalia were being placed in front of them. Satisfying dark green cups with gilt rims. Strange, when one was in a no man's land of the spirit, how objects like coffee-cups and wallpapers and sofas had a sort of incidental clarity which drilled the physical brain, making an abnormal awareness of shapes and textures, while eluding the mind. (He had learned this eight years ago. He still remembered being told of Emily's death against a precise background.)

He poured them both coffee. There was a plate of tiny biscuits, and Eleanor took one and started to eat it. Humphrey thought she was unaware of her gesture.

He asked her if she had seen Jonathan.

"I—" Eleanor choked on the mouthful of biscuit. She was several seconds in paroxysm, gasping, coughing, her eyes squeezed shut. After drinking half her cup of coffee she was able to speak. "Sorry about that, Humphrey, I didn't know I was eating. Yes, I've seen him, we all have. He's wretched, need I say. He's venting it on being angry that David didn't change before going home."

"I wonder why he didn't."

"Everybody does." It must be his imagination that her eyes had again veered away. "He was so sensible always. I can only think it must have been because he was so delighted by all the fun he'd been having. Well, you saw him. He'd never enjoyed himself so much, I don't think. Humphrey . . ."

"Hold on."

This time he took her hand, and they sat in silence, both squeezing, until she was able to smile a brief thanks and take her hand back to pick up her cup. He poured them more coffee.

"Thank you," she said absently, staring across the room, showing him her calm profile. The nerve under one eye was jerking, filling him with a sense of tenderness which was as much to be controlled as the excitement with which it ran parallel. "I didn't know David very well." He suspected she was thinking aloud rather than talking to him. "We got on splendidly, but that isn't necessarily knowing someone. I never knew what made him tick, what he really got excited about. What made him sad. He never really seemed to be sad, but he must have been sometimes. I tried a few times, over the years, to find out. He just used to laugh, and kiss me or something, and tell me he was absolutely ordinary."

"When he was a little boy," he whispered, fearful of interrupting the flow.

"When he was a little boy he was quite uninhibited about his likes and dislikes and not wanting to do things he didn't like doing. But that's not what someone's like, either. I mean—it was only preferring cake to bread and butter and wanting to go out in the rain and so on. As he grew up . . . I didn't think about it all that much, but sometimes it baffled me."

"Your mother and father, did you ever talk about it with them?"

"Heavens, no. There wasn't anything to talk about. It's only now—now that there's no chance of ever learning anything. . . ."

The mystery, thought Humphrey, *the mystery the dead become.* "I know," he said.

"And now it's too late. Oh, Humphrey, the awful feeling that you didn't do enough . . . discover enough . . . take enough pains . . ."

"Don't!" He spoke for both of them. "You mustn't, Eleanor, it's crucifying. And let me tell you, so far as I'm concerned, I've always found your cousin easier to know than your brother," he said truthfully, and saw her eyes alter again, in some indefinable way, making him aware of something he realised he had known.

"You're very fond of Jonathan, aren't you?"

"Yes," she whispered. He sensed another struggle, and took her hand again.

"Don't reprove yourself for that, because David's dead."

"How did you know? Oh, Humphrey, I suppose you—"

"One feels remorse for the most ridiculous things. One has to dismiss it. Really, Eleanor." It was a process which had taken him far too long. Even now he could surprise himself sighing over the words *if only.*

"Thank you." They looked at one another in affectionate concern. He didn't squeeze her hand again in case it reminded her he was still holding it and prompted her to take it away.

"David," she said at last, and against his will he was aware again that her glance was faltering, "didn't seem to need anybody, where Jonathan does. Of course, I've been thinking about him—David—since—since Saturday, thinking about things I'd taken for granted. And I don't believe he needed his family, at least. I began to look back and I couldn't seem to remember him wanting Mummy, for instance, the way I did. I used to pick him up when he was little because he was so adorable and he used to wriggle down as soon as he could and dart off somewhere. I can see now that it used to upset Mummy. But he was always so good-natured and smiling and sunny. Her sunbeam, Mummy called him . . ."

He really ought to stop her. He was being disingenuous in telling himself it was doing her good to talk, he was encouraging her because he wanted to learn as much as he could, try to find out why Eleanor of the honest gaze had hidden a brown-paper parcel in a left-luggage locker and lied about it. . . . He made an effort.

"I think I understand, Eleanor, but I don't think it's something you should dwell on, beat yourself with."

She wasn't listening, she was still following her thoughts. "Funnily enough, I'd say the person David was nearest to needing was Jonathan. If he hadn't seen Jonathan for a day or two in the holidays, he'd be more likely to go round to Jonathan than Jonathan to come round to him. He . . . Oh!"

"What is it?"

Her hand was at her breastbone, her eyes were huge. "A wicked pang of indigestion." She tried to laugh.

"It can't be that mouthful of biscuit. Have you been eating?"

Slowly she focused on him. "I don't really know. That sounds crazy, but it's true. I know Mummy and I've been in the kitchen, sort of messing about. And Aunt Fabia's been over, doing things for us. I don't think we've eaten much because Auntie's been telling us off. Poor Aunt Fabia, she's devastated, she adored David. . . . Oh, Humphrey, I'm going to cry now, but very quietly, I promise you."

The coffee-pot just yielded two more cups. Eleanor did cry quietly, tears running down her cheeks. Humphrey passed her a large handkerchief and waited in silence until she used it discreetly to blow her nose and wipe her eyes. He really did think the weeping would have done her good. He looked at his watch without appearing to.

"I'll have to make a telephone call," he said, "and then we'll sit here without talking until your shell grows back."

"Indeed we won't!" She was on her feet; for the first time since he had seen her that morning there was something of her old manner. "I'm fine now, and you're going to be late for your meeting, if you haven't already missed it. I've been dreadfully selfish, you should have said—"

"I haven't missed my meeting," he said truthfully. "It's in Piccadilly and I shan't be more than five minutes late. Where are you on the way to?"

She looked away from him. "The City."

"Green Park tube takes one everywhere these days. Or the bus if you're not in a hurry."

"I'm not, I told you. And I know my way about London."

"I'm sure you do." He didn't want them to part while she was in this sudden mood of defensive independence. "Forgive me for forgetting for a moment that you've grown up."

This fact was not one he ever did forget. But his white lie had the desired effect.

"Oh, Humphrey . . . You've been wonderful, I can't tell you. Fate brought you this morning at just the right moment."

A moment too soon, he thought, with a queer sense of regret which briefly prevailed over his desire for enlightenment.

"I'm glad if I've helped." They were on the pavement now, and the sun was illumining the steady openness of Eleanor's face. A face that would age well, he thought, having such bones. "Not that anyone can, really. Distract perhaps, but not really help. Anyway—" he took her arm to draw her aside from the path of three youths who would obviously be shambling abreast across London, whatever the obstructions—

"if you suddenly feel you might like to hear me say 'Yes, Eleanor, I know, it *is* like that,' please be in touch."

"Thank you, Humphrey. Dear Humphrey." She smiled at him, and he was ashamed again at the shaft of happiness. Particularly as he saw the sudden pain in her face. "The inquest's tomorrow morning. It'll only last a few moments, apparently, because it'll be adjourned for further inquiries. In the meantime, Humphrey, they're cutting David up."

"Don't. And David isn't in that body."

"D'you believe he's somewhere else?"

"Yes," he said truthfully. His beliefs had nothing, really, to do with church services—he liked to visit churches when no service was being held—but with a constant vague excitement that his life was a staging post. "I hope you do."

"I want to believe it." Again, a look he was unable to fathom. But he would never want to know everything any other human being thought and felt. "The funeral's on Wednesday, half eleven at St. Saviour's Chapel. The police have said we can have him by then."

"It's the coroner who releases the body. The police are working very hard, Eleanor. I know Maurice Kendrick, and I've never seen an angrier man."

"Oh, Humphrey, I wasn't really getting at the police."

"I know, dear. And you'll be glad when the funeral's over, it's always better then." He hesitated. "Eleanor, I have two tickets for Covent Garden for Thursday night. *The Seraglio.* Would you feel you could come? David would approve as much as he would have approved of the Ritz this morning."

She looked at him this time without expression, and for a moment, and with a sense of shock, he saw David in her face. "Yes, Humphrey," she said. "I'd like to come."

He pressed her arm. "You'd better go now."

"Goodbye, dear kind Humphrey." She leaned up to kiss his cheek, then turned and walked swiftly away in the direction of the nearest entrance to Green Park tube station. He was still staring after her when she turned round, just short of the jutting red-and-blue notice. Annoyed at himself for his clumsiness, afraid of losing her confidence, he forced himself to wave an extravagant farewell to indicate he had been watching out of concern rather than suspicion, and was relieved that she responded. Then felt he had to turn and plunge the other way, so that he didn't see whether or not she disappeared underground.

CHAPTER 8

On Monday morning Kendrick was reminded of something he had temporarily forgotten: that there were things as bad to wake up to as murder. With murder, at least the victim's sufferings were over. He had surfaced naturally, before his alarm, and the recall of what he had to get up and do crept over the mindless innocence of his first waking moments, his grateful awareness that his migraine had gone, like a physical poison. He had to force himself out of bed and through the processes of dressing and having breakfast, resenting the signs of Indian summer in the pale blue sky and mild sunshine. The first thing he was glad about was that it was the father who opened the Holden front door. There was no surprise in his face—only, as the day before, the sorrowful courtesy Kendrick found so painful.

"Good morning, Superintendent. Please come in." Holden senior shut the door and they looked at one another in the rich gloom cast by the stained glass panels. The father's face was slashed diagonally in red and green. He said, "You want to see Bunny again? He hasn't left for school yet."

"Good, I hoped I'd be in time. Mr. Holden, we've now questioned all but two of the people who were at the Douglas party—" he'd found on his brief visit to the station that they hadn't been able yet to catch up with the French boys—"and there is no one who saw David at the end of the evening except with your son." Hurt again by the brief moaning sound the man made, Kendrick hurried on. "In the circumstances, I'm afraid I have to ask him to come with Sergeant Grant and myself to the station to answer a few more questions. And—we would like to have a look at his car to see if David was ever in it. It could be that Bruce gave David a lift but is now afraid of saying so, because of not having mentioned it at once." He hesitated. "One other thing, Mr. Holden."

"Yes, Superintendent?" Vague sounds issuing from the back of the hall were getting louder. "Come in here, will you?"

The top part of Kendrick's brain noted that the Holdens must have lit a fire the night before—the ashes in the grate were higher and had changed shape. The idea of Bruce Holden being responsible for David Douglas's death, and thus for the Monster murders, was attracting substance only because of the total absence of any other recognisable human being, and the chief constable, contacted even earlier, had agreed with Kendrick's suggestion that, particularly in view of the reasonable attitude on the part of the boy's father, it would be better in the first instance to ask for a search but not a search warrant.

"We were wondering, sir. . . . It would greatly assist our investigation—and your son, too, if he isn't involved in this business—if you would allow us to have a look round his room, and round the house and garden. I'll be frank with you—" he wished the calm face would give him some indication of the impression he was making—"I haven't got a search warrant, I don't want to apply for one, but if you would allow a very discreet presence, plain clothes of course, as with the car . . . As I said, sir, it would assist your son as well as our investigation."

"I see that, Superintendent. My wife won't be happy, but I agree with you that it would probably be for the best." The light which the day before had shone on the son's temple now showed the tic at work in the father's cheek. "When would you want—"

"As soon as possible, sir. As you'll appreciate . . ." Searches of suspect premises should be carried out before suspects or accessories had a chance to dispose of evidence. Kendrick saw the sudden horror in Holden senior's eyes, and read it as a sudden awareness of the possibility that his son after all . . . and his wife, out of a mother's loyalty . . .

"Of course, Superintendent. I understand." The possibility, to Kendrick's relief as well, seemed to have been successfully dismissed. "Perhaps you would agree to leaving your sergeant here while I make a few arrangements. I should like to come with Bunny to the station if there's no objection?"

"None, sir. If your son agrees."

"I must ask my sister if she will come and stay with my wife. And be present during the search. This is a protection for your men, I believe?"

"It is, sir."

"Yes . . . I must also ring the school. An upset stomach, perhaps."

"That should fill the bill. You have my assurance of course, sir—as things stand—of absolute police discretion as regards the action we are taking."

"Thank you, Superintendent."

"I'll ask Sergeant Grant to come in. And if I may telephone for another car . . ."

"Please do. Behind you. Bunny's having breakfast. Do you want to see him?"

"At the station." He forced himself to another question whose answer he dreaded. "How is your wife?"

"Not very well, Superintendent. She's highly strung, and inclined to suffer over matters less distressing than this one. But she's had a few hours' sleep. Mary will look after her. . . . I'll bring Bunny's car keys with me to the station, if I may. Then your people can simply come and take it and not trouble my wife. The garage is locked and no one can possibly—"

"That's quite in order, sir." He found himself wishing Bruce's father had been less admirable. Back at the station, he went at once to make further inquiries about the French boys, but they had still not been contacted. "We know they took the ferry yesterday morning, sir, but after Le Havre they melted away. Both of them live near Lyons, and were planning on making another week's holiday out of a slow journey south. Secondary roads, long days in the open. The boys' hosts don't even remember their car number, but we've been able to contact their parents and they'll surely be ringing home."

"We'll have to hope so." But the odds were so much against the boys having anything different to say from what had been said by the other Douglas guests.

The further questioning of Bruce Holden took a long time, because of Kendrick's insistence that his youth, and the fact that they had no more to go on than unique motive and unrivalled opportunity, called for frequent stops for rest and refreshment. Kendrick hated each moment of it, observing the increasing agitation of the boy's facial nerve, the way his eyes grew redder and smaller. It was worse, once the statement about the party was signed, superintending the questioning of Bruce on his whereabouts and activities the nights of the Monster murders, trying to turn his own instinctive excitement into compassionate regret each of the four times it was established that Bruce had been ostensibly at home and in bed the night a girl died. On two of the four nights, Bruce told them, he'd come home towards midnight after dropping a friend off—a different friend each time, which meant an inspector and a sergeant going out on two verifications. Kendrick decreed that the two boys be approached on the pretext of seeking corroboration of a claim by their friend Bunny to have noticed the same possibly suspicious character on the street on each of the nights concerned, and told the father and the son this was the way he was going to play it. Both boys greeted Bruce's imaginary sighting with the astonishment Kendrick expected, but gave him the incidental corroboration of the alibi up to midnight which he had sought.

In neither case quite late enough—each girl had died in the early hours of the morning.

So everything was possible, and there was no shred of evidence.

In one of the breaks he went back to the Holden house.

He knew the doctor who was coming down the stairs as the CID sergeant let him into the hall.

"Is this really necessary, Superintendent?"

Last time they had met, at Rotary, it had been what would Maurice like to drink. Kendrick saw John Wright's attitude, now, as a sort of judgement on him for inflicting injury which might permanently damage an innocent (he had been trying not to let the thought through) and as such, in a strange way, he found himself welcoming it.

But he must voice his justification.

"Think about Seaminster just now, John. Think of parents and daughters." He held the doctor's eye through the bands of colour which suffused his face from the glass in the front door. "The nature and scale of these crimes may have forced our investigation out of the usual bounds, but it's had to. D'you think I'm happy about this? For the boy's sake please keep quiet about what you've just found out."

"No press involvement, then?"

"Dear God, no. That's my real nightmare now. I haven't a leg to stand on. But I assure you it's for the boy first and foremost that I dread it."

"Yes, well . . ."

"Let me come out with you a moment." Kendrick took the shrug as unenthusiastic acquiescence and accompanied the doctor to his car, making sure that part of the shrubbery screened him from the road. His photograph was appearing in the papers so regularly now, and semi-regularly on television. It was a distinct handicap. "You're here because of the mother?"

"I am." The doctor hesitated, scanning Kendrick's face. "If it makes you feel better, I'll tell you I think she's the type to flip rather easily."

"Thank you, John. I thought that, too, and the father implied . . . Has it happened?"

"It's been necessary to administer a strong sedative. Put her to sleep, not to mince words. Her sister-in-law's with her; she seems to be as calm and strong as her brother. What a contrast! Strange how people . . ." The doctor pulled himself up. Deciding, thought Kendrick sadly, that he was in danger of unbending too far to someone who had all at once become alien.

"It's the boy I'm really worried about of course, John. Perhaps you can have a look at him later?"

"Whenever that may be."

"I know. We're taking a long time because we're working very slowly, with tea and sympathy. No, I'm not being facetious. I feel pretty sick. I thought I'd be over the moon at the scent of a suspect at last, and I'm anything but." He was relieved to discover that he was speaking the truth. If there had been one point at which the Monster's timetable had failed to fit the possibility of Bruce Holden, he would have been profoundly thankful.

"Hm. If nothing crops up I hope you'll let him go to school tomorrow."

"Of course. At this stage nothing whatever must appear to be different—"

"If he's fit enough, that is. All right, Maurice, I have to get on. I don't envy you."

"Who could?"

"I'd rather you didn't talk to Mrs. Holden."

"So would I. I shall have to eventually unless things resolve themselves, but I promise you I'll leave it out today. John—" he put a diffidently detaining hand on the doctor's arm, aware of being suppliant, uncomfortably suffused with memories of the earliest part of his career—"what sort of boy?"

"A very normal, ordinary, average boy," said Dr. Wright severely. "I've attended the family for most of his life and there has never been anything out of the way." He got rid of Kendrick's hand by feeling in his pocket for his car key.

"Let us hope," said Kendrick, stepping slightly back from the car, "that my men have discovered there's just no way in which Bruce could have left the house in the night undetected. Goodbye, John."

But what the inspector had to tell him, apart from the negative fact that there was nothing at all in the boy's room, or in any other part of the house they'd been able to examine, to connect him with the Monster murders, was that once his parents had gone to bed Bruce could have crept downstairs without being seen or heard, and out through front, back, or patio door.

"To make it that much easier, sir, his room's on its own on a sort of half-landing. On its own apart from a utility room and a second bathroom, that is. He'd only have had to sneak down the last bit of staircase. The sister-in-law has often slept here, and she told us right out that Mr. and Mrs. Holden shut their door at night and don't need to come out at all, because of having their own loo off their bedroom. It couldn't be easier so far as the logistics are concerned. She's said she thought they might have been disturbed if a car was ever taken, but she had to admit there was nothing to stop the boy just walking out of the house and away at night without anyone knowing anything about it." Although he and Kendrick were standing in an empty hall with a full view of the staircase, the inspector lowered his voice. "So far as the wife's concerned, sir, there's a bit of a history of nervous trouble. Pity she's had to be mixed up in this."

"It is a pity, Inspector. For the whole family."

A pity something so disagreeable was having to be made out of what might turn out to be nothing to do with them. Or might not. He had to remember that, as well. He wished he wasn't remembering so clearly the boy asking him, eye to eye, if he'd have been likely to say he could have killed David if he *had* killed him. . . .

"We'll be having a look round the main bedroom now the mother's asleep, sir. Everywhere else we've just about covered. There's nothing. Nothing in the bins, and no evidence of anything having been burned, inside or out. Not that the Monster would need to get rid of anything, never having given us a clue."

"That's right, Inspector." There had never been so much as a speck of human substance, clothing, possessions, which hadn't been attributable to the victim. "But if he's saved press cuttings, kept a diary . . ."

"I hadn't thought of that, sir, but yes." The young, fresh-faced inspector contrived to look chastened and cheered at the same time. "We haven't found anything like that as yet, but I take your point. There's nothing written by the boy as far as we can see, apart from some old school exercise books. Doesn't seem to be the writing type. Nor the reading, for that matter. Not many books at all in his room, and no murder stories. There are quite a lot of books downstairs, including a few Agathas and such like. Clothes and shoes all in order, nothing appearing to have been stashed away, nothing abnormally creased or dirty. No evidence in the garden of anything having been recently buried, but we've not finished out there as yet. All right if we carry on?"

"Yes, but cut it as short as you can without skimping."

When he got back to the interview room he found father and son half-way through the latest cups of tea. He had left it to the father to decide whether or not to tell the son about the police in the house, and he took him out of the room to thank him again for his co-operation.

"Everything seems to be in order, sir, and my men have almost finished."

"Thank you, Superintendent. I've told Bunny. However careful your men are, he might notice something. . . . What happens now?"

"Nothing, I hope. And that your son will go to school in the normal way in the morning. You know you have my assurance of total discretion by the police as things stand. And of course we continue to pursue our inquiries in other directions. I must stress, sir, that despite what has gone on today we have no grounds beyond motive, opportunity, and the appearance of things for connecting your son with the murder of David Douglas. So that so far as the other murders are concerned, of course—"

"I understand, Superintendent. It is not the least dreadful aspect of this dreadful day," said Holden quietly, "that I find myself hoping for another Monster murder. I realise that my son will now be kept under surveillance at night. And that if there are no more murders you will have one more negative reason to suspect him of the five which have already taken place. And to continue the surveillance indefinitely."

"It's a wretched business," said Kendrick, unable to deny and unwilling to confirm. "I hope with all my heart it will soon be resolved in a way which proves your son has no connection with any of it. There is one thing I should like to ask you, sir." Kendrick was aware of tension as he spoke, making him realise how his coming question had been disturbing his subconscious. "Do you, your wife, or your son know any members of the Seaminster police force personally?"

The man's smile hit him in the solar plexus. "The mark of the Monster, Superintendent? I've learned from your public announcements that it was on the boy's body. I don't know any policemen in Seaminster personally. Last night I asked my wife and my son that question, and they both assured me they know none, either."

"You know no one—" this was even trickier—"who works for Forensics? The Scene of Crimes Officer and his assistants are civilians. Likewise the mortuary people."

"I asked that question, too, and had the same answer. My son must have committed all the murders, or none of them. I am convinced, Superintendent, that he committed none."

"Thank you, sir." For a few seconds Kendrick returned the steady gaze, convinced in his turn that Holden was speaking what he believed to be the truth. "We'll go back now, and I'm afraid I shall ask Bruce these questions, too. Then you'll both be taken home."

There was an additional small pang in seeing that the boy was smoking. "Not my idea!" the sergeant and the WPC said in immediate chorus. The father leaned over and gently took the cigarette from between Bruce's fingers, crushing it out in the ashtray which was innocent of any other stubs.

Kendrick motioned him to sit down, sat down himself, and asked the last few questions which had been clarifying themselves under his activities of the past hour. The boy answered in the negative, and without visible agitation, those about possible contacts in the police or Forensics, but his father had prepared him. . . . For the final question Kendrick put his elbows on the scratched table-top between them and leaned forward, noticing for the first time the worn initials cut into it on the side of the interviewee, appreciating absently the sleight of fingernail which must have gone into its execution.

"Tell me, Bruce, did you kill David Douglas?"

"No! I swear to you I didn't!" There was a further pang for Kendrick, that in twenty-four hours defiance had turned to despair. "When he laughed I ran out of that room and out of the house and into my car and I never saw him again." Bruce Holden had said this, in almost the identical words, each time Kendrick had asked him, and he had asked him at regular intervals throughout the morning.

"I'll get someone to take you and your father home now, Bruce." Once he'd checked that his men had finished and left the house. "All that's happened today is a secret between your family and the police. You'll both tell your mother that, won't you? And I do very strongly advise you not to say anything to your friends when you go to school tomorrow." His experience had taught him that vanity could take seriously self-jeopardising forms. "Not, I'm sure, that you'll want to—"

"I'm to go—to school?" The boy had jerked up his head in astonishment.

"Of course. In view of how and when David died, and of the other deaths which have taken place in Seaminster, we've had to do what we've done today. We've finished now."

"But you'll still go on suspecting me!" The glimpse of normality had brought back some spirit.

"We don't suspect you, Bruce. We don't suspect anyone. You're simply the only person we're able to question, the only person as yet who is known to have had a hostile connection with a Monster victim the last thing before the victim's death. And you've been honest enough to tell me that David as David wasn't your favourite person. But that's all. Think about it in that light when you get home, and you'll see that we had to do what we've done today."

Kendrick felt a surge of gratitude towards the amorphous deity in which he thought he believed for enabling him to put it so honestly and yet so reassuringly. And for very slightly clearing the young unhappy face at which he was staring.

"So—that's all."

"Yes. And if you've told us the truth it'll continue to be all." If the boy started to think about being watched, there was a wise man at home who would know the best thing to say. "By the way, you left your pierrot hat at the party. Did you miss it?"

All morning the blush had failed to come so suddenly and spectacularly. "It fell off in that little room." The boy had to clear his throat to be able to go on speaking. "When I . . . Just before David pulled off the wig . . . When I ran out I didn't think about it, and I didn't think until I got home and started to take the costume off." He paused, and Kendrick knew he was thinking, if only for an instant, of something other than the nightmare he was having. "Gosh, I'll have to give it back to Phil, he lent it to me. Is the hat . . . ? Did anyone . . . ?"

"The hat's safe. Jonathan Douglas was bringing it to school today to give back to you. He'll bring it again tomorrow, no doubt." He paused. "We have the suit for the moment, but we'll let you have it back very soon. I shouldn't attempt to go back to school this afternoon, try and rest. The hat, by the way, was found in that little room where you say you lost it." There was no doubt the little room had played a part. But as climax or prelude to Bruce's misguided evening?

He said goodbye to father and son, on the further assurance that they wouldn't have to wait long, then went to the Incident Room to ask for someone to take them home once it had been ascertained the police had left their house. Then told everyone in the room not to get excited about Bruce Holden, and to know nothing about the boy's visit to the station or their colleagues' visit to him. Also, of course, to depute the first of what must become Bruce's nightly tails. Which, reflected Kendrick gloomily, would go on and on into the future if there were no more murders. What had Holden senior said? *I find myself hoping for another murder.* Kendrick had found himself hoping, from the start, that the Monster would not be young.

At four o'clock he brought to the surface Humphrey's theory about the nature of David Douglas, and his own idea about testing the impact of it on David's family. He drove himself to the Frederick Douglas house in his own car.

The daughter was there as well.

"I've got a partner," she told Kendrick, when he was sitting down with them, "and it's not very good being in the gallery at the moment. I went in earlier but people were treating me as a special case just by trying so hard to be ordinary." She laughed disagreeably. "And I'd rather be with Mummy and Daddy."

Kendrick wondered if that were true, the pain in her eyes when she looked at her parents was so patent.

"Do you think," he asked gently, as he received back from the

mother a second cup of the tea she had insisted on making, "that your
son could have been so pleased with the success of his disguise at the
party that he would have deliberately gone home dressed up and alone
as a sort of ultimate challenge?"

There was silence for a few seconds in which he heard the daughter
catch her breath. Eleanor Douglas turned her disconcerting eyes on
him.

"Yes," she said. Almost, it seemed, in triumph.

"You say that from your knowledge of your brother's character?"

"If David left Aunt Fabia's in girl's clothes, he did it deliberately."

Kendrick looked at the other two faces, each of which, on the same
instant, was acquiescently lowered.

"Thank you."

He felt inclined to trust such a judgement, to believe that David
Douglas had intended to walk as a girl into the derelict garden in Birch
Road, alone or at the side of Bruce Holden.

CHAPTER 9

Kendrick made it to Humphrey's by ten to eight, and that was after
having gone home to change and have a leisurely bath. The unfamiliar-
ity of the routine made him stand suddenly still in the bathroom doorway and calculate that he probably hadn't gone through it once in the
past three or four weeks. Baths had been snatched at bedtime or on
getting up, and at night he'd taken off the clothes he'd put on in the
morning. Agreeably aware of his aftershave, he told himself as he drove
to Humphrey's that he mustn't fall into the trap he'd warned his men
against last thing before leaving the station: to let the sense of urgency
slacken now that there was somebody to keep an eye on. To feel a false
confidence that there would be no more deaths.

"No kitchen for you tonight," said Humphrey by way of greeting.

Kendrick noted the unaccustomed colour in his cheeks, although it quickly ebbed, and the way Humphrey's pale blue eyes, after one penetrating look, veered aside.

"How are you, Hump?"

"I'm all right, Maurice, I'm fine. Went up to London this morning for a meeting. Long and tedious, but I was glad of the distraction. Met Eleanor Douglas on the train, as a matter of fact, and dallied with her over a coffee. I think she was glad to talk."

Humphrey led the way to the sitting-room, beyond whose windows the walled garden glowed in the lights he had installed so that he could go on looking at it after dark. "Sit down, Maurice. Sherry?"

"Please. Miss Douglas say anything interesting?" The question was reflex, and he immediately regretted it.

"How d'you mean, Maurice, interesting?" Humphrey used a damask napkin from a table drawer to wipe up the drop of sherry which had slopped from the glass he had started to pick up.

"I suppose I mean about her brother, any more clues as to his character."

"Yes, of course. Try this." Humphrey set the glass down on the three-legged table by Kendrick's chair. "She talked about him quite a lot. But only to tell me how little she really knew him—how little any of them knew him. I've never heard her say that before, but as soon as she said it I knew just what she meant, somehow. Looking back, David was almost too easy and cheerful and dispassionate to be quite real—especially as he was only sixteen. . . . Oh, *Maurice!*"

"Sit down, Hump. The Victorians would have put something on the tombstone to the effect that God had retrieved his own."

"Except that there wasn't anything at all saintlike about David. Not in the least."

"That wouldn't have deterred the Victorians. . . . I'm sorry, Hump. I think you and I both have a tendency to be facetious when we're disturbed. This is the worst business I've ever had to deal with. I know, of course, that I'm going to do some talking about it before the night's out, but I'll try at least to postpone it. Which won't really be difficult—I can't tell you how good it is to be sitting here like this, with no duty to upset you or monitor what you say."

He saw the flush pass again over Humphrey's face. "I'm glad to hear that, Maurice. Anyway, I'm upset enough as it is, and I'm unlikely to

say anything else worth your taking note of. But you must know by now
that I shan't mind how much shop you talk."

"I do know, yes. . . . The garden still looks good. I'd like a house
like this, but there aren't any."

"Not quite like this, no," agreed Humphrey complacently. "But there
are two or three similar sorts of little places at intervals along the cliff
between the bigger ones, and I'll keep a lookout."

"I could have run straight out of the bungalow," said Kendrick,
"which it was my instinct to do, but I made myself wait, and then it
became less urgent, of course. But I'd still like to move, I think."

"Because the bungalow feels too big, or because of Miriam? Forgive
me, Maurice, I shouldn't—"

"Both, I think. The garden's certainly too big for a policeman as busy
as I am at the moment, even with Rowlands one day a week. I like to do
the creative things myself anyway, or at least some of them. I suppose I
should be thankful this awful business has come while the garden's
going to sleep. The leaves, though . . ."

"This garden's small enough not to get on top of me and become a
chore instead of a pleasure."

"A symphony in gold and brown," said Kendrick without thinking
about it, then immediately aware, as at other times, of the vague and
cliché-ridden quality of his language compared with Humphrey's.

But Humphrey said, "Oh thank you!" as if he had received the ultimate in compliments, and both men sat a few moments in silence,
looking out on the sandstone wall which Humphrey had covered in
bright-leaved plants and creepers but not smothered because of the wall
itself being beautiful, and the patterned path wandering between the
small sections of grass. Kendrick, to his chagrin if he hadn't been so
protectively fond of Hump, had never yet been able to detect a daisy or
a dandelion in that grass, and didn't think there was even any moss. No
gardener, either, but the garden *was* very small, and predominantly
shrubby. Kendrick felt better than he'd felt for a long time, sitting back
and sipping Humphrey's excellent sherry. Not because Bruce Holden
had appeared on the scene, even though he had to guard against a
return of the excitement that someone with a face had at last broken
into the blankness of his search—rather, he thought, because of the
relief that today's special discomfort was over and the boy left in not
too bad a shape.

Relaxing made him realise how weary he was. He would also have to guard against falling asleep after dinner, although he knew that if he did Humphrey would put some music on the record-player and be glad for him that he was able to drop off. But it would be disappointing for Hump, who was probably looking forward to further expressing the horrors of the Douglas tragedy almost as much as he was himself. For Kendrick there had always had to be one person, and now it couldn't be Miriam. . . .

"I gave them your number, Hump, just in case. But I can hardly imagine anyone needing to use it tonight."

They dined by the light of red candles, drawing the curtains against the moonlit sea because of Kendrick realising that Seaminster's currently most photographed citizen would be forming part of a *tableau vivant* to passers-by. Humphrey, following avocado pears and an apology for the ease of their preparation, presented a casserole of great succulence and subtlety, a filmy pudding, and some Stilton. They sat a long time over the meal, having no difficulty in keeping off the subject which was foremost for both of them, perhaps because with each glass of claret it was easier to flow from aspect to aspect of other matters which they had in common.

Humphrey maintained his embargo on the kitchen, insisting on Kendrick going back into the sitting-room to await the coffee. Kendrick went instantly to sleep, waking as Humphrey set some brandy by the coffee-cup steaming on the table beside him. He felt refreshed out of all proportion to the healing qualities of a catnap—then saw from a glance at the mantel clock that Humphrey had allowed him three-quarters of an hour. No doubt the kitchen was immaculate, and he had been tiptoed in on several times.

"Thank you, Hump, I must have needed that, I feel wonderful. Well, I could do, if I didn't keep thinking about what I had to do today. The lad you saw dancing with David—Bruce Holden—I had to take him in for questioning because among all the Douglas guests there wasn't one who saw David at the end of the evening either by himself or with anyone else."

"What does the boy say?"

"That he left the house on his own in a fury when he realised David was David. He's stuck to that the whole time. I don't think there's any doubt David was playing a rather unkind game. And eventually, according to Bruce, he got him into a room on their own and pulled his wig off just as Bruce was going to kiss him. If Bruce's story's true, that is—and we've no evidence whatever to suggest that it isn't—simply the fact that David asked for trouble and was then found dead after being seen with nobody but Bruce. Bruce says he stormed out of the house and into his car and away home. No evidence of David anywhere in the car, I heard that just before I left the office. But of course that doesn't really tell us much. It was a fine night and Bruce could easily have suggested a stroll. The worst part, Hump, is that it came over the radio that David's murder bore all the marks of the Monster, and then it was obvious to Bruce and his family what the implications were. To make matters more complicated, the mother's an hysteric and the father a saint. While the boy seems—well, just so straightforward, all the reactions I'd expect from a young man whose strongest suit wasn't his modesty."

"Maurice, how awful for you." Humphrey spoke faintly, dazzled by his sudden inward picture of Eleanor among the left-luggage lockers.

"And I had to have two bites of it." Kendrick stretched his long limbs with conscious enjoyment in the comfortable chair. "The so-called routine questioning on Sunday turned sour because of the mother having heard the radio—and then of course when everyone at the party had been questioned and not come up with anything, I had to bring him in this morning."

"So what now?"

"One of my men standing in sight of the Holden house during the hours of darkness. Unless and until there's another murder. And the chief superintendent giving regular pep talks to his men not to relax their vigilance in other directions. It's been a bit hard for me myself, Hump, not to make too much of the fact of at last having someone in my sights who was actually known to have had hostile contact with a Monster victim within hours of that victim's death."

"The death was absolutely to the Monster pattern? Forgive me, Maurice, I'm not trying to get you to tell me—"

"Ye-e-s. The Monster mark was executed more tentatively than in any of the other cases, but that was to be expected if the Monster was beginning to have doubts about his victim's sex. There's no doubt at all that it *was* his mark. There is, of course, a chance that the murderer was someone who knows the Monster's signature, but that's something I'm just about discounting."

"If it was someone who knew the Monster's signature—that would probably mean, wouldn't it, that David was killed because he was David?" Humphrey got up and drew the curtains over the golden garden.

"It would, yes."

Humphrey drew an interior curtain over one train of thought. "And it could also mean that it might be one of your men, or their nearest and dearest. Or a mortuary attendant, or—"

"I take your point. And I think I'm grateful to you for putting it into words. You've made me realise that I haven't wanted to face the implication, it's a pretty uncomfortable one. But thank heaven there's really no need to think about it. Time, place, style—all in line with the Monster."

"More coffee, Maurice? And a little more brandy? May I ask you if *you* think it could have been Bruce Holden?"

"Coffee, yes please. And a very little brandy. I know it *could* have been Bruce Holden. It's very much a physical possibility, including his superior brawn. But I don't *feel* it was. Certainly all my instinct cries out against the idea of Bruce being the Monster, although I suppose I can just imagine him losing his temper in a sudden sexual rage at his humiliation, and strangling David before the red mist cleared. And he did admit that David as David wasn't one of his favourite people— they're both at St. Saviour's. Were. But we can't get away from the Monster's signature. I had to ask, of course, if Bruce knew anyone in the police, or a mortuary civilian, and got a no. From the father as well, who appears to be just about the most honest and reliable man in the world. One thing, Hump . . ." Kendrick stopped to drink coffee.

"What's that?" Humphrey wished he could feel as relaxed as his friend so obviously was. But Maurice had a lot of relaxing to catch up with.

"I don't want it to be Bruce. I shall really be glad if something turns up to prove it couldn't be. I was afraid at one point . . . The policeman in me, the longing to bring it all to an end, might really want to pin it on a schoolboy rather than a nobody. I'm relieved to find I'm still human."

"Of course you are!" Humphrey gave a short sharp laugh in his relief.

"You can always come to me for reassurance on that point. And I understand there having been a bit of a struggle at first."

"I shall get stick," said Kendrick gloomily, but too languorous and temporarily contented to feel what he was expressing, "if this ever comes out. It's dead secret, Hump. Not just because I haven't a leg to stand on so far as evidence is concerned. More, I assure you, for the sake of the boy, who will go back to school tomorrow as if nothing has happened. I had a foretaste of how things could be for me when I went to the Holden house today. We were searching it, which was an additional bit of misery, but the father was marvellously co-operative. John Wright was there seeing to the mother, and reacted to my arrival as if he'd just kicked over a stone and discovered a nest of maggots. I knew how he felt, of course. He was a bit mollified when I'd persuaded him I was unhappy and that Bruce wasn't to be branded in public."

"I'm so very sorry, Maurice. When I think of that party . . . Forty-eight hours ago I was there, yet it's *aeons* gone. Time is such a tricksy thing, it operates on so many levels one can't—"

Humphrey's discourse was cut short by the imperious note of the telephone bell, sounding from beside his chair. Kendrick gripped his hands together, aware of each muscle in his body tautening, almost praying that it wouldn't be for him. But after a few seconds of listening Humphrey said, "Yes, he's here, I'll hand you over," and Kendrick found himself standing beside Humphrey's chair.

"Sit down," Humphrey whispered, before smiling reassuringly and carrying out the coffee tray, pulling the door to behind him with the crook of one long thin foot.

Kendrick perched on the edge of the vacated chair, snapping his name into the receiver.

"Good evening, sir. I'm sorry, sir—"

"What is it, Peter?"

"There's just been a call in, sir. They've found another body."

Rage and disappointment were so keen he felt the instant pumping in his temples. But Bruce Holden's father could be reassured.

"Where?"

"In that bit of wood off Villiers Street. The other side of town, near where—"

"I know Villiers Street. The Monster?"

"Well, sir, not as you're meaning it."

"I don't know what *you're* meaning, Sergeant." He made a rare foray
into sarcasm. "I suppose it was another transvestite?"

"Well—yes, sir."

"*What?*"

"I'm sorry, sir, I should have said right away, but I didn't quite know
how. . . ." Kendrick had never heard his Sergeant Grant so bemused,
but it didn't sound like the slight alcoholic fuddle of his own brain. "It's
not a murder victim and it's not a young man. It's a man of about fifty,
sir, dressed up like Old Mother Riley. There was a knife nearby which
Forensics—"

"All right, Peter, I'll come at once. He'll still be *in situ,* I hope?"

"Oh yes, sir, the discovery's only just been made. Shall I meet you
there?"

"If you will, Peter. Thanks for not wasting any time."

Kendrick tore out to the kitchen, grabbing his coat from the hall as
he passed the pegs.

Humphrey was at the sink. Nothing was out of order except the
coffee things, sparkling upside down in the drainer.

"A big development, Hump, I've got to fly. I'm glad we were allowed
to have our dinner and then some time."

"So am I. Keep in touch." As he passed Kendrick in order to hurry
and open the front door, Humphrey found the situation familiar. It
must have taken place at least once before.

"Of course. It's been the best evening for weeks. I'll try to talk to you
tomorrow."

Kendrick was glad to see the low full moon, so brilliant the light
from the elegant street lamps was puny. It was eleven o'clock on a
Monday night and he exceeded the speed limit through back streets
without encountering a single other vehicle, smiling despite himself as,
at one sharp corner, his tyres squealed with fictional stridency. He drew
in behind the three cars, boxed in by Sergeant Grant before he had
closed his door.

"That was good going, sir. I got waylaid—"

"Come along, Sergeant."

Once again it was a constable who stood where the trees began. They
had to wind among them behind Sergeant Grant's torchlight for several
minutes before seeing other bobbing lights. The Scene of Crimes Officer

and the doctor straightened up to greet them. The screen was in place, the photographer must have come and gone.

"Good evening, sir," said Detective-Inspector Riley from his position outside the area of most significance. Kendrick found himself reflecting irrelevantly that as good manners continued to crumble, those in the police hierarchy might well be the last to disappear. "This is a rum go. The SOCO will tell you."

Again Kendrick joined a Scene of Crimes Officer behind a temporary screen.

"My hat doesn't fit this job, Superintendent. Natural causes. Coronary, on a preliminary look." The moonlight showed Kendrick the doctor's confirmatory nod. "But there's blood on one of the hands and signs of a struggle, as if someone got away. And there's this knife. Seems like there's blood on the tip." The SOCO's assistant held out a small plastic bag in illustration, the light he was holding wavering as he did so over the body on the ground. They were in a clearing and the moon was dwarfing the artificial light as it had dwarfed it on the cliff road. Looking down, Kendrick saw a bulky body on its side, enlarged perhaps beyond its obvious size by the voluminous long dark coat. Man-size black shoes protruded from beneath it, and the felt hat and grey wig partially rolled away from the head brought back the memory of David Douglas's two hairlines so that he felt his gorge rising.

"Hat and wig all in one, sir. There was a heavy scarf—more like a muffler—half over the face, but obviously put there by the dead man himself." The SOCO indicated another, larger, plastic bag propped up against the screen. "Altogether a rather fishy picture, I'll say that before I've looked any further."

Kendrick had stopped listening. "The photography's done?"

"Oh yes, Superintendent."

"Then you can turn him over. I want to see him full face."

"Of course. Jenkins!"

"And get the hat and wig out of the way, will you?"

Hat and wig were accommodated in an even larger plastic bag, while Kendrick stared with increasing surprise and discomfort at the face now revealed to be surmounted by neat grey-brown hair. It was suffused and distorted by the manner of death, but there was no mistaking it. He had thought with horror of one day looking down in recognition at a young woman, but never at the Monster. . . .

"I know him," he said heavily.

"Superintendent?"

"Charles Hutchinson, Beckwith Avenue. I think it's number thirty, and I know it's a tree name, the Beeches, or the Elms, or something like that."

"There was a Yale key in the coat pocket, Superintendent. That was all there was."

"All right, no need to show me." Last time he had looked at the face on the ground it had been grinning as its owner told him a joke, and John Wright had been grinning, too, as the three of them had a final brandy at the bar following the annual Rotary dinner. June, was it? July? As Hump had said, time was a tricksy thing.

"All right, Basil," said Kendrick to the SOCO. "I'll leave you to it here and see you or another of your ilk at whatever it is Beckwith Avenue. I expect I shall be there for some time. Come with me, Peter. Inspector, get some men round to Thirty Beckwith Avenue, will you, and to cover this ground."

As Sergeant Grant's car followed his through the deserted streets, Kendrick began to think about the time of death, wondering if Charlie Hutchinson could have made his grotesque way across town to die later in the same night he had killed David. Again, he mustn't get excited without proven cause. Transvestism was generally a harmless perversion and Charlie's might just have included liking to walk abroad, and perhaps he had taken an apple with him and decided to cut it up and eat it in the clearing where he'd died. Perhaps it had stuck in his throat. It was understandable that he wouldn't have wanted any marks of identification on him when he went out dressed up.

Charlie was a widower, had been for some time. Children? None around, but when Kendrick pushed at his brain he thought he remembered some sort of early tragedy surrounding an only daughter.

His temples were pumping again as he drew up outside No. 30 Beckwith Avenue. The pre-war house was in darkness, but moonlight and street-light revealed the name *Beechcroft* hung on two short chains from the entrance to the porch. He was sure now it was the right house; he'd either picked Charles up here sometime, or brought him home. Sergeant Grant, however, rang the bell and used the knocker when they reached the front door, repeating the processes before successfully applying the key.

The house, immediately they stepped inside it, had for Kendrick an air of being uninhabited. After doing no more than put his head round the doors to the tidy downstairs rooms, he ran upstairs and pulled out drawers and looked in cupboards for evidence of the daintier side of a transvestite's life—feminine underwear, dresses, shoes.

There was none to be found, merely tidy piles of the good and conventional men's clothes Charles was always to be observed wearing. There was, though, a scrapbook under a stack of bed linen in the wardrobe of the room where it was clear Charlie slept, together with a diary. Kendrick put them gingerly on the bed and started to turn the pages. When he began to laugh aloud Sergeant Grant came flying across the landing to join him.

"What is it, sir?"

Kendrick, kneeling by the bed, rocked back on his heels gasping. "Just evidence on a plate, Peter. Just everything cut and dried after weeks and weeks of nothing." Not forgetting himself even in his near-hysteria, Kendrick put out a careful finger towards one of the books, not quite touching it. "This is a record in press cuttings of the Monster murders. This—" he moved his finger above the other book—"is a diary, in which there is a sort of asterisk and the word 'tonight' in red on each of the nights a murder was committed. We've found the Monster, Peter, and after all the poor wretched men in the street we've interviewed and sometimes grilled, he's turned out to be my respected acquaintance—Seaminster's respected citizen—Charles Hutchinson, one-time secretary of the local Rotary, magistrate, well-known local architect. . . . Why didn't we give *him* the third degree, Peter, why didn't we?"

"Steady on, sir. You look dreadfully pale. Shall I see if I can find some brandy?"

"No, Peter, I've drunk brandy already tonight—I was actually relaxing when you rang me. But I don't think I can blame the brandy for the impact of this. Charlie Hutchinson! I wonder the shock of David didn't kill him, but perhaps it started the process which ended with the next would-be victim. Blood on the knife . . . but no body. Perhaps the signing of the victim was more important than making sure the victim was dead. Oh, Peter, we're going to advertise! We're going to beg one young lady to come forward and bare her breast. We're going to be able to sort out the cranks from the genuine on this one, Peter, we're—"

"With respect, sir, the knife would have got bloodied if it had glanced off the victim's arm, say. But we'll advertise, of course. Ah, here's someone, sir. I'll go and let them in while you just—"

"I'm all right, Peter, but thanks for the drop of cold water, I needed it. Yes, go and let them in."

Kendrick wasn't far behind Sergeant Grant in the hall. He wasn't more than a few seconds on the stairs, but it was enough for him to realise that despite his shock over Charlie Hutchinson and a thought far back in his brain that he must be sure, in the future, not to make benevolent assumptions about the well-heeled and influential in the community, he was more eased in his mind than he'd been for weeks. Bruce Holden was young, and he was free.

"Hello again, Basil!"

"I handed over, Superintendent, I wanted to be the one here."

"And there's lots to show you," responded Kendrick jovially as he led the way upstairs. "By the way, I forgot to ask you. About the time of death. Was it the same night that he killed David Douglas, or was it last night? I don't imagine it was earlier this evening." The SOCO had stopped abruptly, not quite at the top of the stairs, and Kendrick turned impatiently round. "Come and see what we've got here. You'll hardly believe—"

"I'd forgotten, Superintendent, that you hadn't stayed long enough to hear the doctor's report. That last murder—the boy on Saturday night/ Sunday morning—this chap can't have had anything to do with that. There's no way the doctor can make the hour Hutchinson met his Maker any later than the Thursday night or very early the Friday morning."

CHAPTER 10

Kendrick was at the chief constable's house by seven-thirty and taking coffee with the chief constable in his breakfast-room, having personally brought the news that the blood on the knife was human and of a different group from the blood of Charles Hutchinson. So far as the Monster was concerned, they had travelled in a night from nothing to everything. Four out of the five murders were solved, and the press conference which for several weeks they had been resisting was now to be welcomed.

"I'm not as happy as I thought I'd be, sir."

The chief constable was looking at him keenly, and Kendrick waited in hope. If he didn't have to explain, his unhappiness would be shown to have a basis understandable by other people. And he would be able to ask a favour.

"That last murder and the Holden boy, eh?"

"Yes, sir. D'you think, sir," said Kendrick with grateful speed, "that we might continue with the same absolute secrecy so far as the boy's concerned? Obviously we'll want to give some reassurance that we've someone in our sights for the Douglas murder but with the complete lack of evidence . . . I know certain of the party-goers will start thinking, now—and talking, of course—about Bruce Holden, but we don't have to go along with it, do we? I'll tell you honestly that so far as I'm concerned the fact of the boy not being the Monster makes him a much better psychological bet for the Douglas killing—David Douglas was certainly playing a sadistic game and Bruce Holden was wounded in what for even a pseudo-sophisticated youth must be a pretty tentative sexual pride. Also I should say he's hot-headed by temperament, but there isn't a shred of evidence and he's young and if he didn't do it . . . What do you think, sir?"

Kendrick sent his eyes on a tour of the bright objects in the chief constable's breakfast-room, most of them matching, telling himself in a variation of the traffic lights game that if he was looking at something sympathetic when his superior spoke . . .

"I think I'd be prepared to go along with that, Maurice." Kendrick's eyes had been on the only natural objects in the room, some yellow chrysanthemums in an orange pot. "So long as you hold an internal conference first, and make absolutely sure the non-committal stance on the fifth murder is a uniform stance. And a plain clothes one, too, of course."

The chief constable didn't laugh at his own little joke, and the relationship between them was such that Kendrick didn't laugh, either. "Of course, sir." The chrysanthemums, small single blooms with white hearts, exploded in a suffusion of pale gold as one of the morning's edgy clouds sneaked on and the sun struck the big square window. "And I'll see the Douglases and the Holdens as a matter of priority with the bad news and the good."

"Bad news, Maurice?"

"Well, sir . . . So far as the Douglases are concerned it could bring in a personal element, couldn't it? It could mean that David Douglas was killed because he was David Douglas." He thought of Humphrey turning his back and walking over to the window as he said those words. "Not simply because he looked like any pretty young girl in the world. Because he'd upset Bruce Holden, for instance. Which is the bad news for the Holdens, too. On reflection, I don't know that there's much good news in it for either family. All right, the Holden boy won't be suspected any longer of a series of madman's murders, but he's rather more likely, as I've said, to have committed just that one."

"Yes, I see." Kendrick thought the chief constable had started to lean back before recollecting he was on a long-legged bar stool. Probably his thighs were aching, too. "And you, Maurice? You won't be indulging in the general relief that it's an entirely good thing for Seaminster?"

"I haven't lost the wider view, sir, I promise you." He hoped that was true. "There's another priority. We've got to try and entice in the presumable young woman who came into contact with that knife. We don't exactly need any more corroborative evidence against poor Charlie Hutchinson, but the girl might be in need of medical attention, and Charlie might have poured out a stream of explanatory matter, believing the ear receiving it would soon be deaf. Does it justify shock tactics, sir? One of Forensics' photos? Obviously a photo of Charlie in his normal guise with artist's embellishments would provide a better likeness, but one gathers that with the hat and the muffler his face was scarcely showing."

"If you think the best impression of the Monster will come from the death photos, then use them by all means. And we've got to realise, Maurice, that the right photo could bring in a whole lot of evidence from the public at large as well as from this last wretched girl if she exists—I seem to remember that following one of the murders there was a report of a woman having been seen near where the body was found, at just about the time it was thought the murder was committed. I don't care how shocking you are, so long as you give the best impression."

"Thank you, sir. There's just one more thing. The Monster's signature. I'd like to go on keeping that a secret—I don't want to make it easier for young Holden under further questioning, or for anyone else. And if it doesn't get out we'll be spared a stream of bored and publicity-conscious young women coming in with bosoms freshly and specifically flayed. The press will appreciate that they're helping us by keeping quiet on that aspect of things, even if involuntarily."

"Yes, Maurice. I think that's wise."

"Thank you, sir." Kendrick got to his feet, surreptitiously flexing grateful legs. "I must be going; the inquest on David Douglas opens at ten. This is the sort of day where everything should be dealt with simultaneously."

"Judicious delegation, Maurice." More slowly the chief constable hauled his bulk down from the other counter stool. "If you've had a weakness over this business—and I'd have to look pretty hard for it—you've been a bit reluctant here and there to use help."

"Yes, sir. Thank you." Kendrick wondered how many bosses there were who could make a criticism sound like a compliment. "The Douglases and the Holdens I feel I must see myself, but of course I'll get the chief inspector to set up the internal conference and the press ditto. Twelve noon, say, for the press? The inquest will be a formality at this stage. Will you want to be at the press conference?"

"I don't think so, I'll leave it to you." The two men grinned at one another. "And if my curiosity gets the better of me, it will still be your show. Any chance of having the photos and the spiel ready by then?"

"They must be. That's the obvious first. Which I'll delegate."

On a further exchange of grins Kendrick hurried out to his car. The sun was obscured again, and he shivered in a foretaste of winter. Looking up at the house as he opened his door, he saw the chief constable's maturely attractive wife, her hair still tousled from bed, drawing back the curtains from an upstairs window. It took him most of the drive back to Seaminster to subdue the memory of how well she had got on with Miriam and his recurrent longing to know if she and Miriam were still in touch, but when he reached the station he needed only twenty minutes to agree to the illustrations to be used on the Monster publicity handout—one photograph of Charlie's body with hat and wig, one artist's impression of him standing in his female gear—and the wording to go with it. Then another twenty or so to delegate the setting up of the two conferences.

It was nine o'clock and he ought to have plenty of time to go and see Bruce Holden's father. Holden senior's office would undoubtedly be the best place, and Kendrick suspected he was a man who would come early to work. At any rate, he could wait as unobtrusively as possible for the man's arrival. But Holden was already at his desk and gave Kendrick instant access.

"What can I do for you, Superintendent?"

Holden had got up and come round his desk with his usual courtesy and his face was as calm as ever, but Kendrick was unable to disregard the signs of strain and suffering in the tightness of the skin, the sunken narrowness of eye. Even, it seemed, a loss of flesh.

"I've come to tell you," said Kendrick, averting his gaze as he took the proffered comfortable seat, "that a man has been found dead who is without any doubt the Monster. You will have known him, sir; he was an architect, too: Charles Hutchinson."

"My God, Superintendent . . . Yes, I knew him."

This was the first time Kendrick had seen overt distress in the face in front of him. He must speak again, and quickly, before he saw relief.

"Mr. Holden, I'm afraid I also have to tell you that Hutchinson died before David Douglas. The latest time his death could have taken place is very early on the Friday morning—that is, about forty-eight hours before David was killed. That means—"

"I see what that means, Superintendent." Holden's face had resumed the impassivity with which it met personal setback. Kendrick thought of Holden's wife. "Bruce will now be suspected of only the latest murder. But you will feel rather more inclined to believe he committed it."

"I've always found it personally very difficult to believe Bruce could have been the Monster." Kendrick was still finding it impossible to give this man the lie direct. "We shall now be forced to reconsider Bruce's denial that he had any contacts which would have enabled him to discover the nature of the mark which the Monster made on his victims, and I regret that we shall have to talk to him again. In the meantime, however, we shall be withdrawing our overnight watch on your house and—"

"And the anonymity I've been so grateful for?"

"No, we're maintaining that. I'm holding a press conference later this morning and I shall say merely that we have someone helping us with our inquiries into David Douglas's death. That doesn't mean we shall cease our inquiries in other directions. We still have no actual evidence against Bruce."

"But psychologically you feel—"

"Bruce quarrelled with David a short time before David was murdered. And it's more likely that Bruce killed David alone than that he committed all the murders. As you yourself implied."

"I would agree with you, Superintendent, if I wasn't convinced of his total innocence." Holden smiled, making Kendrick drop his eyes. "It's a funny thing, I feel as though we'd lost a form of protection. The idea of Bunny being responsible for all those lunatic murders was so absurd it seemed in some strange way to be his defence. Now it's simply one normal young man provoked by another and possibly losing his temper. And his self-control."

"And proof having to be found that he could have known the Monster's mark. To say nothing of our having yet to establish a physical connection. But I did want to assure you, before you heard the news, that the possibility of Bruce's involvement in David Douglas's death will continue to be a guarded secret."

"Thank you, Superintendent. I very much appreciate what you're doing and the fact that you've come to tell me. Will you have coffee?"

"No time, I'm afraid. The inquest on David Douglas is opening at ten. It will be adjourned for further inquiries."

"I see. . . . I haven't taken it in yet about Charlie Hutchinson. Is there anything you can tell me which is going to be common knowledge?"

"I hardly know anything myself as yet. There's a feeling, I suppose, that we can go into the whys and wherefores of Charles Hutchinson at comparative leisure. And that the press will be only too pleased to undertake the job for us anyway."

"Of course. The unsolved murder is the priority. Thank you again, Superintendent."

"Not at all, sir. I'm very sorry about it all." Kendrick's sense of dissatisfaction made him realise he had been hoping for a sign of weakness, at least of unreasonableness in some area, to make his admiration of the man less painful. "How is your wife?"

"No worse."

"I thought it would be best to talk to you and ask you to talk to her, and to Bruce. Make use of broad shoulders."

"I'm glad you did that, Superintendent. Please don't let me keep you any longer."

The day, at short of nine-thirty, had already given him two relentlessly attentive hours, and he decided to secure himself a short break by walking along to the court—his car was parked far enough from Holden's office for there to be little likelihood of a connection being suspected. The inquest was, of course, something he could properly delegate, but he never liked to pass up on the possibilities for observation arising out of official events in the wake of violent death—such as there being one unlikely presence, although today this was something he could scarcely expect, a coroner's court offering none of the rear dark corners afforded by churches and even crematoria chapels—the truth about one murder early in his career had come to him when he had spotted a figure in a corner back pew at the funeral. (That glimpse, Kendrick had always thought, was what had taken him from sergeant to inspector.)

His walk, through sudden dramatic contrasts of sun and gloom, wasn't the snatch of refreshment he'd hoped for, punctuated as it was by reminders that he could no longer go anonymously about Seaminster. Notoriety rather than fame, thought Kendrick ruefully, as the second pair of middle-aged women turned away from him with hostile eyes to whisper. Well, if he walked the same route tomorrow morning they might even come up to him and shake his hand, without consideration of the fact that the Monster had given himself up rather than been caught.

That this reflection failed to flood him with the joyous relief he would have experienced only four days earlier made him acknowledge the fairness of the chief constable's oblique reference to personal priorities —to have to remind himself to be glad the Monster menace was over was to be obsessed with solving the continuing mystery of David Douglas's death. He must discipline himself into the frame of mind in which he should be instinctively revelling. He was doing all he could to protect Bruce Holden in the absence of evidence against him, he couldn't do any more. . . .

To Kendrick's relief, the only member of the Douglas family in the coroner's court was the father. At least an inquest was preferable to a funeral, where the whole family was forced on parade at the time they most wanted to be down a burrow. Kendrick saw no one he didn't know, or easily found out about. There were no press people, but they were doubtless preparing their weaponry for the conference their editors would already have told them to attend. Anyway, the fact that nothing was said concerning Charles Hutchinson and the Monster murders was of no significance—even without the unwelcome discovery about the time of death, there would have been no mention of them at this stage. Most important of all, there was nothing in the formal statement of death and the cause of it, the release of the body and the adjournment of the inquest, to disquiet Frederick Douglas in advance of Kendrick speaking to him.

He caught up with Douglas on the way out, to ask if he could immediately come and see him.

"You've something to tell me?"

As with Holden, the evidence of suffering was involuntary in the face, in lines and tension and suddenly more obvious bones.

"Yes, sir."

"I'm going home, Superintendent. Will you follow me there?"

"Of course, sir." Kendrick was aware of a mixed reaction. It would be more uncomfortable to see how the wife, and possibly the daughter, too, received his news than merely the father in his office, but there would be greater chance of an inadvertent piece of assistance.

Frederick Douglas's car was in the court car park, and Kendrick watched him drive off. His ten-minute walk to his own car would give the family time to brace themselves, the women to put on good faces in both senses. As he walked he toyed with the idea of driving via the station and picking up a WPC, but decided that this would be to make too much of the information he had to hand on. When he saw Humphrey's car on the Douglas forecourt he was entirely glad he had come alone: Humphrey's presence would be far more comforting than that of a policewoman, and far less dramatic.

"Good morning, Chief Superintendent Kendrick."

It was the daughter on the doorstep. Kendrick hadn't imagined she could look more fragile than she had looked the first time he had set eyes on her, but in some indefinable way she did. "Please come in, we're expecting you."

She seemed to drift into the room ahead of him, rather than plant her feet, and went immediately to sit down where she had sat the last time he had called, on impulse to ask them what David might have done. The mother and father were in what Kendrick found himself thinking of as their usual places, and Humphrey on the fourth easy chair. Both men sprang to their feet, and Humphrey made for the door which Kendrick continued to block.

"Good morning, Mrs. Douglas . . . Humphrey . . . There's no need for Mr. Barnes to leave, if you're agreeable. What I've come to tell you will be common knowledge by lunch-time."

"I see," murmured the tiny woman in the big armchair. "Do sit down again, Humphrey."

"Stay, Humphrey," said the daughter.

"In that case . . . thanks." Humphrey strode back to his seat, almost overshooting it, trying not to look anxiously at Eleanor.

Frederick Douglas put out a hand towards the sofa. Kendrick briefly smiled, but remained standing.

"Last night," he said, "we found the Monster's body. He had died of a heart attack, and he was dressed as a respectable elderly woman." Kendrick could see Humphrey's eyes on the daughter's face, as if they were fixed there by a string. He followed the string with his own eyes and saw the dawn of relief relax the thin line of mouth into soft full lips in one dramatic move. Turning to the mother's face, he decided to leave Charlie Hutchinson for the time being. "There is no doubt that this man committed the four murders of young women. But there is no doubt, either, that he died during last Thursday night, almost forty-eight hours before your son. I very much regret that this means your son's killer is still at large and that—"

Kendrick was looking at Humphrey as he spoke, as the owner of the least painful face, and Humphrey leaping from his chair seemed to synchronise with the moaning sound the girl made, rather than follow it. Quickly turning, Kendrick saw Eleanor Douglas slump with ashen face across her chair, as limp as a fabric doll. Humphrey was on his knees beside her, propping her into his arms so masterfully neither the mother nor the father was doing more than lean forward.

"Eleanor. Eleanor!"

The pale hand tapped the pale cheek, and then Humphrey had pushed the head down against the knees, continuing to stroke the cloudy dark hair. Kendrick, to his irritation, found himself feeling like a voyeur. When Eleanor Douglas's head came up, still assisted by Humphrey, her eyes stared unseeing across the room.

"Eleanor," said Humphrey, "it isn't so much more terrible."

"It is much more terrible." Her voice was mild, without expression.

"It could mean," faltered the father, "that David was killed because he was David," and Kendrick for a few seconds was occupied with the phenomenon of his own involuntary shudder.

"By someone he knew," whispered the mother.

"I also wish to inform you," said Kendrick, hearing the official voice which was sometimes so useful in dispersing emotion or hostility, "that we have someone helping us with our inquiries." The daughter shot her huge eyes in his direction.

"Someone . . . you've got someone. . . ."

"Helping us with our inquiries," repeated Kendrick. He had never been more grateful for the euphemistic phrase, it had the layered significance of poetry. "I'm afraid I can't say more than that at the moment."

"You're concentrating in one direction, Superintendent?" Again, Frederick Douglas cleared his throat as if otherwise he wouldn't be able to speak.

"No, sir. Unless and until we actually make an arrest, we continue our inquiries in all directions."

"Who is the Monster, Superintendent?" Eleanor Douglas was sitting upright, no longer relying on Humphrey's arms, but Kendrick noticed she was holding his hand. He wished fleetingly and unofficially that he had also noticed which of them had inaugurated the gesture.

"Charles Hutchinson, the local architect," he said, glad to observe the various evidences of distraction caused by the extraordinary nature of his disclosure.

"Charlie Hutchinson!" As with Holden, there was more expression in Frederick Douglas's face than Kendrick had yet seen there. "That's terrible, Superintendent. You're sure—"

"Quite sure, sir."

Frederick Douglas looked across at his wife. "Charlie, dear, that's terrible, isn't it?"

"No wife," whispered Marie Douglas. "No wife to suffer."

"The only daughter died young. . . ." Kendrick and Frederick Douglas spoke simultaneously, and as each made a gesture to the other to carry on, Eleanor Douglas's voice came harshly into the brief silence.

"Perhaps that's why he did it."

"Only last week," said Frederick Douglas, "we had a drink together in the club. Dressed—as a woman you said, Superintendent?"

"Yes. He was found in that bit of wood off Villiers Street. There was a knife nearby with blood on it, and we suspect he had been with another intended victim, who escaped when he had his fatal coronary. We're preparing posters and press handouts to try and get this girl to come forward." He made a noticeable gesture out of consulting his watch, although he knew there was plenty of time. But he wanted, now, to get away. "We're holding a press conference shortly, and all these details will be on the news and in your papers later today."

"And—the details of David's murder?" asked Eleanor Douglas.

"No details," he said gently. "Merely that we are continuing to make inquiries, with which a man is at this stage assisting us."

"Don't you think *we* are entitled to know more, Superintendent?" Miss Douglas was suddenly on her feet and Humphrey scrambling to his.

"Not at this stage, no," said Kendrick steadily, returning her gaze. "Not until we decide—if we do—to ask the Director of Public Prosecutions if they agree with us that someone has a case to answer. I'm sorry."

"Oh, I understand," she said, almost with impatience. "I'll see you out, Superintendent."

"Thank you. Mr. Douglas . . . Mrs. Douglas . . . Humphrey

. . ." Humphrey, Kendrick thought, was starting to edge towards the
door, but the mother put out her hand and asked him not to go.

"Of course not, no," muttered Humphrey. "Goodbye, Maurice."

Eleanor Douglas led the way to the front door in silence, but as he
turned on the step to face her, Kendrick found his eyes caught again in
the steady hazel gaze. He saw it as a challenge to him to continue the
conversation he had just broken off, but he resisted it.

"Goodbye, Miss Douglas. I'm sorry to have brought disturbing
news."

She gave a sudden sharp laugh, disconcerting him. "Disturbing! Yes.
You know Humphrey, Superintendent."

"Yes."

"Did you know his wife?"

"Yes."

"You can't say any more than yes while David's murder is unsolved?"

"I'm sorry." There was something shocking to him in the unnecessary elaboration of her sarcasm. "Humphrey Barnes is an old friend,
and I've known him since before he was married."

"Has he got over her death?"

It took him a few seconds to realise she was talking of Emily.

"The fact that I'm not answering these questions has nothing to do
with my being a policeman."

"Of course not, it was inexcusable." She leaned against the doorpost
as the prop of her aggression fell away. "I'm sorry, I wouldn't have
dreamed of asking if I'd been—myself. No sleep . . . Please forget it."

"Of course, Miss Douglas. I understand. I hope with all my heart we
shall be able to wrap up this dreadful business soon."

"Dreadful business, yes . . . Thank you, Superintendent."

Driving back to the station, Kendrick found himself wondering
whether to tell Humphrey what Eleanor Douglas had asked him. In
view of Humphrey's recent performance on his knees, and the fact that
curiosity usually meant interest, he was very tempted. He'd keep it in
reserve, at any rate, and if he did pass it on he'd do it to offer Hump a
stimulant rather than to tell a tale.

National and local press were both well represented, crowded into
the largest room the Seaminster station had to offer, the one-time drawing-room of the Victorian house, the moulded cornices of its high ceil-

ing long ago picked out in blue and gold by a police constable on holiday.

The press representatives, thought Kendrick, were slightly disconcerted by the abundance of good things poured out for them without their having to angle for them. A palpable sense of relief, even euphoria, was soon spreading through the room, but Kendrick was aware that collective ingenuity, unexercised by the main subject of the conference, could well concentrate on the area where there was as yet no success to report.

He had decided to leave to his audience the onus of comment on the fact that only the four deaths of the girls had been solved. It came, when he was almost being lulled by the general goodwill, from a female representative of a national daily.

"You say that this Charles Hutchinson was responsible for the murders of the four girls. What about the murder of the boy on Saturday night?"

"He was not responsible for that murder," answered Kendrick, in what he hoped was a ready, even a conversational, tone. "He died during the night of Thursday-Friday, forty-eight hours before David Douglas was killed."

The general murmur was inevitable, the general movement of heads and feet and chair legs.

"So that," continued the woman, "the murder of the boy could well have had a personal motive."

"It could, yes," agreed Kendrick amiably. "I can tell you at this juncture only that we have someone who is helping us with our inquiries."

"Helping you with your inquiries?" almost echoed a crouching bearded figure at the back.

"That's all I can tell you on this one at the moment, I'm afraid. You know the rules. I shall hope to have something further to say very shortly."

"The murder of the boy was thought to be a Monster murder." The London woman had a nose like an eagle's beak and predatory hands to match. Each time she spoke Kendrick disliked her more, and had to make more of an effort to appear to be listening calmly and politely. "Which means that the body bore whatever mark the Monster put on his victims. So whoever killed the boy had found out what the mark was. Not an easy thing to do in view of police secrecy."

"Can you tell us now, Chief Superintendent, what the Monster mark was?" A local lad, flushing as he heard his own voice, probably the youngest person in the room.

"I'm sorry, we feel we must continue to keep that information secret until the Douglas murder is wrapped up. My last questioner has virtually told you why." Kendrick, delivered if only temporarily, beamed on his tormentor. "It's important that the killer of David Douglas, whoever that may turn out to be, should remain in the position of having to conceal his knowledge of the Monster mark, and of being capable of being betrayed into revealing it. Also, by withholding information about the mark we can be certain of the genuineness or otherwise of any young woman who comes forward claiming to be the intended victim at the time of the Monster's death."

"Assuming the blood-stained knife was used to make the mark," supplied a much more attractive younger woman.

"Assuming that, of course," agreed the chief inspector at Kendrick's side.

"Was the appearance of the boy's body identical with that of the four girls?" persisted the first woman, who then, realising what she had said, blushed and looked down at her notebook as the laughter swelled. It went on for quite a while, as the meeting recovered its sense of relief and thankfulness, and Kendrick could see that it broke the woman's spirit.

He took pity on her to the extent of eventually answering the question she had meant to ask. Untruthfully, remembering the wavering lines of the cross on David's breast, he told her yes, he understood what she had intended to say, the murderer of David Douglas had left the boy's body in just the same case as the Monster had left the bodies of the girls.

The meeting broke up, as Kendrick had hoped it would, with satisfaction still the chief general emotion.

CHAPTER 11

Doreen saw the poster just as she was going to climb onto a bus, and stood suddenly still under the shock of it so that the man on her heels bumped his chin against her head and there was a sharp moment of ill-feeling in the queue of tired workers behind her.

"I'm sorry, I'm sorry." Doreen, as she half turned round, found herself clutching her coat across her, even though it was all buttoned up, as if the people in the queue would otherwise be able to see her unique connection with the words and picture on the hoarding beside them.

THE MONSTER IS DEAD!
And it is thought that his latest intended victim is alive. If you saw this person in this position on the night of Thursday, 27th October, the police urge you to come forward.

The bus was still filling up, and from the window seat she secured on the near side she could easily see the blown-up photograph of that huge man-woman who since Thursday night had so regularly occupied her dreams. She must have imagined the big black feet moving; they were still at the angle she had seen them and would always see them, poking out from under the skirt.

There was another picture underneath, of the man-woman standing up, with more words appealing to anyone who might have seen the Monster at any other time. But the top picture, and the first set of words, they were appealing just to her. *Doreen, the police urge you to come forward.*

She'd had a feeling right from the start that she ought to go to the police. Even knowing as she did that she would lose her precious independence—she couldn't defy her mum and dad—she'd probably have

gone with a bit of encouragement from Ray, but Ray had backed up her
first instincts to lie low, put TCP on the cuts, take a Valium at bedtime,
and go on as if nothing had happened. He'd smiled and said he knew he
was being selfish, because he'd be as upset as she would if she had to go
back and live at home, but whenever she'd said that even so perhaps she
ought to go to the police he'd stopped smiling and got really het up at
the idea, really—almost—bullying her out of it. And from the moment
he'd seen the cross the evening after, he'd been—well, he'd been sort of
turned on by it, although she hated to put it that way, even in her mind.
Certainly he'd started going home later and later, and although Mrs.
Crale hadn't said anything, Doreen knew she must have heard Ray on
the stairs and must have thought he might as well have stayed the night
for all the difference it made. . . .

"Fares, *please!* You asleep or something?"

Doreen apologised again, catching sight as she did so of another
identical poster in another prominent position. It was only then that it
occurred to her to be glad that the terrible creature—in the night, once,
she had even found herself wondering if it was entirely human, had got
up to look at her breast and see if there was any satanic mutation of the
cross upon it—was dead and gone.

He is dead and gone, lady.

The line drifted across her mind. She didn't know where it came
from; she must have memorised it unknowingly at school and kept it in
her subconscious for this moment.

Doreen, the police urge you to come forward!

Come forward she would, on so compelling and personal a summons,
whatever Ray said. And surely even Ray, when they met that evening,
would bow to the official command of the posters he, too, was bound to
see.

It was when she started to prepare her bit of tea that she realised how
nervous she was. She was remembering more and more vividly just how
het up Ray had been at the mere idea of her going to the police, how he
had made her swear that she wouldn't, and she kept dropping things.
Since Friday she'd taken a Valium at bedtime, but she shook one from
the bottle when she'd eventually managed to make herself some toast
and marmalade and tea, and took it with the tea. One thing which
ought to be bucking her up, she'd be able to go out now on her own,
after dark, something which had been impossible since she'd got home

that night. And she'd be able to go to work down the alley where the boy whose name had probably been Kevin had tried to mess her about. Silly, it really was silly, not to be able to go down that alley, even in daylight, when what had happened to her that night hadn't had anything to do with Kevin, hadn't even happened there, but that was how it had been. Well, it would be all right now.

Wouldn't it?

They were going to a disco and Ray was coming for her. As Ray had been since Friday it was hardly worth getting herself all dressed up, hardly worth doing her hair properly, putting lipstick on at all carefully. She was getting herself sort of roughly ready, of course; she'd never want Ray to think she was waiting . . . expecting. . . . And really, if she was absolutely honest with herself she did think she'd rather wait until later, until they got back after the disco and she asked him if he'd like to come in for a cup of coffee. That way, the whole evening was a sort of a preparation, the touching and looking at odd moments. Not, since Friday, that it hadn't happened when he came in at the end of the evening, too, and that was absolutely all right, but really and truly she'd just as soon—she'd rather, if she was honest— meet Ray all fresh and ready to go straight out and only sort of start getting excited as the evening went on. She was a bit worried, too, that she wasn't going to be able to get into the mood in the early evening if he went on—well, expecting her to. And she couldn't relax properly anyway at that time of the day, with Mrs. Crale likely to knock at any time to ask her something, or to suggest she and Ray pop in for a sherry on their way out. It was a relief to know that this evening, at least, Mrs. Crale had gone out for her supper. Doreen did like Mrs. Crale and she didn't want to lose her friendship or her respect. Or both.

She wasn't a bit hungry and so she ate the toast very quickly, to get it over, giving herself indigestion. The indigestion was like a little lump in the middle of her chest which she could swallow past. This was the third time she'd had it now, in one week, and it felt quite familiar. In fact it never really and entirely went away, but it did go very small and then she could almost forget about it. She could easily have asked Mrs. Crale for some magnesia tablets or something—she knew she had them —but somehow she didn't feel like meeting Mrs. Crale at the moment unless she couldn't avoid it. She knew she would blush or drop her eyes or do something silly and unnecessary if Mrs. Crale so much as looked at her hard with that sort of knowing glance she had. And if Mrs. Crale actually said something about hearing Ray so late . . . It was silly and unnecessary because Doreen didn't have a bad conscience or feel ashamed of anything in her life (except about not going to the police). She just felt it would be better if she and Mrs. Crale didn't put certain things into words, and once Mrs. Crale got used to hearing Ray's feet very late on the stairs she probably wouldn't want to say anything anyway, and then they could go back to Doreen putting her head round Mrs. Crale's kitchen door to see if she could share a pot of tea, and Mrs. Crale ringing Doreen's bell chimes for the same reason. . . .

She was even more nervous clearing the tiny meal away than she had been getting it ready. She couldn't pretend any longer that Ray would be anything but very angry when she told him she was going to the police in the morning, after all. She could, of course, go to the police without saying anything to Ray, but that didn't fit with her ideal of total loyalty, total honesty. She'd committed herself to Ray—that was why she didn't have any conscience about him staying so late—and having done that she couldn't possibly just go off to the police station without telling him she was going to. And even if she did, he would be more angry afterwards, not just at what she'd done, but because she'd done it without telling him, without giving him a chance to persuade her not to.

She wouldn't let him persuade her, but she was very, very anxious that the rather new sort of Ray who seemed to have come into existence since that awful night shouldn't be too dreadfully angry at what she was determined to do. Her first thought had been to let the evening go through to its usual pattern, and then tell Ray when he brought her home. That would obviously be the most sensible way to play it, but she knew she wasn't going to be able to, she knew that the moment Ray came into the hall of the flat she would start telling him what she had made her mind up to do—what the posters had commanded her. There was, of course, just the chance that the posters might have persuaded Ray, too, but somehow she didn't have much faith in that possibility. Ray had been so absolutely and even—well, even violently, opposed to the idea of her going to the police, she didn't really imagine that any amount of posters, however persuasive, could make him change his attitude. Well, she wouldn't change hers, either. It would be so much more sensible, though, to spend the evening with Ray in the usual way, without quarrelling, and then tell him when he brought her home. . . . The circular argument was going round in her mind for the umpteenth time and her doorbell was ringing; she had just managed to hear it above the pumping of her heart. Doreen went draggingly down her little hall, her hand held instinctively (as so often, since Thursday) against the breast which had destroyed the even course of her life.

"Hello, Ray."

"Hello!" He looked at her sharply as she stood back to let him in. Even without her telling him what she had decided to do there was tension, now, between them. Even if she didn't say anything at this stage, the evening wouldn't be like their evenings had been only a week ago. (The man-woman was an enormous gap in her life, so that thinking about how she and Ray had been before that night was like thinking about something which had happened years and years earlier.)

So she might as well tell him now. It wasn't as if she would spoil something which could have been really good, really relaxed. And anyway, if she didn't tell him she would probably have to . . . Ray would expect (he was already taking off his jacket), and this evening she couldn't possibly . . .

"Did you see those posters, Ray?"

"They were big enough." That was why he had looked at her so sharply, of course. That was why the tension in the room was something she could almost run her fingers along, like wires, even before she'd said a thing.

"The first message and the first photograph—they were addressed to me."

"They were addressed to the girl who was there when the Monster snuffed it. Any girl, so far as they're concerned, in Seaminster or out of it."

"You know what I mean, Ray." To her fury her voice was weak and faltering, when inside she had never felt so strong, so determined.

"And what do you mean?"

He had crossed the room so quietly and quickly he had her cheek pinched between his fingers before he'd finished speaking, before she'd seen that he'd started to move.

"You're hurting me!" The superficial pain was excruciating, and to her surprise she found herself chopping down on his wrist with the side

of her hand, so that he let go. "It's my duty now to go to the police,"
she said, holding her hand against the protesting side of her face, knowing she couldn't have put it worse, in a way more likely to get his back
up.

"Your duty," he said sneeringly. "Your duty! I've told you I don't
want you to go to the police, and that's your duty, your duty to me.
Unless you're not the faithful little thing you keep telling me you are.
Unless going to the police isn't the first thing you've decided to do
against me—"

"It isn't against you, Ray!" She moved backwards, facing him, and
sat down on the edge of her bedroom chair, half expecting—fearing—
that Ray would follow her across the room, but he stayed where he was,
glowering at her. "How can it be against you? You weren't even in
Seaminster that night!"

"What's that got to do with it?" He was across the room now,
crouching down in front of the chair so that they were face to face, and
the anger in his eyes almost felt hot. Anger and . . . something else,
which for an absurd moment she thought looked like fear. "What's that
got to do with your going to the police, that I was in Seaminster or
wasn't in Seaminster?"

"Nothing, Ray, I only meant . . . I was only trying to show that it
doesn't affect you in any way at all, your not even being here that
night."

"You're too right, I wasn't here. But that doesn't mean that it doesn't
affect me. Doesn't affect me that my girl goes and shows her boobs to a
roomful of policemen. Please, sir, excuse me, sir, the Monster used me
for his model on Thursday!"

"Ray . . . please . . . You make it sound like my fault, as if I . . .
It'll help them to find out more things, what time it died and so on, and
I expect they're worried about me—about the girl they think was there
when the Monster died. Well, there *was* a girl there, and it was me, and
I've seen their posters and I've got to go and tell them what I can. I
can't understand why you're making such a fuss about it. The Monster's dead. It—he—can't retaliate, and all I'll be doing is telling them
about what happened during the last ten minutes or so—it was only ten
minutes, I looked at my watch, and I'd looked at it after—after I'd said
good night to Len and Barbara." Dear God, she'd nearly said something about Kevin or whatever his name was. If Ray ever got to hear

about *that*, in the mood he was in . . . She almost wished that she'd told him about it right away. It would have been laughed off by now and she wouldn't have to watch her tongue. On a cold shaft of dismay, plunging all the way down her back, she hoped Len and Barbara would go on watching their tongues, too, wouldn't let anything slip out. "I can't believe it was only ten minutes, it felt like ten years, but that's all it was, and that's all I'll have to tell them about and then I expect they can close their files. Ray, dear, please try to understand how I feel."

He'd got up and gone to sit on the bed, encouraging her to hope that the rage in him had died down, that she could appeal to his imagination. It occurred to her for the first time that maybe he didn't have much imagination.

"The last murder," he said, quite lightly, calmly, his hands dangling relaxed between his knees, so that her heart gave a leap of hope, "the murder of the boy in drag, the Monster didn't do that murder, although the police had thought he did, believing he had a girl. But the boy died two nights after the Monster cut you up."

"Did he, Ray?" She was pleased to go along with him, keep his thoughts away from her and what she had made up her mind to do, if only for a few minutes. "I hadn't thought about it. I haven't really seen a paper since then, or listened to the radio." *Or done anything except work and worry and have you.*

Ray was actually half smiling. "There's no need for you to think about it, no need for either of us to think about it. I was away again the night the boy died, and you were in here taking it easy."

"Yes, that's right, Ray. It was wonderful to have had you home on the Friday night, but I was greedy and I was wanting you to be here with me on the Saturday night, too. I know you've got to be away sometimes, I'd never grumble, you know that, but on Saturday night, feeling like I did, I did wish you'd been here with me."

"I wish I had been, darling, I wish I could have been, but you know how it is. If I'd put things off I'd have lost business, and you told me you'd wash your hair and do a few things about the flat, and we were going to have all Sunday and the boys asked me to stay over—"

"Of course, darling," responded Doreen, eager and grateful. "I know. You'd had a busy day of business—poor you, having business on a *Saturday*—and you were tired and the boys suggested you stay the night and relax with them. I was glad for you, I wasn't expecting you, and as you said, we'd arranged for Sunday. I *did* wash my hair," she said, shivering without knowing she was going to, "because of still feeling dirty even after washing it on Friday morning. I'd have washed myself inside as well as outside if I could have done, the way I felt after—"

"I know. I know." He was across the room again, crouching in front of her, but this time to insert his hand inside her blouse and cup her breast, the one where the nipple had been cut, which she was afraid had gone a bit septic and which hurt horribly when he took hold of it, as he had done now. "I'm sorry, darling, I didn't mean to get so steamed up, but we want to forget all about all this. It's nothing to do with us, nothing at all. The Monster's dead and no more girls are going to be killed or hurt and you going to the police isn't going to do anything for anyone, except keep it all going for you just when you're beginning to forget it, get over it."

His voice and his eyes were steady and hypnotic, or trying to be, but in her pain and her disappointment she pushed her thighs against the chair so that it shot backwards across the carpet and the unbearable friction of Ray's fingers came to an end.

Doreen shot to her feet, feverishly trying to fasten the tiny buttons of her blouse.

"I'm sorry, Ray, I thought you'd understood. I'm going to the police. You talk about me beginning to forget, get over it, but I can't until I've done what I have to do. I'll never live comfortably with myself again if I don't go to the police now. I'm sorry, Ray."

She stopped, cowering away from the expression on his face, then waiting in a sort of resigned paralysis for him to scramble to his feet and come over to her.

"You pig-headed bitch!"

She braced herself for what she knew had to come, somewhere far off surprised and even impressed by the unflinching way she was now standing. His hand stung one side of her face and then the other, once, twice, three times, then she was flying across the room and landing face down on the bed, listening to her deep sobs of outrage and pain, then the slamming of the front door.

"Ray! Please!" She appeared to be calling out to him, yet after crawling across the bedroom floor, crying hysterically and helping herself along by the wall and pieces of furniture, when she reached the front door she put the bolt on so that he couldn't get back in again with the extra key he'd had cut.

She lay, then, on the hall floor just inside the door, glad of the draught through the letter-box onto her sore, burning face, deciding not to wait until the morning to go to the police. She hadn't got her watch on and she didn't know how long she lay there before struggling to her feet and going slowly into the bathroom to pull the light cord and see the effects of another act of violence against her.

Both sides of her face were a funny shade of red, sort of bricky, which she supposed meant that bruises were coming, and one side looked a bit bigger than the other. Desperately she began splashing cold water on it, which improved how it felt but not how it looked, so that when she had very carefully and gently dried it, she put on a lot of powder. Her left breast felt too tight but she didn't look at it, she shrugged into a jacket, picked up her bag, and started for the front door, pausing as she reached it on the dreadful thought that Ray might be waiting actually to prevent her from carrying out what for some reason he had chosen to see as her threat.

And Mrs. Crale was out.

But so long as Ray wasn't lurking in the public parts of the house, Mrs. Crale being out had its advantage. Doreen could telephone for a taxi without having to say anything to Mrs. Crale and without attracting her shocked and inquiring reaction to the state of her face.

It took her a few moments to get up the courage to take the snib off and open her front door, a few moments of feverish self-reminder that all that had happened was that she had made her boyfriend angry by disagreeing with him and he had lost his temper and slapped her, and then she was closing it very quietly behind her and slipping down the stairs and round the corner into Mrs. Crale's big kitchen and the telephone on the wall. She was sure she hadn't mentioned to Ray that Mrs. Crale was out, so he wouldn't have risked waiting for her in the kitchen.

For heaven's sake, Ray wasn't the Monster. Ray was Ray, and the Monster was dead.

She managed to order the taxi in quite a calm voice, and asked for the driver to sound his horn when he arrived. Ray could be watching the front door from any one of a number of hiding places, but she didn't think he could see her in Mrs. Crale's kitchen, peering at the gate from behind the net curtain. If the kitchen hadn't faced the street it wouldn't have been so easy; Mrs. Crale kept her other doors locked.

She seemed to wait for ages, her eyes burning as she tried to see the details of people and gateways and side-streets through the pattern of the net curtain. She didn't touch the curtain, but she couldn't really be sure that Ray wasn't standing very still somewhere very close by, watching the outline of her motionless red face.

She had one moment of intense panic as she saw the taxi drive up, wondering if Ray would leap out and dismiss it, wondering if she had the courage to go out to it. The courage came from a sudden wave of self-disgust, that she should be feeling so afraid about doing the right thing. And Ray could hardly prevent her, in a street full of people, from climbing into a taxi.

He might of course be waiting at the Seaminster police station. But the taxi was stopping right outside the building and there were people— two of them were policemen in uniform—standing on the forecourt. Doreen paid the driver while she was still sitting in the taxi, then got out in a normal orderly fashion and crossed to the steps at her usual pace, but not looking to right or left. Inside the station, she went straight up to the counter and leaned her elbows on its worn shiny top in relief.

"Yes, miss? What can I do for you?"

The man in uniform was so friendly and smiling and reassuring, if the counter hadn't been between them she might have let her head drop against his uniformed chest and begun to cry. As it was, her voice was suddenly out of control.

"I want . . . Can I please . . ."

"Yes, miss? Take it easy, now."

"The posters. There are some posters up today. About—about the Monster." Saying the word was like reciting a wicked spell; it brought back the memories, all of them, clear and confused at the same time. Suddenly she needed the counter to prop her up. The desk sergeant saw the oddly coloured anxious face dramatically whiten, except for an area to each side which seemed to flare suddenly black and red against the pallor. Subduing his excitement, he came round to the front and gently took the girl's weight.

"You're all right, miss, come in here with me now and sit down a moment. You'd like a cup of tea?"

"Tea . . . Yes, please."

"That's the ticket." The desk sergeant freed one hand in order to snap his fingers and order tea and a WPC from a hovering constable. Then, as unobtrusively as possible, he helped Doreen across to the interview room and sat her down in the usual place.

"Sorry there are no soft chairs, love. You all right?"

"I'm all right," said Doreen, finding herself happier than she'd been for days. "I just want to tell you . . . Those posters . . . I'm the girl who was with the Monster. I wasn't sure he was dead but I suppose I knew he was, really, and I suppose I ought to have stayed, or got someone to go and help but I couldn't. I couldn't stay, I just had to run away, and then I didn't tell anyone. I know I ought to have done but I was afraid my mum would make me go and live at home again and anyway I think I knew that he wouldn't be going after any more girls and I'm very sorry I didn't . . . couldn't . . . and Ray didn't want me to, Ray tried to stop me. . . ." This was the worst part of all, and Doreen put her hands up over the burning patches on her face and burst into lovely, releasing tears.

When the WPC came in the desk sergeant, at arm's length, was awkwardly patting Doreen's untidy hair.

"WPC Thomson, I'm glad to see you. She needs some comfort. It's all right, love," he said to Doreen as she tried to flop against him. "Here's a nice lady to see to you. Get her to undo her blouse," he said in a quick whisper. "She says she's the girl the posters are asking for. I'd say her distress was the real thing, at least. Let her have a few sips of tea first."

The tea came as WPC Thomson was taking a chair round the table so that she could sit close enough to Doreen to put her arms round her. The desk sergeant went out and put a DO NOT DISTURB notice on the outside of the interview room door. After Doreen had gulped some tea, WPC Thomson said gently, "Show me, love," and made a token move towards the buttons on Doreen's blouse.

With the instinct which seemed age-old, Doreen's hands flew protectively to her breast, and the WPC waited patiently while she began to smile uncertainly and her spread rigid fingers relaxed and started to unfasten the buttons.

Doreen's young flesh had had almost five days to heal, but the wavering outlines, reinforced by irregular small blood clots like beads, were unmistakable, as was the infected state of a nipple.

"Thank you, love." WPC Thomson made a show of helping Doreen to cover herself up. Then she went to the door and opened it, removed the notice, and called across to the desk sergeant, who came at once to join her outside the door she had softly closed behind her.

"I should say she's the one. Just what we'd expect. Can you get the chief superintendent? I don't think he'd thank us for getting anyone else. And a doctor," she continued indignantly, as if the desk sergeant, merely by being a man, had had a hand in things. "It isn't all healing up as it ought to be."

CHAPTER 12

When it came to it, Kendrick found himself attending David Douglas's funeral out of respect for the Douglas family rather than as an added opportunity to look for enlightenment about David's murder. On Wednesday morning he was so engrossed with Doreen Daly and her obvious fear of the boyfriend who had changed within a week, he didn't look at his watch until a quarter past eleven, and even then it was an effort to tear himself away from the Seaminster interview room and arrive at St. Saviour's school chapel just before the cortège. The chapel was a blunt wedge shape with only two rear angles, one of them containing schoolboys and the other occupied by Humphrey, huddled into himself and looking even more miserable than usual. What Kendrick thought of as a reserve of boys was being directed to the few remaining empty places, but when he showed his ID he was instantly found a seat near the front, in the last of the variegated pews before the uniform mass of boys began.

Humphrey, who had arrived too early and was feeling cold as well as unhappy, was aware of Maurice's excitement with a disagreeable sensation as of cold water dripping down his back. But why should Maurice's mood—his elation, almost—strike him disagreeably? It was a question he didn't want to answer, and anyway his energies were charged for the entry of David's coffin, for the dual exercise of keeping his emotions manageable and missing no jot of what the Douglas family might be about to give away. He felt indignant on their behalf, that at this of all times they should be subject to public scrutiny, while gearing himself to scrutinise no less proficiently than Maurice himself—Humphrey's awareness of his hypocrisy was adding a sense of self-dislike to his continuing shocked sorrow. Maurice had telephoned the night before, full of triumph that his posters had done their job and brought a live girl into the station with the Monster's mark on her. Maurice had also said something about the girl being afraid of her boyfriend and needing medical attention, but that could hardly be what was making him look so excited—impatient, almost—this morning. The Monster was dead— Humphrey continued to dislike himself, too, because of his inordinate relief at now knowing for certain that the Monster hadn't been at Fabia's party—and any further information about him could only be anticlimactic. Maurice couldn't be interested in the Monster now; it was only some fresh development with regard to David's death which could make even the back of Maurice's head tell Humphrey that it was buzz-ing.

They were here, the organ had changed its note and people were getting to their feet. Humphrey, as he rose, stared eagerly and fearfully ahead of him, hearing the slow shuffle of the feet of the men who were carrying the weight of David and his coffin, then the voice of the school chaplain at the back of the procession. It was another small shock to see that the coffin wasn't being carried by grown men, that it rested on the shoulders of four of David's contemporaries, one of them Jonathan. He saw Jonathan's grim white profile for a moment as the coffin was set down and the bearers separated to each side of the aisle, Jonathan to join his parents in the front pew opposite the pew where Frederick was standing and ushering Marie and Eleanor past him. Pity swamped curi-osity as he saw the faces of David's parents and sister. Marie was so small, so neutral, so much the little woman crushed by grief, Humphrey realized her gaiety had been as much a characteristic of her face as her nose and mouth. Frederick's normally fine features were positively as-cetic, monklike, his tall thin body so frail he found himself imagining

Frederick as the subject of a surrealist picture with the sudden shaft of sunlight shining through him. Eleanor, all black and white from where he was sitting, was yet another shock to him in her simple beauty . . . beautiful simplicity. Savagely he wrenched his mind from its familiar verbal preoccupations. Across the aisle Jonathan's back was as revealing as Maurice's. Jonathan had never had a good carriage, but now his shoulders were squared as if David's coffin had hardly been an extra burden to the one he was still carrying. David and Jonathan . . . It surprised him that his memory of both boys at the party was so vivid, it seemed so long ago.

It hadn't only been modesty which had sent him into this remote pew: The part of it where he was sitting jutted in such a way that his glance was scarcely impeded by the body of the congregation and he was able to look directly, if distantly, at the protagonists (a good word, in a way, with its double meaning of chief character and combatant; each of the Douglases at the moment must be fighting grief). Jonathan's shoulders were still pressed back even though his head was bent. The unrelieved black of Eleanor's back view was pierced as she dropped her head forward and her hair parted to each side of her white neck. Marie's hands were gripping the rail in front of her.

It was no good, he couldn't keep on looking. For the length of the simple service Humphrey either shut his eyes or kept them on the Order of Service sheet to which he intermittently attended. Or the chaplain's face during the short address. It must have made it easier for the chaplain that there were so many positive things to be said about David—his prowess on the games field, in school plays, in his studies (with a sad smile and a ghost of a twinkle, "if and when he wanted"), his general popularity. Curious, though, how vague a picture one ended up with—a bit like those jolly prototypes in television advertisements of mothers and housewives and do-it-yourself fathers and schoolboy sons. He thought, as he had thought so many times, of what Eleanor had said over coffee at the Ritz.

The chapel appeared to be full, Maurice had only just got a seat. The bulk of the congregation was made up of schoolboys, with just three or four pews at the front containing women and men other than schoolmasters. Humphrey decided that as many boys had been let in as would fill the place once the extent of the outside attendance had been gauged. They would have begun with the boys in David's form, then gone on to the boys just above him and then those just below. He hadn't realised that the trivial chasing around of his mind had been a defence ploy. He'd all at once succeeded in disciplining himself to concentrate on the service, and as a result he could feel tears pricking behind his eyes. But tears for dead youth were proper, even from grown men. Tears for men and women who had lived their lives were merely for the mourners, at finding themselves bereft. Even with someone as young as David, though, his abiding belief that there was life to go on to should ease his lamentations. But they were, of course, as much for Marie and Frederick and Eleanor.

It was over, thank God it was over. He could see that Maurice was fidgeting, wishing he didn't have to wait for the family and the coffin to go out first. The family would be going with the coffin to the crematorium, so he'd sit by the sea for twenty minutes or so, before presenting himself at the house as Eleanor and Marie had invited him. Or talk to Maurice, if he wasn't in as desperate a hurry as his body movements were signalling.

Both parts of the Douglas family were coming up the aisle behind the coffin, facing him now, nearer and nearer. Humphrey had one horrified impression of the pinched stoicism of their faces (white except for George's, which was red, and Fabia's, which was pink and cream), then he was looking down at his hands on the pew back in front of him.

"Hello, Hump."

"Maurice! Oh, I'm glad that's over."

"Yes. Are you going to the crematorium?"

"No! Back to the house, though, they asked me. Can you spare a few moments?"

"Not really, but if you want to fill in time I'll drive you round the corner and you can walk back for your car."

"That's wonderful, Maurice. We'll just have to hang about a few minutes, until they've gone."

"I suppose so."

Frederick, Marie, and Eleanor were standing outside the chapel, waiting to greet the congregation as it emerged. Humphrey's admiration, that they should have elected to carry out the worst, and the optional, part of their ordeal, was a painful sensation. But surely all those masters would hold back the mass of the boys until the family, having greeted David's special friends, had left their post.

David's special friends? No one had ever mentioned any.

He rather mumbled his way over the handshakes. When Eleanor said that she would see him at the house, he was glad she was able to think of something so unimportant, before he was glad she had thought of him.

"I could tell by your back you were excited," he said to Maurice as they drove away. "Surely not just because you've found the Monster's last intended victim? It can't have any bearing on David's death?"

"I'm not so sure." Maurice had turned two corners and drawn up beside a relatively unspectacular prospect of the ubiquitous sea. "As I told you, her boyfriend turned really nasty when she said she was going to the police in response to the posters. She should have come much earlier, of course—it happened on the Thursday night—but she'd been afraid of losing her flat in town and her independence if she let on she'd been in such really bad trouble. The boyfriend was apparently away that night, and then again the night David died, but I haven't talked to him yet. I shall have to." Kendrick was almost smiling in his enthusiasm. "Well, Hump, I want to, of course. I'm intrigued, because this girl really is out of her mind with fear. The boy actually knocked her about when she said she was going to the police—you've only got to glance at her face to know that *somebody* did, and rather recently—and she told me he'd never shown any signs of violence before. Also—I had to prise this out of her with the help of a WPC—he got an instant obsession with the poor girl's br—injuries—that's the nearest I've got to spilling those particular beans, Hump, forgive me for drawing back, but I've made my men swear they won't tell *anyone.* Anyway, he's been pretty permanently turned on, it seems, since her misfortune. She came in in a really panicky state, and by the time she'd got over it a bit she realised that the one thing she wanted after all was to go home to her mum and dad. This simplifies things for us, as you'll appreciate. She's obviously afraid that her boyfriend will attack her again, and more violently, when he realises that not only did she defy him, he's going to get our attention because she did, and we have to suppose she's right. Now that she's decided she wants to go home, we simply tell her to stay there for the time being. Her injuries want treatment anyway, so she'll be better off away from work for a few days—at least until an injunction's been taken out preventing the boyfriend having access to her. The thing that's really intriguing me—the girl told me her boyfriend had drawn her attention to the fact of David having been killed forty-eight hours after her own ordeal, then made a point of reminding her he was away that night, too."

"I see." He didn't know whether he was relieved or dismayed. "It doesn't sound all that significant to me, Maurice, really. Forgive me, but—"

"The boyfriend would have known the Monster mark."

"Yes. Of course." Again that dual reaction of relief and dismay. "Have you heard from those French boys?"

"No. I almost forget about them. But all the time somewhere I have a faint hope that they might have been more observant than Bruce Holden's compatriots. Everyday things *do* tend to have more impact when one's abroad."

"Yes. Oh yes," responded Humphrey encouragingly, realizing he shared Maurice's hope of a way out for the Holden boy, and that once again he didn't want to work out why. "But you'll be going for this other young man now? I mean—"

"Going for him, yes, of course I will. It can't—dear Lord, it can't—be as difficult to discover if he really was away the night David died as it's proved to be to discover whether Bruce Holden is telling the truth. And if he was away, then that's that. If he wasn't, I shall really start to get excited. The girl, by the way, is being quite naïvely co-operative."

"Good." His spine was cold again. "I mustn't keep you any longer, Maurice. And if I stroll back for my car now, it'll be just the right time to get to the house."

"They'll all feel better now," said Kendrick, encouraging in his turn. "You know that, don't you?"

"Yes. Except that Emily wasn't murdered."

He didn't really want to go back to the house, he didn't want Marie to have to have anyone back. He was pleased, again largely for unselfish reasons, to discover that he was one of only half a dozen friends. He had been in the house for several minutes before realising he was also glad that none of them were young men.

Eleanor came and sat beside him, trying, he thought, to cheer both of them up so that he felt more and more uncomfortable about what he knew he must do the next night, the night they were going to the opera. It was worst of all when she said she was glad they were going.

"Yes, well, as I said, David would approve."

"Oh yes." She had broken the meat pie on her plate into several pieces, none of which she was eating.

"I'll have to meet you in town, Eleanor. I've got to go to London in the afternoon." He had to keep reminding himself of her extreme reaction when Maurice had told the family that the Monster had died too early to have killed David. And, of course, her behaviour by the left-luggage lockers. "I'll meet your train. Can you manage the five-thirty?"

"Quite easily." If his conscience hadn't been pricking, he'd have rejoiced for her that she was able to smile at him. He realised as the smile quickly faded that he was no longer able to enjoy the slight fullness of her lower lip, her mouth since David's death had changed so much. "At least David has ensured that I needn't pull my weight at work just now."

"I wish you wouldn't talk like that, Eleanor." He couldn't wish it in silence, he found it so disturbing—not least because it seemed to be uncharacteristic of the Eleanor he thought he knew, and each time a sarcasm came out it somehow made him think of her behaviour that morning at the station. . . .

"I'm sorry, Hump." Now she sounded so weary his heart smote him. The sarcasms were probably her defence, just as his trivial word games were his.

"It's all right, dear." He had found her hand before he knew he was reaching for it, and to his surprise, there in her parents' sitting-room with Marie's wet red eyes on them, she offered a return pressure and sustained it. It was he, at last, who withdrew his hand, as Jonathan appeared and thrust two plates out at them.

"A ham sandwich, Mr. Barnes? Or would you prefer a sausage roll?" Jonathan's shoulders were still squared, his voice was soft and level and his face expressionless, so that Humphrey had to make an effort of the imagination to remember the way he had looked and sounded the night of the party, when they had sat briefly together in the marquee. "Funeral baked meats, etcetera. At least there aren't any marriage tables in the offing, are there?"

Jonathan's eyes were resting serenely on his own—Humphrey didn't think the boy had blinked since he had appeared in front of them—and he found himself suddenly aflame with embarrassment, which intensified at the idea of anyone in the room being aware that he had been absurd enough to experience an involuntary personal response to Jonathan's casual remark. It *was* casual, surely. Palpable in the atmosphere was a sense of trauma which, if it in fact existed independent of his imagination, could make this stricken family say and do things out of character, beyond logic. Sometimes embarrassment showed in his pale face as a momentary pale pink; he'd seen it in the mirror. But nobody except Jonathan seemed to be looking at him, and Jonathan's gaze had a far more distant objective.

"Jonathan did *Hamlet* for O-levels," said Eleanor, almost in her normal voice and to his intense relief. "But in all fairness, he *is* more at home with the arts than most scientists."

"Liberal education," said Jonathan, turning suddenly and just catching a sausage roll as it jerked off one of the plates he was carrying. "I've always hoped I'd manage it." He smiled, so unexpectedly and humourlessly Humphrey was the victim of another small shock and thought longingly of going back to his office. As Jonathan turned away and Eleanor bent her head in silence to her plate, his mind turned almost enviously to Maurice, clear of the scene, pursuing his unnerving enthusiasms. It would surely be accurate to imagine Maurice now enjoying himself, but he had only the vaguest mental pictures of the surroundings in which Maurice would be indulging this unfamiliar sensation. He had never set foot inside either the Divisional headquarters or the Seaminster police station.

Kendrick, awaiting an answer, with an appearance at least of patience, from the young man who at his instigation had earlier been brought in, looked round the interview room and imagined his friend Humphrey, if ever taken on a tour of the station, trying to say something complimentary about its bumpy grey walls and linoleumed floor. In his new, ebullient mood he was able to find the reflection amusing, actually have to repress his reaction to it to prevent any suspicion of a smile from reaching his mouth.

The constable in the corner coughed and scraped his chair—the linoleum had worn near the wall and one of the chair legs was on the stone floor underneath. Kendrick brought his gaze back to the man on the other side of the table, his dark head bent, his mutinous glance apparently on the hands enlaced in front of him, the fingers intermittently twitching.

"Perhaps you didn't hear me. I'm asking why you had to hit your girlfriend in the face because she wanted to do her civic duty."

"Civic duty!" The pale face came up sneering. "Your Monster was dead; it said that on the posters, too. Why should Doreen have to go through it all again so that you could cross a few *t's* in your files?"

"But that was what she wanted to do," said Kendrick quite gently. "You can't have had any doubts about that."

"Doreen doesn't always know what's good for her." *Good for her?* The boy was conventionally handsome, in a sullen mould which made Kendrick think of his own earlier days and James Dean. He was constantly aware of the barely suppressed rage. "She gets carried away."

"Carried away? Behaving sensibly and responsibly? It won't do, Porter." Kendrick sighed and got to his feet. He started to pace the small area, watched by the constable but not the boy, whose eyes were down again. "You overreacted in a way which makes you interesting to us, just at the moment."

The head shot up again. "I wasn't in Seaminster when Doreen was cut up. And I wasn't here when that boy was murdered. Find that interesting, do you?"

"Unless and until I know you're telling the truth." Kendrick spoke at the farthest point from the boy which the room offered him, then flashed round and went to sit down in one rapid movement, leaning confidentially across the table until he induced a slight recoil. "We'll start with the more recent event, the death of David Douglas last Saturday night. When did you leave Seaminster on the Saturday?"

The head came up again, slowly this time. "I've told the other bloke. If your sidekick had written it down, you wouldn't have to ask me again. I left about eleven. I didn't actually look at my watch as I drove off, so I can't say more than that. About eleven. Why doesn't he write it down?"

"You can write it down yourself, eventually. For the moment I'd just like you to go through it again. And quite possibly again. And even, it could be, again after that. Although if you tell the truth now we may be able to make do with that."

"I've told the truth already."

"I'd like you to tell it again."

"With my lawyer here."

Not for the first time, Kendrick regretted the popularity of police series on television. "I'd better remind you, Porter, that I'm in a position to charge you with causing grievous bodily harm. Now, let's hear it again."

The head jerked. Like the head of an animal feeling the first, loose coil of the lasso on its back, thought Kendrick.

"If you've got the time . . ."

"I've all the time in the world," Kendrick assured him. "Give."

"I often do business on a Saturday." The suddenly light, almost casual, tone made Kendrick wonder about the nature of the business. Extra-curricular activities of a kind Raymond Porter would prefer to keep quiet about, most likely. Kendrick regretted his sudden sense of impending disappointment that Porter's punishing desire to keep his girlfriend away from the police could have been put down to no more than the nature of his weekend business.

"Away from home?"

"That's it." The comparatively compliant attitude was still evident. "I'm in the garage business—you know that—and Saturday's the day I meet up with opposite numbers and compare trends and the week's business. You know."

"Not really," said Kendrick. "That's why I'm interested in you telling me. Where d'you go?"

"Midchester, mostly." The tongue tip furtively moistening what must be dry lips could have been licking a one-up to Kendrick on a tally board. "It was Midchester this time. Most of the boys—my opposite numbers—work in Midchester, though sometimes we get together different places."

"And where in Midchester did you get together this time?"

"Here and there."

"Not good enough, Porter."

"All right. Saturday I went to White's garage on the Caley Road—you can check up."

"We are doing. Then?"

"There were five of us. We went on to a pub for a drink and a sandwich. The Duck and Cabbage. You can—all right, I told the other bloke."

"How long did you stay there?"

"Can't say exactly. Anyway, we were at this car auction by half three and we went straight there." There was a gleam of triumph. "You can check that out all right."

"Good. After the auction?"

"We went back to White's garage for an hour or so, just to tidy up the loose ends." The eyes, which were unusually large and blue, slid aside. "You can check, Mr. Chief Superintendent. It got a bit sort of less businesslike after that. We went on to another pub—the Farmer's Arms at Heathley—and stayed there until we got hungry—I suppose it would be about eight—I've told them already—then went back to this bloke's house—Ben Gerrard, I've told them—and his missus made us all fish and chips—she often does, she's really decent—and by the time we'd got that down, and some more of the drink we'd brought in with us, I wasn't in the best shape for driving back to Seaminster. Phyl Gerrard said I oughtn't to and I knew she was right, so I took up her invite to sleep on the sofa. I've done it before on a Saturday; it opens out into a bed, very handy."

"So you performed a public duty yourself, Porter, refusing to drink and drive."

"That's it. No point in asking for trouble, is there?"

"None at all, I'm glad you see it that way. Doreen wasn't expecting to see you that evening?"

"No. I did sometimes go back on a Saturday in time to go to a disco, but as I said, I sometimes kipped at the Gerrards', and anyway she was all in, I'd seen her the night before, the night after she'd had that do, and I thought she ought to have a day in bed. On her own. We'd arranged to spend the Sunday together. I rang her from the Duck and Cabbage. I told them that and you can check."

"Doreen has told us she received a call from you."

The sneer was there again, an unpleasant small shock. "Regular little copper's nark, isn't she?"

"An injunction is being sought preventing you from approaching her, Porter. I advise you very strongly from now on to keep away."

"Don't worry, Superintendent." The anger was still piling up. But if his, Kendrick's, luck really had changed, Porter wouldn't be in a position to disobey his advice.

"When you get back to your digs very late," said Kendrick, "is your landlady likely to hear you?" He was staring into those limpid eyes, and they didn't falter. Porter shrugged. Kendrick tried not to see it as a gesture of confidence.

"She has done, she's called me a dirty stopout. But I wasn't back till about ten on Sunday morning."

"She saw you arriving?"

"Yes." Again the flash of triumph. Kendrick encouraged himself with the reflection that it had been absent from about ninety per cent of Porter's narrative. "She said I looked as if I'd been on the tiles and I said she was being less than fair to me."

That had been easy enough to check, immediately after the first time he'd been taken through it. The landlady had confirmed the bit of badinage as well.

"Thank you, Porter. What time had you— Come in!"

The tap on the door was followed by the upper body of another police constable. "Inspector Riley's here, sir. I wouldn't have disturbed you, but he thinks you'd like to—"

"That's all right, Constable." Kendrick followed the constable outside, closing the door, trying to subdue his excitement.

"Something for me, Riley?"

"Well, sir . . . He was at the pubs and the motor auction as he said, and in the same company. As you suggested, I got on to Mrs. Gerrard rather than any of the men, and she went through the classic routine of being a bit hesitant, and then suddenly absolutely sure. You know the sort of thing. I could swear she was lying when she said Porter had spent the whole night in her house. Before she got all positive she showed me the sofa he was supposed to have kipped on and said he'd lain on it until he'd slept it off and then . . . then she was all at once assuring me he'd stayed there for the rest of the night. The first part of it was true, I should say, but after that . . . I took the decision, in fact, sir"—Detective-Inspector Riley was coming to the point which would explain why he was looking at the station floor as if it were covered in jellyfish—"not to approach the men at all until Mrs. Gerrard's had a chance to think things over. Of course there's the chance she may telephone her husband and then he'll do his best to stiffen her up. But she may just think about it on her ownsome and come back to us. There was no particular urgency about getting onto the men, sir, was there? I hope I haven't—"

"I think you've been rather intelligent, Frank. We'll give it an hour or two. Meanwhile I'm inclined to try a bluff in there, suggest the lady's already come across."

"As you think, sir. Thank you, sir."

Smiling in relief, Inspector Riley beat a retreat, and Kendrick went back into the interview room.

He tried to cover the short space to the table in a portentous manner, but the act was lost on Porter, whose head was down again over his hands. When the silence was beginning to get Kendrick down, Porter raised his eyes.

"Ah," said Kendrick, "you're ready for us to continue. It's not really so much of a continuation, Porter, as a coming to an end. I'm afraid that when your friends—your business contacts—learned that it was a police matter they told the truth. You sobered up at the Gerrards', but you didn't stay there all night." The white face stared at him without expression, but to Kendrick's surprise a sudden brightness of eye indicated the nearness of tears. Please God they weren't the tears of despair at not being believed when speaking the truth. "It's a serious matter," he said more gently. "If you have nothing to do with David Douglas's death you'll help yourself to prove this by telling the truth. I appreciate you may have had a reason for pretending you were away from Seaminster that night which has nothing to do with the murder. But I think you would be wise to tell me. Now, what time did you leave the Gerrards', and where did you go?"

"Must have been half past eleven, quarter to twelve." Kendrick had to lean forward and down to catch what was hardly more than a whisper. "I've got this new girl. Out of my class but she fancies me. It won't last so I didn't want Doreen bothered, and that's why I told her I wouldn't see her on Saturday. I told her on the Sunday I'd been all night with the Gerrards." *But before the murder, he'd merely told her he wouldn't be seeing her.* "It seemed simpler, somehow. The Gerrards and the other boys had agreed to back me up; they thought it was a joke. Then when I read about that murder and Doreen said she was going to the police—I reckoned the story that I stayed in Midchester all night was the best one all round. Not that I thought the little bitch'd have so much to say about me as well as about her adventures in the woods."

"Remember what I said to you about Doreen. So you arrived back in Seaminster about twelve, twelve-fifteen."

"Must have done." Defiance, which was the mask of fear.

"And went straight to your new girlfriend. Where does she live?"

"East Cliff. Posh, yes, I said. And not so far from Birch Road, you're thinking. Better go and have a look in my room."

"We are doing. Your landlady will be showing us round."

"To see fair play? You won't find anything."

"It's been four days."

"Isn't that slander, Mr. Chief Superintendent?"

"It's just a statement of fact," said Kendrick, suddenly anxious to bring the interview to an end. "Write down the particulars of your new girl for the sergeant, and then you can make a formal statement."

"I'll make a statement. I'm not saying anything about the girl."

"It won't read like chivalry to us, Porter." Tiredness had pierced his elation and he lurched wearily to the door, to confront Detective-Inspector Riley once more, just raising his hand to knock.

"Any joy?" asked Kendrick, closing the door behind him.

"I should say yes, sir. Mrs. Gerrard's just been on, to tell us she's thought it over and felt she should tell us the truth. Porter kipped on the sofa until about eleven-thirty, then disappeared into the night."

CHAPTER 13

Humphrey went to London next day at lunch-time, although all that was essential was for him to be there in time to meet Eleanor off the five-thirty train from Seaminster. There was, he had realised, the slight danger that she might decide to go up to town by an earlier train and that, if he left it until, say, the three forty-five and she was on it, he would have no explanation to offer for his behaviour, to say nothing of the possibility of encountering her somewhere in Seaminster during an afternoon on which he was supposed to be elsewhere. These, however, were not the chief reasons for his reluctant departure by the one-fifteen: He took that train, and consigned himself to an uneasy couple of hours wandering about St. James's Park, from an absurd sense that he ought to do what he had told Eleanor he was intending to do—spend the afternoon in London. He hadn't told her anything beyond that, so walking in the park instead of sitting in his Seaminster office was to spare her the lie direct.

At least it was a fine day, more like September than November, and his favourite park was beautiful, the lake sparkling beyond a lazy fall of the last gold leaves, the sun gold on grass and tree-trunks, the air warm enough to have encouraged a variety of people to walk slowly or sit in the deck-chairs whose summer tenure a flexible authority had extended into sympathetic autumn. As he walked, sat, and fed waterbirds, sparrows, and pigeons on buns bought at a teahouse, Humphrey considered and rejected a range of possible reactions to Eleanor's inevitable casual query as to how his afternoon had gone, feeling ultimately more comfortable with the decision to play it as it came. At a quarter past four his insides reminded him that he hadn't really had lunch—he'd only managed to play with the substantial cheese roll his secretary had brought in for him before he left the office—and he went back to the teahouse and sat outside it drinking tea and playing this time with a Danish pastry. Anyway, he'd ordered smoked salmon sandwiches and wine for the long, civilised Covent Garden interval.

His agreeable situation appeased him despite himself, until he began wondering, with the sense of anxiety which had become inseparable from the thought of Maurice, how his friend was proceeding with the fresh slant to his investigation. He'd been out the night before having dinner with his brother, so he couldn't be certain Maurice hadn't telephoned him with the news that his new suspect was looking more and more promising. Or—a goose walked over his grave—that something had happened to make it obvious he was on the wrong tack. And he wouldn't be there if Maurice telephoned tonight.

He carried his speculations on a last tour of the park, in the end almost running to the tube, but of course emerging onto the station concourse with time to spare. Resisting the temptation to go back to the left-luggage lockers, he spent it in the bookstall nearby, and was standing at the barrier, composure outwardly regained, as the small crowd appeared from the Seaminster train.

Eleanor was in the centre of it, looking, he thought (with allowance for the difference in dress), as Anna Karenina had probably looked on

the station platform that last time, her face so pale and weary. . . .
Remembering that Anna had left the platform only to plunge beneath a
train, Humphrey was assailed by a sense of horror so searing it was still
on him when Eleanor had given up her ticket, passed through the barrier, and arrived to stand in front of him, smiling for a moment in
which she no longer looked tired.

"Humphrey! I knew you'd be waiting, of course. You look as if you'd
seen a ghost. Have I been travelling with a bit of your murky past?"

"Not the past, Eleanor." *The future?* He couldn't see the future as
being any longer than the evening. "Thank you for coming."

"I wanted to come, Hump chump."

She was dressed almost sombrely in a skirt and jacket of some brown
silky material over a plain blouse, and he approved the sense of fitness
which would offer a reminder of what had happened, even though none
was necessary. He himself had chosen his darkest suit and most lacklus-
tre tie.

"How are you?"

"I think I'm all right. How was your afternoon?"

He felt himself shrugging. "Much as expected." None of the possible
responses which had occurred to him in the park had been so totally
truthful. "Have you been to the gallery today?"

"For a short time this morning. In a way I find it easier to be there
than to be at home. Mummy and I . . . We're almost . . . well, almost *embarrassed* together. Each time we look at one another we're
signalling the whole awful thing again. Can you imagine—"

"Yes." He didn't need to imagine, he could remember. Going to stay
with Emily's sister and cutting the visit short because of neither of them
being able to bear the view of the other's grief. "Come along. We're
early, of course, but that was the latest possible train."

He was watching her sidelong as they moved away. Past the bookstall, the entrance to the left-luggage lockers . . .

"I had another look at the books," he said, "because of being too
early as usual, but the stock seems to be exactly the same as it was on
Monday."

His hand was lightly at her elbow and there was no doubt that her
arm stiffened. She murmured, "Yes," and quickened her step, whether
by instinct or intent there was no way for him to tell.

But the time was not yet.

They went on the tube to Covent Garden and walked about the two levels of the elegant small shops. Eleanor drew him into a picture gallery which seemed to be full of prints and watercolours of ordinary objects—windows and doors and tables—grown baleful, and a large stock of perverse postcards. Eleanor knew the girl who was serving and whom Humphrey saw as the colours and textures of the pictures made flesh. He had begun to enjoy his surroundings, to the extent of actually buying a postcard, when, strolling together, he and Eleanor turned a corner onto another bright picture, of a boy spreadeagled on an empty infinity of ground.

Hands flying together, they leapt back. Eleanor said, in a passionate whisper, "It's no good! It'll never be any good!"

"It will, it will." His heart as well as his conscience smote him at the thought of the immeasurably worse thing he was to do against her. It was becoming more and more of an effort to remember her reaction to the news that the Monster couldn't have murdered David.

"To forget for a moment! It's dreadful."

"It's nature. Not that one really does forget. Not *forget.* Other things come in front, that's all. Or you can see it as successive seasons of fallen leaves." For heaven's sake, he spun words and images round himself like a—like a shroud. And he was about to press on. "The old leaves haven't gone, they've just been covered up, and—"

"Thanks, Humphrey." They were out of the gallery, and still hand in hand. Humphrey had only just noticed, and decided Eleanor hadn't.

"There's nothing I can do to make you thank me for it," he said miserably.

"Oh, but there is. You having had the same experience . . . Well, not the same of course, much worse, forgive me." He had to look away from her. "But losing someone. And sharing how you felt. And—and— just being there, being you . . . Oh!" Eleanor looked down at their hands, then unclasped her own. "You're easier to be with just now than anyone else. Well, you must realise that."

"I hadn't realised it. I can't really imagine . . ." He was pleased to see the slight colour in her face, although it was probably just that she had embarrassed herself.

"*Yes*, Humphrey." She took his hand again, to squeeze and release. "Look! No need to say listen!" she shouted, as they were enfolded in the rich blasts from a saxophone which was being played in the open space at one end of the shops by a man who at the same time was working a small drum by treadle and illuminating himself in the dusk with an Anglepoise lamp curved above his head. He wore a shiny-backed waistcoat and a bowler hat, and was surrounded at a distance by a fringe of people, several of whom kept looking pointedly about them as if, Humphrey thought, loath to acknowledge themselves an audience.

"It's gorgeous sound, isn't it?" said Eleanor. "Each note's reproaching me for appreciating it."

"David would laugh at you." He had spoken before knowing he was going to. But he stood by it. "He'd say you were ridiculous."

"He would, wouldn't he?"

There was a detached, reflective note in her voice which made him turn and look at her. Her eyes were fixed above the performer's head and despite the intermittent light he could see an expression in them of something more than grief. Apprehension?

Whatever it was, it reminded him of something he didn't like.

"I think we might go into the theatre now. Have a drink. I don't know what you've had to eat today, but I've ordered smoked salmon sandwiches for the interval and I'm going to see that you have your share."

"Good old Humphrey," she said, he thought absently.

Standing by the bar she was aware of him again, and told him her mother and father were going away.

"On Saturday. To the Cotswolds. Which they discovered before David was born, and before I was, either. I've had to persuade them, but I'm certain it's a good idea. It'll be easier for me, too."

"But you won't stay at home on your own?" he asked, aghast.

Briefly she smiled at him. "It wouldn't be so dreadful. Well, perhaps at the moment. Anyway, I'm going to stay with Marian, my partner. There are two children, and a husband who never takes anything seriously. They asked me, I didn't."

"You wouldn't."

"Marian Foster," she said. "Mrs. J. S. Foster. Seaminster 0682. It's in the phone book of course if you don't remember."

"Thank you, Eleanor." He hadn't time to enjoy the surprise of learning she wanted to keep in touch with him before being swamped by regret at having to tell her that he was going away, too.

"Ah, I see. When, Humphrey?"

"On Sunday. I'm driving up to Edinburgh for my annual fortnight."
"Yes, you *would* have an annual fortnight. Several different sorts of annual fortnights, probably." She was briefly pink again, and again there was something in her eyes which he didn't recognise, but this time it intrigued rather than repelled him, even though he knew it was tinged with hostility.

"It seems you know me depressingly well. Anyway, I'm driving up on Sunday, because of there being almost no motorway lorries that day." He paused and smiled at her. "I always do that, too."

"*Humphrey.*" She half smiled back. "I'm sorry. I'm prickly just now. But it isn't only that. You don't know. I'm selfish but I'm sorry you're going away. I'm trying very hard to get Mummy and Daddy to stay three weeks. So when you get back, Seaminster 0682."

"I shan't forget, I shan't have to look it up." He was disconcerted to find himself deciding he would really rather be ignored by Eleanor than courted as a sympathetic uncle. Although what other kind of relationship could he aspire to with her, for goodness' sake? He hadn't known he had so much vanity. Shaken by his reactions, he tried to sound enthusiastic at the idea of being *in loco parentis.* "Will you have dinner with me the night I get back? I hate cooking after a journey, so you'll be doing me a favour. It will be a fortnight on Sunday, whatever the date is. Can you keep it?"

"Of course, Humphrey."

"Book somewhere for us then, please." The bell was ringing, and they joined the slow drift out of the bar. "I'm glad *The Seraglio*'s a comedy."

"David would have approved? No, *no,* Humphrey!" she added immediately, before he had time to flinch, reminding him of her remorse, to the extent of stamping her foot, when at the Silver Wedding party she had appeared to lump him among those guests of her parents' generation who had to be doled out a dance. (He found the memory not very far below the surface.) "I may be prickly but I wasn't getting at you then. I was thinking of David. . . ." Again a look he didn't understand. "I'm sure he *would* have approved," she said briskly. "And as for me, I've supped enough on horrors, or whatever the quotation is."

" 'I have supped full with horrors,' " he supplied, then wished he had managed not to.

"I don't know anything about this opera," she said, as they sat down and he handed her a programme.

"It's preposterous but fun when well done. Weber said Mozart never again produced a major work so thoroughly imbued with the spirit of youth and happiness." He hesitated. "It's a love story, really. The heroine's name is Constanza, and Mozart was just marrying his own Constanze."

She didn't answer as the lights went down, but when the prolonged applause died away at the end of the first act she turned to him. "That was lovely. I didn't think I would have liked it so much." She went on over the sandwiches, after she had eaten two and he had slightly relaxed his vigilance, "I haven't listened to music—what *you'd* call music, Humphrey—since I left school. I suppose you know about pictures, too."

He had to smile. "Not much about very modern ones. And I'm ashamed I've never been to your gallery. Although it's only because of shyness, honestly."

She stared. "Shyness? You, Humphrey?"

Of course, uncles were not expected to be shy; it was an affliction far removed from their detached, avuncular natures. But he went stubbornly on, "Me. Yes. I can feel shy."

"When, I wonder?" The favourite niece was practising, casting her eyes down, then suddenly, provocatively, upwards.

"When—when I do anything I don't normally do." He spoke a little sadly. That hadn't been what he had wanted to say, but it was the truth.

"Ah yes." She patted his hand as if to say "Never mind" and he felt sadder still. "That's you, isn't it?"

"I suppose it must be, by now."

Eleanor laughed, and the better part of him rejoiced to hear her. "Don't look so tragic, Humphrey. I like you to be as you are."

She would, of course. Uncles ought to be stodgy and predictable, to fill their traditional roles. "Thank you," he said.

"Honestly." Her face clouded. All evening it had been like an April sky. "I think I'll ring Mummy."

"When you've had another sandwich."

While she was away he did his best to adjust himself to what seemed to have flowered as her innocent need of him. Temporarily? That he must certainly be prepared for. It was almost a relief to leave the subject alone and start worrying about what he was going to do when they got back to the station. He said nothing in the second interval, or at the end of the performance, merely keeping them moving at as steady a pace as possible through the departing crowd, along the pavement to the tube. On the tube she had her most sustained burst of cheerfulness since David's body had been found, turning a knife in him. They were up the steps from the underground, just on the concourse, when she commented on their slight speed.

"I know you like to be in good time, Humphrey, but we really have got heaps of it. More than a quarter of an hour, and we've both got tickets."

He cleared his throat, leading her even more rapidly in the direction he must go. "I know. But I had a whole lot of papers with me this afternoon—for the meeting—" there, in the end, was the lie—"and I didn't want to carry them round with us all evening, so I popped them into a left-luggage locker. Such useful things, aren't they? I'm glad they've started to let people use them again, since the bomb scares died down."

He burbled on for a few seconds beyond his awareness of her sudden weight on his arm. Until, in fact, he had to stop because she was no longer moving. In agonized reluctance he turned to look at her. "What is it, Eleanor?" He was horrified to hear his innocently concerned voice.

"It's nothing, I was just faint for a moment. You know I haven't been eating much. I'm all right."

"Shall we find a seat?" She looked so suddenly terrible, he was weak himself, with remorse. Her pale face was ashen, and her eyes were supping on those horrors she had so recently dismissed. Her whole weight was on his arm but as he asked his question he felt it lighten, assisted by an almost painful circling of his wrist by her hand.

"No, no. Just take no notice. It'll pass. It's passing. . . ."

There had been no way of telling whether the locker she had used was still occupied—he hadn't been near enough or at the correct angle to pinpoint it—but he had chosen one as close as he could to where she had appeared to be standing on Monday morning. He felt her sag again as he led the way towards it.

"Here we are!" He heard the false joviality of his voice; he had never felt less jovial. "Poor Eleanor, I'm sorry I haven't got the car." He was torn in half by his two preoccupations: his desire to know the truth, and his real concern for her. "Lean on me, if you like, while I'm—"

"It's all right."

Her voice was strange, not merely feeble, and when he had his locker open he turned round to her.

She was standing against the lockers opposite, and there was a look in her eyes which sent an icy finger down his back. Fear. Furtiveness. He'd seen them before, but now there was an extra element. Suspicion. So strong, as he forced himself to hold her eyes, it was enabling her to draw herself away from the support behind her.

"Humphrey," said Eleanor, in a hard unfamiliar voice, "please tell me what you're doing."

"What I'm doing, dear?" He was shocked, again, that he could sound so tenderly puzzled when his swamping emotion was fury with himself for having overdone it, pushed his luck too far. He had to force himself a second time, to be able to go on. "You can see what I'm doing, I'm retrieving my papers."

"Of course. Yes, of course, I'm sorry, Humphrey." She had slumped back against the lockers and the suspicion had left her eyes with the fear and the other thing he could hardly bear to name even in his mind. Gone, he was certain, not dissembled, and weak with relief he, too, leaned back, bruising his spine on the open door. The stab of pain seemed to clear his mind. He picked up his briefcase and took her arm.

"Come along," he said cheerfully. "We've still got plenty of time. I'm glad you had those sandwiches."

"Only because you made me." She looked better, and there was no pressure on his arm as they reached the barrier. "Let's walk up to the top. There's still time and there won't be so many people. Stop looking so worried, Humphrey. I'm not going to throw a fit. I'm not even going to have the vapours again."

But as the train began to move she suddenly turned to him in the seat they shared, digging her fingers even more uncomfortably into his arm and almost hissing into his ear.

"Humphrey I'm desperate, I don't think I can hold on. I don't think I can bear it. Humphrey, please. Hold me. Hold me, Humphrey, cover me up. Don't let me go mad."

"Eleanor . . ."

He was disgusted with himself, even as he did it, that he should first look round to see if there was anyone to observe them. And even if there had been, surely he would still have done what she asked?

"Thank you, Humphrey." At least she didn't seem to be aware of any delay. He felt her body almost burrowing against him, the body of a small animal trying to escape the perilous surface of the earth. He should be grateful that it was being given to him to be the uncle, the comforter, the solid presence.

Her arms were round his neck now, he thought she was sobbing dry sobs. She was whispering as a sort of incantation. "It's so awful, so awful. If you knew, if you knew, if you knew . . ." Over and over again.

"I do know, Eleanor." It really was as well there was no one to see them, with Eleanor writhing against him. On this particular train there could quite easily be someone he knew. Probably was, farther down.

"No, no, no!" She drew her head back indignantly. "You don't know, you can't know. Oh, Humphrey, you're the only thing that's real, that isn't a shadow." Her anguished face blurred as her head dropped towards him again. Her cheek was against his as he made small encouraging sounds, was moving, covering his mouth. No, not her cheek, her lips. Eleanor was kissing him, fiercely, even energetically, as—in one shocked second he admitted it for the first time—she had kissed him so often in his dreams. He was kissing her. . . .

No!

Almost roughly Humphrey struggled his hands up to her shoulders and pushed her away from him, an uncomfortable melange of selfish and unselfish emotions. He didn't know anything about Eleanor's private life. Whatever she had hidden in the locker could have been to do with an affair of her own, something she didn't want the police to find if they were looking round for clues about David.

An affair?

Eleanor had kissed him; perhaps she kissed easily. Though even if she did—and why should the possibility fill him with such pain?—surely he as her uncle was the last person to be concerned. He should be glad to think that the brown-paper parcel might have nothing to do with David's death.

Her face was in focus now, looking almost as if she was asleep, her eyes closed, her mouth, despite its recent activity, remote, unaware. And when one was asleep one sometimes had silly dreams. He had once dreamed of a flirtation with the elderly unattractive filing clerk in his office. . . . For heaven's sake, had she fainted?

"Eleanor! Oh, Eleanor . . . dear . . ."

"Humphrey . . ." Her eyes were open, she was staring at him in a sort of bewilderment, then gently withdrawing to lean back against her own side of the double seat. "I'm sorry."

"No, Eleanor, no!" he said, anguished. "*I'm* sorry, I—"

She ran her hands over her frame of hair. "Thank you for understanding."

What ought he to have understood? He realised the train had stopped, started again, without any movement round them in or out.

"Your friend the chief superintendent," she said. "How is he getting on? It wasn't as straightforward as he'd imagined." She was facing him, but her eyes were turned away.

"No." His heart leapt at the opportunity she had given him, then plummeted before another prospect of trial which must be exploited. "He's much more cheerful these past couple of days, though. He appears to have found a new and very likely suspect."

He made himself smile as he spoke, and determinedly went on smiling as he saw fear again in her face, so strong and sudden for a moment he thought she would be unable to control it.

"A—new suspect?"

There had been several seconds before she spoke, and it had hurt him to compound her shock by waiting in silence.

"Yes. Someone who claims to have been elsewhere at the time. So he's still got an alibi to break."

"I see."

And Humphrey saw relief, as unambiguous as the fear it replaced, followed, deep down behind the wide eyes, by an access of what he could only call dread. Instantly he partook of it.

"Are you managing to sleep?"

The question was the first thing that occurred to him as an alternative to staring into her face.

If possible the dread intensified. "No, Humphrey," she said in a whisper, "I'm not able to sleep."

It would have been inappropriate, at that moment, to give her the anodyne assurance that eventually she would. Instead he took her hand, overcoming an initial new wariness, and held it in silence until they reached Seaminster.

On the platform, outside the station on the walk to his car, it was cold, and she crossed her arms and crouched over them, moving a little apart from him.

"All right?"

"Yes."

On her doorstep, her key in her hand, she turned to him.

"I won't ask you in, Humphrey. Mummy and Daddy—"

"Of course not." Anyway, he didn't want to go in. Buffeted by various primary sensations, he was as tired as if he had spent the evening combating a gale.

"You go away on Sunday."

"I'll ring you."

"I know you will. Thanks." She yawned. The sort of nervous reaction he had seen in cats.

"Before I go away. Thank you for coming tonight."

"Thank you for asking me. Humphrey?"

"Yes?"

"Good night. Thank you. Really."

She opened the front door, so that after she had kissed his cheek she was able to flit instantly inside.

CHAPTER 14

"I beg your pardon?" The haughty beauty looked at Kendrick as though he had just crawled out from under the nearest stone.

"Raymond Porter," repeated Kendrick. "He tells us he spent last Saturday night—the night of twenty-ninth/thirtieth October—here with you in your house, arriving about twelve-thirty. Are you prepared to confirm his statement?"

"His statement, Inspector?" Kendrick was sure she was aware of his rank and, unlike Fabia Douglas, was deliberately demoting him. "I think you must mean his impudent lie. Perjury actually, isn't it, when you swear a false statement? Raymond Porter tried to chat me up in my local a few weeks ago, and found out my address. My only contact with him since has been a few words at my front door before I closed it on him. He *did* ring my bell on Saturday night, which is as near as his story comes to the truth. I thought he was merely out of his class, but he must be out of his mind as well."

Perhaps he was, thought Kendrick, denied access to this tall blond creature with the confident husky voice and perfect length of leg. Perhaps he had lurched about the quiet roads of East Seaminster in his frustration, and come upon David Douglas tempting fate.

But if it had been like that—already, in his head, Kendrick had begun the dialogue with himself which he considered the due of every last one of his suspects—would Porter have offered Miss Samantha Budd as his alibi? Would he have taken a gamble on her being of a temperament so eccentrically quixotic?

Yes, answered Kendrick, if he was in a corner and the alternative was to say he'd just been roaming around. And it had taken a day and a half to get the woman's name out of Porter, a measure of his desperation.

Or of an unexpected sense of chivalry? He could have had inordinate sexual confidence, and read the lady's rebuff as merely the prelude to her acceptance of him. Looking into the proud indignant face, Kendrick gave Porter higher marks for self-confidence than for realism.

Unless he was telling the truth . . .

Then Miss Budd would be lying, and of course (his heart sank at the prospect) his men would soon be in the pub round the corner, talking to the landlord and staff, trying to establish the real nature of that encounter. If she was lying, she was putting on a first-rate performance. If only he could direct the fingerprint team up to her bedroom. There was still a long way to go on Raymond Porter. And there was still Bruce Holden.

Thinking of Bruce's pathetic description of how David Douglas had behaved, Kendrick allowed himself to wish that the body of the Monster had lain undisturbed long enough for it to have been impossible for the Path people to have pinpointed the time of its death to within a week, let alone two days.

"What time was it, Miss Budd, that Raymond Porter came to your front door on Saturday night?"

"Goodness, Inspector, I can't remember! Half past twelve? One? All I'm sure of is that I was in my dressing-gown and ready for bed."

"You were alone in the house?"

"I was." Her eyes flashed, but she relaxed as he murmured, "No housekeeper . . ."

"Not at the moment." He could see that this time he had made the right sort of suggestion.

"So you opened the front door in your dressing-gown, after midnight, to a young man you hadn't invited to your house."

"I did not, Inspector." Miss Budd's full height surpassed that of Sergeant Grant, but she was wearing very high heels.

"You said you closed the door on him."

She bit her full red underlip. "That was when he came once during the day. Not that I let him in then, either. On Saturday night I saw him through my spyhole, and told him through the letter-box to go away." She said, almost with impatience, "These things tend to happen to me, Inspector."

"I can imagine they do. Thank you very much, Miss Budd, for being so helpful. I really am sorry we've been forced to intrude on you with these routine inquiries. But you'll appreciate that every least lead has to be followed up . . ."

"Of course, Superintendent." Miss Budd was actually smiling at him, showing him many immaculate teeth.

". . . in a matter of murder." She would put two and two together anyway. It was already determined that the previous Saturday night was to be notorious in the annals of Seaminster. His sergeant gave a just perceptible nod.

"Murder?"

She had checked, just. But anyone innocently brushed by the ultimate crime would show a reaction.

"I'm afraid so. Mr. Porter was attempting to establish an alibi. Somewhat foolishly, I must now believe." He smiled at her in disingenuous encouragement. He thought she took a deep breath.

"Very foolishly, Superintendent. Murder . . . I'm sorry I can't help him. But if he killed someone—"

"Mr. Porter is merely helping us with our inquiries," said Sergeant Grant blandly, "in company with others."

"Innocent people frequently have no alibi at all," observed Kendrick.

He paused. "But to have one broken must, you'll appreciate, quicken police interest in the person involved. There is, of course, sometimes the discovery that the motive for attempting to set up a false alibi has been no more than panic. This could be the explanation in Porter's case, although in view of what you have just told us it's curious, to say the least." He smiled again. "We're sorry to have troubled you."

"That's quite all right, Superintendent. Sergeant. I'll show you out." Half-way across her hall she stopped and turned round to them. "Superintendent, it must be the murder of the boy who was dressed up."

"That took place on Saturday night," Kendrick agreed. Miss Budd waited a few seconds, then in the face of their silence walked on and opened her front door.

"Pretty garden," said Sergeant Grant.

Between Miss Budd's front door and her gate was a charming profusion of small conifers and terracotta urns set on multicoloured paving. Right out of young Porter's league, no doubt about that, and it wasn't hard to imagine Miss Budd being appalled at the prospect of such a connection becoming public knowledge.

Characteristically, Kendrick broke off his interior dialogue at a point which was counter to the outcome he thought he would prefer to see. But back in the interview room the young man's demeanour had become so crushed he began to be afraid of developing the same sense of reluctance which had discomfited him from the start of his unavoidable assault on Bruce Holden.

"I've seen Miss Budd, Porter, and she denies ever having let you into her house."

"She—what?" Porter was on his feet, backing into the corner of the room as if to escape Kendrick's revelation.

Revelation? If Miss Budd was as honest as she had presented herself, he would have to have been expecting it.

"Denies your statement. Says that you've never gained admission to her house. That you went round there on Saturday night—at the time you told us—but that she didn't open the door."

Kendrick was silent as Porter sat down heavily at the table and dropped his head on his arms. Eventually he took the chair opposite and leaned across. "Perhaps you'd like to tell me," he said gently, "what really happened on Saturday night."

"I have told you." Porter raised his head and looked into Kendrick's face with a sort of angry defeat. "So what's the use?"

"You don't wish to amend your statement?"

"I don't have anything else to say."

"Take a rest, then," said Kendrick. "And we'll have a talk later on."

"I don't have anything else to say."

"I'll send you in a cup of tea." There was a knock at the door, and the constable, on a nod from Kendrick, got up and opened it. Inspector Crowther's face came round.

"I'm sorry to disturb you, sir, but there's something . . ."

"I was just coming out, Inspector. Important, is it?" he asked when he had shut the door behind him. He had noted the flushed face and bright eyes.

"Well, yes, sir. We caught up with those French boys. The tape's in the Incident Room."

"Let's go."

A statement similar to all the other statements—observations—on the conduct at the Douglas party of Bruce Holden vis-à-vis David Douglas would hardly have so noticeably altered the appearance of the normally phlegmatic Brian Crowther. Kendrick's heart was racing as the inspector stood back for him to enter the Incident Room first. His own Sergeant Grant was by the machine.

"It's interesting, sir, that they should be the only ones we couldn't talk to, and the only ones—"

"Let's just have it, Sergeant."

The first voice came at once, without preliminary. "My name is Bernard Dupuis and on Saturday, the twenty-ninth of October, I attended a party given by Mr. and Mrs. George Douglas at The Willows, Holmwood Drive." The words sounded doubly laborious, being in accented English and obviously being read. "I and my friend Pierre Lestrange did not know anybody at the party, and so we watched people perhaps more than one does gen-er-ally. Quite early in the evening we began to watch David Douglas, dressed as a girl, dance with different men and sometimes we could see that the men thought he really was a girl. Each time at the end of the dance, or soon afterwards, he let them see that they had made a mistake, but after supper he started dancing with a boy who we could see was very interested in him as—*vous voyez*—"the two words slipped past in an entirely different tone—"as a girl. Pierre and I, we were amused by this, we found it funny, and we—" there was a pause and then an even more laborious—"took it in turns—*c'est ça?*—to watch them, while the other one danced. In the end we were so interested neither of us did any dancing and we just watched them. About a quarter to one o'clock they went together into a small room near the front of the house and shut the door. I tried to look through the keyhole but I could not see anything, so we waited where we could see the door and nobody could see us. It was only a very little time when the door came open quickly and the boy—the one who had thought the other was a girl—came running out and ran straight out of the house. Pierre went after him just as quickly, and saw him get into a car and drive away. I stayed where I was, and after a few minutes the boy dressed up came out of the little room and walked quite slowly back towards the marquee. He was smiling, he looked happy. Pierre and I decided to go away from the party then, too, so we didn't see him again. We have been shown photographs of the two boys, and we are certain that they are the same two that we saw."

A pause, some crackling, an encouraging murmur, and then another voice, more heavily accented and reading with less confidence and fluency. "My name is Pierre Lestrange and on Saturday, the twenty-ninth of October, I attended a party given by Mr. and Mrs. George Douglas at The Vil*low*, Hollumwood Drive. I agree with all that Bernard Dupuis has said in his statement, and I am certain that the two boys whose photographs we have been shown are the two boys that we saw at the party."

"The signed statements are on their way to us," said Sergeant Grant, switching off, "but I don't think there's any doubt."

"No possible doubt." If he hadn't left another wretched youth stewing in an interview room, Kendrick's heart would have been lighter than it had been for weeks. "I'll go myself and see Holden senior right away. It's all right, Sergeant, I'll drive myself. I'll also take a proper lunch-hour. If young Porter's going to say anything more, it won't be for several hours."

The first thing he did was to go to the private telephone they'd given him and ring Holden's office. It was frustrating to learn that he would be out for lunch until half past two. Kendrick supposed he ought to ring the mother, but decided to wait. After a walk to the window and back he dialled again.

"Lunch, Hump?"

"Maurice! I wondered if you'd been trying to get me."

"I did ring you last night, but then I remembered you were going to the opera."

"Is there something . . . ?"

"Yes. Yes! But best not on the phone. Can you have lunch?"

"Of course."

"The Three Tuns, I presume?"

"Don't presume, Maurice!" Humphrey's rejoinder came sharp and fast, making Kendrick wonder if he was upset about something. "I am, believe it or not, capable of departing from routine. You suggest somewhere."

Kendrick thought he understood. "How about the Goat and Compasses?" he suggested gently.

"Fine! What time will you be free, Maurice?"

"Ten minutes?" It was, perhaps, a tiny test.

Humphrey took it with a canter. "Ten minutes it is."

He was, of course, there when Maurice arrived, looking perhaps more anxious and despondent than usual. The moment the drinks were in and the food ordered he asked Kendrick what it was he particularly wanted to say.

"We've caught up with the French boys. They saw it all exactly as Bruce Holden described it."

"You mean he *did* run out of the house alone and drive away?"

"He did. I tried to get hold of his father, but he was out at lunch. I'll go round to his office when I leave you."

"I'm so glad." Humphrey discovered that he was, with a sense of relief he didn't want to analyse.

"There's something else," said Kendrick, and with a sinking of the heart Humphrey saw that his elation was not yet fully explained.

"Yes, Maurice?"

"My other suspect is very promising. Very promising indeed." They were in a corner of the old pub, their backs to an ancient wall, but Kendrick lowered his voice.

"He is?" Humphrey took a gulp of lager, as if it might warm him from within.

"Yes. Despite what he's said it looks very much as though he *was* in Seaminster the night David died. We've broken two attempts at an alibi:

one that he slept on a mate's sofa in Midchester, and when that was busted, that he spent the night with a high-class glamour girl not so very far away from where David was found. *She* says he had got her address after seeing her in her local and that she didn't open the door to him. There's the possibility of course that the girl's lying, if only that it's hard to believe anyone would be so stupid as to try and get an alibi out of someone he's unsuccessfully pestered, but his back's against the wall. And if she isn't lying, imagine him reeling round the streets, then meeting David and being pouted at." Humphrey tried not to imagine it. "David Douglas didn't have to meet a madman in order to get murdered—he could have turned a sane man temporarily mad."

"Yes, Maurice," whispered Humphrey.

"And Porter's known to have inflicted physical injury on the woman who's supposed to be his steady girlfriend. I must admit that the coincidence knocks me back a bit—that the Monster himself may have led us to the solution of the one murder that he didn't commit—but it's by far the likeliest thing that's turned up so far."

"It sounds like it," agreed Humphrey faintly. "And forensic evidence?"

"Ah! Trust you, Hump, to bring me down to earth. No more forensic evidence as yet than we got from Bruce Holden. Which is to say that there's none. We've been to Porter's digs, and they're clean inside and out. But of course he's had several days to dispose of any incriminating evidence, and that's a long time. We've got to probe the second attempt at an alibi, of course, find out if the encounter between the boy and the blond beanpole—she's formidable and beautiful, I went to see her myself—was as insignificant as she claims it to have been. If it is—well, Hump, I feel I could be on the way at last."

"Yes. I see. Congratulations, Maurice."

The only time Humphrey's smile really showed, Kendrick reflected, was when he was working at it. So Hump was being complicated. Kendrick knew better than to ask him if something was up. Anyway, it was more than likely there'd been some sort of complex carryover from his foray to the opera the night before with the Douglas girl. Eleanor Douglas could hardly have been her usual self.

"A bit early for congratulations. And, of course, I've got the Bruce Holden feeling all over again, seeing another apparently bewildered youth with his head in his hands." Humphrey made a sharp movement.

"Drink up, it's my shout. And eat up, too, these sandwiches are delicious."

The effort to appear in normal spirits for the remainder of lunch made Humphrey uncharacteristically glad to part from Maurice in the street outside the pub.

It was too early to do what he had known in a flash he would have to do, so he continued limply back to work, glad of the absorption forced on him by two successively awkward clients. It was half past four by the time he got rid of the second of them, and he immediately rang the Douglas West Gallery. Marian Foster told him Eleanor had gone home. "Her mother and father are going away tomorrow, and she's coming to stay with us." There was a pause. "I expect she's told you."

"Yes. Thank you."

He could find some way to be alone with her. And it was in order for him to wish Frederick and Marie a helpful holiday, if not a happy one.

Humphrey told his secretary he would see her on Monday, rang through on the internal telephone to his brother with the same information, and went out to his car.

Marie answered the door to him, and he was ashamed that his response to her open arms, in his mind at least, was tempered by a fear that Eleanor might not after all be at home. But he saw her over her mother's shoulder, before Marie released him.

"I just wanted," he said, as he walked between them into the sitting-room, "to see you before you went away."

"Thank you, Humphrey."

He was dismayed that there was no sign, as yet, of the characteristic Marie, or that she would eventually reappear. She had changed, grown commonplace, and Frederick, extending a hand from his chair by the fire, had aged.

"I'll make tea," said Eleanor. She, at least, was physically unchanged, but he thought there was a reserve in her which he had been unaware of when she had come up to him at the station the night before.

"Not for me, really . . ."

"Please," said Marie, as she sat down with unaccustomed heaviness opposite her husband. "We haven't had any this afternoon. We don't seem quite to remember . . ."

"Of course, I can always drink tea." He had been a fool not to have instantly seen his opportunity. "I'll come out and hinder you, Eleanor."

"How are they?" he asked when they were alone in the kitchen.

She shrugged. "Shattered. We said it last night. When the older generation loses the younger. I'm glad they're going away."

He sat down on a kitchen chair, watching her move draggingly round the room. "I had lunch today with Maurice Kendrick." There was no missing the sudden tension of her body.

"Yes?"

"I haven't seen him so cheery in months. He's found a highly likely suspect—well, I told you—and has broken his alibi." He saw her hand lean out for the support of the dresser behind her, and took a deep breath. He'd told her one lie, and here was the other. "Maurice hopes to be able to make an arrest very soon. Eleanor . . ." He moved towards her, where she stood with head bowed. He saw the tremble of her upper arms, and had to force down his powerful instinct to take them between his hands. "I found it very difficult to look as if I was sharing his excitement. I think you know why. Eleanor, this is agony for me. I'm not going to say anything except . . . If you have anything to tell me, to show me, dearest, I think you should." She lifted her head and he was astonished that there was a warm light in her eyes which died as he watched it. She stared at him without expression, and there was another sort of agony in the sudden realisation that he might be making a mistake. He was appalled that for the first time it had occurred to him that he might be making a mistake. "If I appear to be talking nonsense," he whispered, "I beseech you to take no notice of me. I do talk nonsense, you know that already. Eleanor . . . You either understand me or you don't." Either way, whether he was right or he was wrong, this was, could only be, the end of their association. "That's all I'm going to say."

For a few moments after he stopped speaking she went on staring at him, then, on a deep sigh, let her head drop again towards her breast, and he was aware of the tension going out of her.

"I'll make the tea," she said, and did so in silence. When she had put a few biscuits onto a plate he picked up the tray and followed her back to the sitting-room.

Marie and Frederick hadn't moved, the one staring across the room at the garden, the other with his hands obscuring the newspaper on his knees.

"Eleanor tells me you're going to stay somewhere you've known for a very long time," he ventured when Eleanor had poured tea for them all and her parents had moved biscuits from one plate to another without seeming aware of what they were doing.

"Yes." Frederick cleared his throat. "Chipping Campden. We went there for our honeymoon."

"There shouldn't be many tourists," supplied Marie, turning her biscuit over and setting it back on her plate as if it were a piece of porcelain. "Although there really don't seem to be close seasons for tourists these days, wherever one goes."

"It shouldn't be so bad." He couldn't imagine a time or a mood where they might ever again be less than stilted with one another. "I'm sure it's a good idea."

"We can't escape it," said Frederick sternly. "We can perhaps gather a bit of strength."

"Yes."

Eleanor, he thought, was retaining her new subtle relaxation. Although she had failed to respond to his confused inept words, he had no sense that she had repudiated them. As he finished his second cup of tea he said it was time he left, and she got up and went out of the room. When she came back a few moments later she remained standing in the doorway, making it easy for him to get to his feet and say goodbye. Her parents made no move to rise, and he kissed Marie and shook Frederick's hand where they sat.

He saw that Eleanor was carrying something, and as he noted the size and shape of it his heart began to beat wildly. When they were in the hall she shut the sitting-room door and put the brown-paper parcel into the hand he found he had out ready to receive it.

"It's there, Humphrey," she said. "I hope even now you'll be the only other person ever to see it. You don't go away until Sunday, do you?"

"No. No." If he'd arranged to go the next day, he would have delayed his departure without hesitation.

"I'll come and see you sometime tomorrow. When will you be in?"

"All day." He wouldn't cross the threshold.

"All right, then. You saw me hide it, didn't you?"

"Yes."

"You saw me when I learned the Monster was dead?"

"Yes." She hadn't mentioned his trial of her, but that could mean no more than resignation crowding out resentment. "Eleanor, if you could just understand—"

"I do, Humphrey, I do."

As he drove away, his head was filled with an impression of her empty hands hanging unclenched at her sides.

CHAPTER 15

Told Jon about my encounter with Mary J. after the school concert. Twenty minutes on my coat on the ground inside that old garden off Birch Road. He tried to shut me up but I just went on until he couldn't hide how much he wanted me to. Jon hasn't been with a girl but he'd like to. I know. I made him listen to every last bit of it. He was lapping it up but he wouldn't give me the satisfaction of letting me see. . . .

Jon's been accepted by Mensa. "One of our youngest members." Too clever by half. But good for some fun. For me. That's clever too, isn't it, to have fun with someone as dull and awkward as Jon? I had a good time with him today, telling him what an all-round idiot he is, suggesting he'll need treatment before he can ever be a man. He won't show me that I'm getting to him, but he won't come and see me if he can help it, it's always me going round to him. "Here's David, dear!" Aunt Fabia carols up the stairs or out to that shed of his. "Your cousin and your faithful friend!" Jon comes blinking up to me. "Hullo, David." Never a reaction. Except for that tic by his eye. When there's nobody around Jon but me, that tic gets busy. "Why don't you go round sometimes and see David?" coos Auntie. "Not leave it all to him? A true friendship is give and take." I laugh out loud in my delight, Aunt Fabia asks Jon why he can't be sunny and cheerful like his cousin. But perhaps things are best as they are. If Jon ever let on how it is, to anyone else at least, the game would be

*over. Sometimes I wonder why he doesn't. Could he possibly be
enjoying it too? No, oh no. I don't want Jon to enjoy it, if he did I
couldn't. Jon's just a stick, that's what it is, a dull stick. Just clever,
a clever clot. . . .*

*Mensa at sixteen. But not so clever when you don't do anything
else, don't even try to make people like you. When people like you,
you can do anything with them.*

*It must be an effort not to let me see what I'm doing to him, he
must be all screwed up inside, with the effort of not letting me see.*

*Jon is pathetic. He told me today that on his way home from
evening class last night he cut across that bit of wood half-way up
East Cliff and saw the body of the latest Monster victim. I immediately tested him out by saying that if he didn't go to the Silver
Wedding dressed as a magnificent pirate chief I'd tell the police
what he told me. He said he'd go as a pirate chief. But he wouldn't
tell me what the special mark was on the body, and I don't believe
he saw it, I believe he'll do what I tell him because he's afraid of
being shown up a liar, a pathetic fool. So it's just as good for me
whether he saw the body or whether he didn't, there'll be just as
much scope.*

The childish round script came to an end in the middle of a page, and
the rest of the hardbacked exercise book was blank. Humphrey closed it
on a long shuddering sigh, then threw it across his pale sitting-room
carpet, getting up almost at once to retrieve it and place it on a table
near the door. He walked across to his French window and despite the
windy chill of the day opened it and went to stand among the stone urns
on his small terrace, breathing deep. He'd cast the book from him once
already, across his bed the night before into a corner of his bedroom,
where he'd let it lie until morning, but he was slightly ashamed now of
possibly being responsible for a buckled corner. What David had been,
David had been, and that was no more terrible because he, Humphrey
Barnes, had now read his diary.

Jonathan hadn't let anything show in public, either. Even when he
and David had danced together in the marquee on the night of the
party, Jonathan hadn't registered anything beyond apparent mild
amusement. That was the best way he could hit back, but it must have

taken the most enormous self-control. And not just that evening. And when such self-control broke down . . .

The diary wasn't all Jonathan, but it was all egotism, resentment, spite. *I laugh out loud in my delight.* Yes, David quite often did, and the effect had been pleasing.

There was, reflected Humphrey as he moved about his garden touching things, a cause for thankfulness. If David had lived, the ultimate pain for Marie and Frederick, and without doubt for others as well, would have been infinitely more terrible.

Was it an extra chromosome, or one too few? He could never remember, but it was one or the other. It wasn't, it couldn't be, anything less clinical.

His front doorbell, extended to a small tinkling device above and outside the French window, was ringing. Eleanor, if it was Eleanor arriving at eleven o'clock, had timed it exactly right, giving him time to read and absorb, not enough time to swell his imagination to nightmare in the absence of the facts.

It was Eleanor, Jonathan beside her. Humphrey put his hands on a shoulder of each, before standing aside for them to come in. He led them into the sitting-room and shut the French window against the noticeably invading cold.

"Sit down, both of you, please. I'll make coffee and then I'll listen."

He had it almost ready. When he had set the tray down and poured out, he found a bottle of brandy and two small glasses, put them on the table beside the tray, tried to smile at them, and sat down. Eleanor leaned back in her chair, warming her hands, Humphrey thought, round her coffee-cup. It was clear she had no intention, at that moment, of speaking. Jonathan remained sitting upright and Humphrey, by dint of looking for it, could just see the minuscule flutter of the skin beneath his right eye.

After he had taken a gulp of coffee, Jonathan began tonelessly to speak.

"I don't have to tell you anything, do I, Mr. Barnes, about what it was like up to the time I found that girl?" Humphrey made a dismissive gesture, but Jonathan hadn't really been asking for one and ignored it. "I did find her. I fell over one of her shoes and I looked at the body before I ran away, long enough to see the Monster cross." For an instant the boy shut his large pale eyes, making Humphrey aware of the strained pallor of his face under the untidy hunks of hair. "I knew I ought to go to the police, of course I did, but I knew, too, that the girl was dead and that someone else would find her and that I'd rather it wasn't me getting involved and maybe helping the police with their inquiries because of so often walking about on my own at night. I was a coward, but I was thinking of Mum and Dad, too, and that it wouldn't make any difference to the girl. I know, there could have been clues which wouldn't last but that was what I did, I ran away and I didn't say anything." Jonathan shut his eyes again, and drained his coffee-cup before he went on. "Until next day, and that was the stupidest thing I ever did in my life. I told David. And yes, I was showing off, trying to go one up. I should have stuck to my usual line. For as long as I can remember David's been going for me and I've been refusing to let him see that he's getting there. 'Denying me the satisfaction', that's how David put it. I don't know how I've managed it—he's belittled me, laughed at me, treated me all the time we've been alone together as if I was nothing, and I've never shown any reaction. So I think perhaps I gave as good as I got." Jonathan sat back in his chair, his mouth momentarily relaxing. "He was jealous of me, you see, because I'm rather unusually clever." The voice was without emphasis or pride, merely stating a fact. "He always had to be the tops in everything; it wasn't enough for him to have the looks and the charm, he ought to have the best brains as well, so I had to suffer. Only apparently I didn't. There were times when I almost enjoyed his frustration, though really he's made my life hell. He couldn't abuse me physically, although when we were little he tried—I was as strong if not stronger. But with words, suggestions, insinuations . . ." Jonathan sat forward. "Most of it's in his book, he kept meticulous records. I coped with it. But then I told him about seeing the girl's body, and that was making a bigger rod for my back than David could ever have devised for me on his own. I regretted it the instant I'd told him. It was the first time he'd had anything on me and I knew what he'd do with it. Right away he said I was to go to the party as a pirate chief—the personality he thought the most ridiculously different from mine, I suppose. I don't think he believed me that I really had seen that body, and I wouldn't tell him what the Monster mark was. I think he felt he would keep me to heel because I was afraid of being shown up a boastful liar. What I was really afraid of was being shown up a coward and un-public-spirited. And I was still thinking of Mum and Dad, so he'd really got me."

Jonathan stopped and gripped the edge of the table in front of him. When Humphrey had helped them all to more coffee he took the brandy bottle and poured a couple of tots, putting them beside his visitors' coffee-cups.

"I think I can see how it was," he said gently. "Better tell me now about the night of the party."

"Yes." Jonathan took a sip of brandy. "You saw us dancing, didn't you, Mr. Barnes? David got caught up with Bunny Holden a bit later, but escaped him soon after the disco took over and insisted on having another dance with me—that was important for him, as he knows— knew—how I hate disco noise. Then he told me he was going to hang round Bunny again, who still hadn't caught on to him. That seems odd in a way, but I think Bunny's friends were so amused they weren't doing anything to enlighten him. David of course couldn't resist what for him must have been the fun of leading Bunny on, seeing how far he could go. I think after that I went into the sitting-room and talked for a while—Eleanor was there, she'll remember it." Eleanor picked up her brandy glass, nodding. Humphrey was horrified by the suffering in her face, and averted his own as if he had been prying.

"Then I went and had a look in at the disco but I didn't go much farther than the entrance because of the din and the flashing lights, and I was just turning into the back bit of the hall, thinking I might go and see if I could find anything else to eat, when David came strolling towards me. He was grinning and looking pleased with himself. He said it had been a near thing with Bunny, or something like that, and that fighting him off had made him hungry. We went into the kitchen to-gether and ate bits off the dishes which were on the kitchen table. There wasn't anyone there—the caterers had washed up and left. When we'd eaten all we wanted David said he was ready to go home, but that he wouldn't feel safe alone and I was to escort him. I said that he had his own clothes in the cloakroom, that was why he'd brought them. But it was no good, of course. He just wasn't ready to give up the game he'd had so much success with all evening. Well, you saw him, Mr. Barnes." Jonathan took another sip of brandy. "When I mentioned his clothes, he just said something about the police being interested that I'd seen that body, and I said I'd walk home with him. He said that when I got back I was to take his clothes up to my room and bring them round to him next day; he didn't want a rocket from his parents. I agreed of course." Jonathan suddenly stopped, and, to Humphrey's astonishment, burst into tears. "I shouldn't have been such a coward, I shouldn't have cared whether he went to the police or not, I should have said I wouldn't go with him." It wasn't easy now to hear what Jonathan was saying, but he repeated himself several times over as his groaning sobs subsided. Eleanor, in what Humphrey could not help registering as one graceful movement, knelt out of her chair and put her arms round her cousin until he was quiet again.

"I don't think," said Humphrey, pouring them both a very little more brandy, "that if you'd refused to walk with him David would have changed his clothes to go home. I think he would have walked out as he was and challenged the Monster or any other lurking deviant. That's what I was convinced he'd done."

"I suppose so, I suppose you're right." Jonathan was stony calm again. "But then *I* wouldn't have killed him." Humphrey forced himself to meet the sad, angry challenge of the boy's eyes. "I'll tell you now. We went out of the back door; it leads to another path and gate quite a bit away from the front. You can't see the back path from the front of the house, and it comes out in the direction you have to walk to get to Aunt Marie's. So we didn't pass the house and nobody saw us. As soon as we were in the road David began sort of living the part he was playing, hanging on my arm and saying he was frightened of the Monster. When we reached that bit of wood, the place where he's taken girls—some of that's in the diary; perhaps you saw it—he insisted we go in. He took hold of my hand and he led the way to that clearing." Jonathan screwed up his eyes, and then his whole face, in one ugly transforming second. "And then—he made up to me. He put his hands . . . Those feelings he'd described to me, forced me to listen to, I started to have them. I found my hand touching one of the lumps of screwed-up paper—I knew what they were, I'd made one of them—and as I got hold of it I looked into his face. He was grinning and his hands were more and more . . ." Jonathan shrank back in his chair, lifting an arm as if to protect himself from his memory.

"You must go on," said Eleanor.

"Suddenly—" and suddenly Jonathan was bolt upright, staring again at Humphrey—"it was enough. Suddenly I had to be rid of it. Had to be rid of years in a minute. And I was half suffocated by a feeling of the badness of it. It was almost like self-defence, like pushing a pillow away which was smothering me. But it wasn't, of course. I took my hand off the front of his dress and my other hand came up and they were round his neck, he was the one who was choking. In some strange way I was thinking that even doing what I was doing I wouldn't be able to get to him, but I was, I was wiping the grin off his face, his hands were leaving go of me. He looked fantastic in those shoes but he wasn't at home in them. He stumbled, he seemed to lose his strength as he lost his balance, he hardly struggled at all. When I realised what I was doing I let go and he fell. I couldn't believe he was dead, but he was. He'd fallen on his back with his arms out. Perhaps that's what made me think of that girl. Anyway, I was quite calm by then, able to think clearly. Perhaps it's something to do with being rather specially clever, but I still seemed to be absolutely in control of my mind. The dress David was wearing undid in the front and it was quite easy to pull down. The bits of paper which had made the bosoms were sewn into the dress so they came away with it—I didn't bother about keeping my fingers off the paper because they'd been on at least one half already. I got my pirate knife out and made the cross I'd seen on the girl. That was probably the worst part of all, worse than when I killed him because then I hadn't been in charge." Eleanor knelt forward again, to raise his glass to his lips. "I scuffed my feet around a bit in the soil and grass in case I'd left any shoe prints. I remember standing there after I'd wiped the knife on some grass, hardly being able to believe it had been so easy. I hadn't any qualms about hoping to pin it on the Monster; he was a fiend and he was in so deep already. The most dangerous part was getting back into the house—anybody walking or driving along the road, whether they were connected with the party or not, would notice a pirate chief in full fig. But there wasn't anyone, and I went in again at the back gate and up the path and back into the kitchen, which was still empty. And then I just walked into the hall and started to look for Eleanor—"

"I'll go on," said Eleanor, and Humphrey was forced to turn and watch her face. "Jonathan came into the sitting-room where I was still talking with a few people. The marquee by then was pretty well given over to the very young. I thought he looked a bit pale and serious, but that was natural enough when he was out of his element. No one else would have noticed anything, I'm certain of that. He leaned towards me quite casually and asked me to come out so that he could speak to me in private and I remember laughing when he asked me to go upstairs with him to his room. *Laughing.* Then he told about him and David and the diary David kept and then he told me what had happened." Eleanor shuffled her chair so that she was able to take and hold Jonathan's hand. "He said I was to imagine how I would have felt if David couldn't be found and he hadn't told me anything, and then to act it and when I got home to get hold of David's diary. He told me David used to keep telling him where he kept it locked up and he said he thought I'd find the key in the pocket of the trousers he'd been wearing before getting dressed up. As soon as he got back to the house he'd gone to the cloakroom to look in the pockets of the jeans David had left there, but the key wasn't in them. Well, I did all that. At least Mummy and Daddy were asleep when I got home and I was able to go into David's room and take my time. I found the key, and then the diary where Jonathan had said it would be. I took it back to my room and read it."

Her face, now, was so awful Humphrey had to get up and go over to the French window until she could cover its nakedness. She began to speak again while he was still there.

"At least it made a sort of awful sense of what Jonathan had done. You know the rest. I was afraid, having the diary in the house, even though it was out of David's room when the police took a routine look round. The fact that it was in the house at all seemed to shout out loud. I took it to London and hid it in the locker. Then I got frightened of the big fat red locker key in my bag and I realised how much more unnoticeable it would be simply to put it among my books. Then we learned that the Monster couldn't have killed David—you were there, Humphrey, you saw how I took that piece of news—and then I wondered whether I ought to leave the book where it was. But that afternoon—Tuesday—I slipped up to London again and took it out of the locker and brought it home and put it into a high bookshelf in my bedroom."

"That was intelligent," said Jonathan.

"It was an instinct. When you took me to the Ritz, Humphrey, and we were talking about David, I was trying to realise *him* even more than his death, talking out the things I felt should have warned me. I let you see that I was ashamed of not having known him better, and that was true. I can't help feeling that if I had, I might have helped him."

"You couldn't have helped him," said Humphrey, sitting down again. At least he was sure of that.

"But I was ashamed, too, that I hadn't seen anything, that I was so stupidly unaware of what he was doing to Jonathan."

"You had no idea at all?"

"None."

"It wasn't anything to do with anyone else," said Jonathan, rousing himself to drink more coffee. "It was a private prosecution. Like yours, Mr. Barnes."

"I saw two things," said Humphrey slowly, "which I couldn't dismiss as being of no significance. Heaven knows I tried. All I did about them, Jonathan, was to persuade Eleanor to tell me the truth. There was no way I could do it decently. She was the one I prosecuted." It had been an opportunity he couldn't miss, to try and find out whether his alienation of her was irremediable. But she didn't seem to have heard him.

"That morning we had coffee, Humphrey, I was learning out loud what sort of brother I had."

"I see that. Eleanor."

"What do we do now?"

It had never in his life been so hard to be honest. "Maurice Kendrick can't get clinching evidence against Raymond Porter. Well, of course not. But he isn't as close to making a wrongful arrest as I made out. You could do nothing, Jonathan, unless and until the chief superintendent makes a move."

"So you just wanted to find out for yourself, Mr. Barnes?"

"Yes." He realised that was what it had been.

"You haven't said anything about your suspicions to your friend the policeman?"

"Nothing at all." Not just because they were suspicions rather than evidence. He didn't think he could ever feel it his place to confess another man's crime for him.

"Thank you," said Jonathan. "I wouldn't have let anyone else be arrested, apart from the Monster. We just hoped—when the Monster was no go—there wouldn't be another suspect."

"I've told you. That's all he is."

"And it's too much." Jonathan gave a deep sigh and got to his feet.

The obvious release of tension reminded Humphrey of Eleanor on her front doorstep the night before, after she'd given him the diary. "I want to go and see your chief superintendent. Will you telephone him and pave my way?"

"Yes." How could one be so glad and so sorry at the same time? "But I'll ask you to tell him so far as I'm concerned merely that you came to me first as an old friend. Whatever else I tell him, if I tell him anything, must be up to me."

"Of course."

"Don't say anything yet to your parents, your aunt and uncle."

Jonathan, able now to focus normally on other people, looked at him curiously. "Why not?"

"I don't know." He didn't know. "But wait until you must."

"Auntie and Uncle are away anyway. I'm not often around Mum and Dad, so they won't miss me. I was seventeen yesterday, so they won't have to be there when I'm being questioned. You're suggesting I wait until the actual arrest?"

"Yes. If it comes."

"Oh, it'll come. One thing at a time? Perhaps you're right, Mr. Barnes."

"Let Mummy and Daddy have their holiday, at least." Eleanor was looking at Jonathan with love and sorrow. Humphrey had wondered if she would try to persuade him to wait and see, but she had made no attempt to influence him. "I'll just nip upstairs, Humphrey." She paused in the doorway to pick the diary off the table and slip it into her large bag.

"There's the cloakroom."

"I like your bathroom better." Wistfully he heard her feet on the stairs, less laggard than he would have expected. When she came down, Jonathan left them and went into the cloakroom.

"He won't want me to go with him to the police," said Eleanor immediately. "Shall I stay a bit, Humphrey? We all need to recover."

"It's all right, dear, you don't have to stay."

"Humphrey, I—"

"I appreciate your good manners, Eleanor. But I think you should go with Jonathan."

She picked up the bag she had cast down on a chair. "I'll see you when you get back," she said flatly.

"Of course!" He tried to sound cheerful. "I'll be coming to see your mother and father. And you must all come—eventually—and have dinner with me. I'll—"

"I didn't mean that." She sighed and started towards the door. "Thank you for what you did. It would have been much easier for you, I know, not to have done anything."

"It wouldn't, Eleanor." How kind she was, how considerate, in the face of his deceit. Like himself, she had tacitly allowed the idea to lapse of dinner together the night he got back from his holiday, but he thought it might have been easier if she'd carried it further and told him their friendship was at an end.

When they had gone he went straight away and rang Maurice.

"Jonathan Douglas has just been here with his cousin. To tell me he killed her brother. I believe him. He's on his way now to tell you."

There was a silence, then Kendrick said, "Why now, Humphrey?"

"Because of innocent people. Once he knew the Monster couldn't have done it, it was only a matter of time and courage. Maurice, there are extenuating circumstances."

"You know these people quite well, Hump."

"Lately . . ."

"I'd like to see you when I've talked to the boy."

"I'm going away first thing in the morning. I'll ring you as soon as I get back."

Kendrick said, after a pause, "Of course. Thanks for sending the boy on."

"I didn't. He's seventeen now, Maurice, you won't need the parents. . . . Forgive me, I didn't mean to try and teach you."

"It's all right, Hump. Have a good holiday. You need it."

Already regretting having put Maurice off, Humphrey went upstairs to begin his packing, reflecting as his plodding feet paused on the turn of the stairs that this was the first time in the years since Emily's death that he had approached his trip to Scotland with less than eager anticipation.

CHAPTER 16

Humphrey's hostess had an eye for nuances, and within half an hour of his arrival in Edinburgh was asking him if life was being difficult. He told her it was.

Nevertheless, and to his surprise, he found himself enjoying his holiday, especially the parts of it where his understanding friends encouraged him to go off on his own. The cool windy city seemed to suit his elegiac mood, although by the end of the first week he was trying half-heartedly to throw this off and relearn that there was life beyond Seaminster. He was successful enough, by the end of his second week, to discover that he was reluctant to go home, but still grateful that two business matters which had pursued him to Scotland dictated that he did.

As in so many earlier years, he left Edinburgh on the Saturday and broke his journey at a certain magnificent country inn, reaching his house soon after noon on Sunday. The fact that there was nothing of interest in his post and no messages from Mrs. McNicholl was more of a disappointment than he would have expected, and he unpacked the provisions he had bought on the way somewhat despondently, preparing a small meal for no other reason than that it was lunch-time. He was sitting by the French window with a cup of coffee, wondering whether to try to get hold of Maurice, when his doorbell rang.

He hardly approved of the excitement which had him jumping to his feet, but he still went running across the hall.

On his doorstep was Jonathan.

"Hello, Mr. Barnes. May I come in?"

"Of course . . ." Humphrey closed the door and led the way into the sitting-room. "But, Jonathan . . . I thought . . . Please sit down."

"That I would be locked up by now? I thought so, too, Mr. Barnes." The boy was superficially composed, but Humphrey thought he looked even less well than he had looked two weeks earlier.

"You went to see Maurice Kendrick?"

"Oh yes. And went again. And again. Mr. Kendrick was very good. He only came to the house once and easily persuaded Mum and Dad it was about my bike—an official reprimand for all those times it's been impounded."

"So?"

"I'd been too clever, Mr. Barnes. I'd been so careful to try and cover my tracks I'd succeeded. Nothing at the scene of the crime, nothing on me or my clothes, no one seeing me with David or—after."

"The pirate knife . . ."

"I'd taken that to school and got something out of the lab and got it clinically clean."

"But Jonathan . . . The Monster mark."

Jonathan laughed, sounding somehow too old. "Don't you see? He *expected* me to know it. The family all knew it. Once Uncle Frederick had been shown David's body it was inevitable. I've no way of proving I knew it *before* David was killed. Even the diary wouldn't have helped me there; I never told David."

"The diary!"

Jonathan looked Humphrey hard in the eye. "The diary's disappeared."

"Disappeared . . . Eleanor picked it up off that table when you were both here. I saw her."

"She says she meant to, she thought she did, but she didn't have it when she got home. Perhaps she put it down on a chair in the hall. Or perhaps . . . Mr. Barnes . . ."

"No, oh no, Jonathan. I swear to that. I haven't seen the diary since I saw Eleanor pick it up."

"All right, I believe you. I didn't even think about it at first. I forgot it when we left here that time, I never thought of asking Eleanor for it. I'd no intention of using it, I didn't want the police—anyone—to learn about it, most of all not Auntie and Uncle. And I didn't think I'd need it, I just thought telling them would be enough. . . . Mr. Barnes, the police won't arrest me, they don't even want to see me any more. The diary might have convinced them, but without it there's nothing else I can do."

"You don't think your mother . . . Eleanor's mother . . ."

"*No!* If Eleanor or I'd had it, we'd have guarded it with our lives. But each of us was thinking it was with the other. D'you think it could still be here without your knowing? Forgive me, but I just can't think of any other explanation."

"I suppose it could be. I went away the next morning and I've only just got back. My daily's been in a couple of times and might have tidied it away. She's inclined to tidy books and papers, but she's not the type to read them."

"May I have a look round then, please? By the way, Eleanor's coming up any minute. She said to tell you she's booked a table for tonight and wants to give you details. I'll just go and look."

Jonathan was out of sight in the hall and Humphrey was sitting down abruptly on his chair by the window, his legs weak and his mind whirling. Eleanor was coming, Eleanor had booked a table. . . . He didn't after all want to sit down and was on his feet again and moving about the room, looking in a desultory way for the thin, hardbacked book. Not—at a glance—where he had last seen it, not with the telephone directories or the little pile of journals. Not added to the books on the shelves. Not down the side of a chair . . .

The bell rang again, and Jonathan called out. "I can see Eleanor through your spyhole, Mr. Barnes. Shall I let her in?"

"Let her in, yes."

Humphrey precipitated himself at the sitting-room door, then forced himself to slow down and move forward at his usual pace.

"Eleanor, how lovely . . . And I've only been back an hour." The prospect of an evening with her meant he could, as he should, concentrate on the matter in hand. "Jonathan's told me about the diary."

"Yes." He thought she avoided his eye. "I picked it up, I thought I put it in my bag, then when it wasn't there, I thought I must have put it down again and that Jonathan had taken it."

"I've hardly been in the house since then, so if you'd both forgotten it I could quite easily not have noticed it."

They spent a quarter of an hour or so looking round all the downstairs places where Humphrey's daily might have tidied away a hardback exercise book, and drew a blank.

"I just can't think," said Humphrey, as they stood around the kitchen while he made them coffee.

"It doesn't matter as much as it might have done," said Eleanor, sitting down at the table. "I went to that superintendent friend of yours myself when he told Jonathan he didn't want to see him again, and I asked him if he was going to arrest anybody else. After humming and hawing he said he wasn't. Of course, he must *believe* what Jonathan told him, even if he can't find any reason to *accept* it. Oh, Humphrey, I'm glad we took your advice not to say anything to the parents. What made you say that?"

"I told you, I didn't know. Perhaps I suspected somewhere in my subconscious that Jonathan had covered his tracks too well, and that they would never need to be told."

"I'm glad about *that,*" said Jonathan, with an obvious, involuntary shudder. "But. But—I shouldn't get away with it. I shouldn't!" He had sat down, too, but jumped to his feet and started flinging about the kitchen.

"I don't imagine you will," said Eleanor. "In yourself, I mean. You've sentenced yourself already. Darling, you've got to remember that if a court had sentenced you, it wouldn't have been for ever. You mustn't let it be for ever. You *mustn't.*" She caught his hand as he went by, and after a struggle he stopped by her chair.

He muttered, "I wonder you can touch my hand."

"That will be enough of *that.* Oh, Jon darling, it must be terrible." Eleanor grabbed both his hands and held them against her.

Jonathan smiled, a wild, wide movement of his mouth. For a moment Humphrey was afraid it would turn to hysterical laughter, but Jonathan swallowed hard and shook his head. "It is. I think it'll be worse still when I've taken it in." He pulled gently and she let him go. "I'm going to walk. Don't worry, I'll be home for supper. And I'll go to the States as soon as I leave school. Harvard or Princeton. An early brain drain." He turned in the doorway. "I can guess what's happened to the diary. Thanks, Eleanor."

Eleanor stayed weeping in the kitchen while Humphrey saw Jonathan out.

"You can never weaken, you know," said Humphrey as he opened the front door. "You can never feel you've just got to talk about it. Except to Eleanor. And of course," he added diffidently, "to me. You can always talk to me. But never, never to anyone else. If your uncle and aunt—"

"I know, Mr. Barnes, I know."

"You do, of course. Forgive me."

"You were quite right to speak. It would be unthinkable for Aunt Marie and Uncle Frederick to learn about David. Don't worry."

In Jonathan's twisted smile Humphrey for a horrified instant saw the whole of his dissembling future.

"I'm so sorry," he muttered.

"So am I. I might talk to you sometime, Mr. Barnes, I might need to."

Watching him grow smaller along the cliff road, Humphrey was vaguely assuaged to see that his shoulders were still square.

Eleanor was in the hall as he closed the front door. An uncle would have comforted her with an arm and a chaste kiss, but he was unable to bridge the small gap between them and stood in dumb anger at himself while she blew her nose and wiped her eyes.

"I do know where the diary is, Humphrey," she said as she pushed her handkerchief into her sleeve.

"I'd begun to think you might. Under your mattress, I suppose?"

"A much better place than that. Come and see."

She led the way up the staircase, and before they reached the top he remembered hearing her feet on the stairs the last time she had visited him and noting their unexpected energy. They had had a purpose.

"Here . . ." By straining on tiptoe she could just reach the top shelf of the books which reared the length and height of one landing wall. "I'm sorry, Humphrey."

"Don't be. It was a good place."

"I thought so. Will you destroy it for me?"

"I'll hope to be able to," said Humphrey, "when I've seen Maurice for myself. I'm not doubting your word, Eleanor—and I think you're tremendous for having bearded him—but I can question Maurice a bit more searchingly, make absolutely sure Jonathan will never need it."

"Of course you can. May it stay on your shelf for the time being? I know it's not a nice thing to have about the house, but I'd be so grateful and I'm sure it won't be for long."

"That's all right." He took the book from her and returned it to the place she had found for it. He was slightly amused to see that it had been resting against a volume entitled *What Is Truth?* As he turned back to her his confidence vanished.

"Jonathan told me you'd booked a table . . ."

"Yes. The Lobster Pot's the nicest place open on Sundays." She led the way downstairs and back into the sitting-room. "I booked it for eight. Can you call for me at Marian's at a quarter past seven? Twenty-seven, Poplar Road."

"I know. Eleanor . . . I didn't think you'd ever want to speak to me again."

She moved across the space between them and stood in front of him. "Hump chump, don't you see you're the only person I *can* speak to?"

"Well, if you want to talk about the diary and so on—Jonathan—then I suppose—"

"Humphrey!" She had moved to the window, where she turned to look at him. "I'm so desperate for Jonathan, and I've got a great big empty, dirty hole where David was. If it wasn't for you I don't think I could bear it."

If it wasn't for you.

The heady and unaccustomed sense of there being time ahead was still with him, and he could afford to put the dazzling words aside.

"Eleanor, why didn't you tell me?"

"How could I know that you'd want to be told? It was only when you came to the house that last time. In the kitchen . . . I knew then that you wanted to know."

"Why did you think I wanted to know?"

"For yourself," she said simply, coming back to stand in front of him.

"Oh yes, oh, Eleanor . . ."

"Did you ever suspect me?" she asked lightly.

He tried to pull himself together. "I didn't suspect you—or anyone in your family—in the usual sense of the word. I just knew that you had a terrible secret about David's death. Oh, Eleanor, you understand, you can see why I did what I did."

She was looking at him now very seriously. "I hope I can. I hope it was because you . . ." She was back at the window, looking over her shoulder, and he managed to join her there. "Humphrey," she said softly, "you don't help me. You don't help me at all. You're the only person I can ever really talk to about *anything*. Don't you *see?*"

"Eleanor, I . . ." His garden was shimmering before his eyes, as if the November murk had been suddenly transformed into a heat haze. He was aware of Eleanor moving sharply beside him.

"Perhaps I've made a mistake." Her voice was quite different, hard and cold. "Perhaps you don't want me in your perfect little house, cluttering it up, interrupting your routine—"

He had turned and was letting his hands press against her shoulders as they had so often longed to. "Of course I want you, Eleanor, even more than I want my routine." His clown's tendencies were showing again, but perhaps that wasn't a bad thing; it might pre-empt any possible risibility in the concept of an ardent middle-aged lover. *"Dearest Eleanor.* But how could I possibly have imagined that *you . . ."* He still couldn't imagine it entirely, yet he felt he had always known that this moment would come.

"Well, I do."

"For how long, beloved, beautiful Eleanor?"

"Oh, months. I was so furious at the dance, when I knew I'd made you think I was dancing with you for duty and really it was absolutely the opposite. Then when I looked for you after supper you'd gone . . ."

"Well, I did think that I'd had my ration of you." After all, they were being able to talk over one aspect of that evening as if it had been an ordinary one.

"I knew you did. Do you want another wife, Humphrey?"

"I want you. But I think you ought to be absolutely certain—"

"Will it be the same, or different?"

"Different. We're different people. I as well as you. But, Eleanor, I really think you ought to give yourself—"

"That must be the most marvellous thing a widower ever said to a spinster bride."

"Eleanor, I'm serious. You're twenty-five. I've been wrong to let you see . . . It's only because you're so upset. Once you begin to feel—"

"I adore you, Humphrey." She had taken hold of his hands where he had let them drop from her shoulders, and put them together behind her back. This time he returned her kiss for slightly longer before drawing away.

"I think, Eleanor, we ought to modify our rapture. If only to match the reactions of your mother and father."

"Hump chump! Mummy and Daddy will be delighted. They've half said as much." She drew right away. "But perhaps you aren't sure, yourself. Perhaps you're having second thoughts about an alliance with the Douglases—"

"That's frightful, stop it! I'm sure, Eleanor."

"I don't want to take you over, Humphrey, any more than I want to be taken over myself. I like space round me, too, I'm independent."

"I know, I know. Come here!"

It was she, this time, who eventually broke away. "I must go now. I don't want us to go upstairs yet, and if I stay any longer . . . Be there at a quarter past seven, won't you?"

"Yes. Oh yes."

Kendrick was raising his hand to the front door as Humphrey opened it. He and Eleanor greeted one another with a wary gravity.

"A remarkable girl," said Kendrick as they stood on the step watching her drive away. "She came to see me."

"She told me." Finding he had involuntarily laid his new happiness aside and was full of doubt and anxiety, Humphrey realised how much he valued Maurice's friendship. "Is it true, Maurice?" he asked when they were in the sitting-room. "Have you let the boy go?"

"Yes."

"Because Jonathan—"

"Porter's second alibi," said Kendrick, taking a chair which looked out on the garden, "decided to support his story. She evidently thought better of her original repudiation of him, and called on me to tell me she *had* let him in when he came to her door. It must have cost her something, but I wasn't entirely surprised as I'd noticed she was a bit thoughtful when I mentioned murder. It was a switch to honesty which worked better for him than the change of heart of his mate's wife where he dossed down in Midchester."

"Yes . . . So what now, Maurice?"

Kendrick yawned and stretched, but Humphrey knew there was a keen eye on him. "The inquest won't be resumed for a week or so, but it'll be a verdict of wilful murder against person or persons unknown. The file will stay open."

Which Jonathan would know. A sword of Damocles. He had to speak of him.

"Jonathan Douglas was here this afternoon, too. He told me you'd finished with him."

"Yes, Hump. Nothing to support his story."

And no fear, any more, that Marie and Frederick would ever know about their son. Except that Maurice . . .

"Whatever Jonathan said to you about David, Maurice, I hope you'll feel you can forget it for the parents' sake."

"As things are—yes, of course. By the way, it was Eleanor Douglas who did the talking about her brother. Jonathan said very little. Until I told him I didn't want to see him again, and then he started going on about a diary the dead boy had kept, which he said would prove his motive. But he couldn't produce it. Mention it to you, did he, Hump?"

"Yes," said Humphrey. They stared at one another. "You don't think there's someone still out there, do you, Maurice?"

"I don't think anyone will ever appear whose story we'll be able to substantiate." Kendrick got to his feet. "I must be on my way. There's something else brewing now, would you believe it, and I'm unlikely to make Sunday supper by my fireside. I'll see you properly during the week. I just wanted to let you know what the Douglas pair came to tell you. And to see if you enjoyed your holiday."

"Thank you, Maurice. I enjoyed my holiday but I'm glad to be back." He was glad, too, of his realisation that the friendship was secure, that Maurice had come as near as he ever would to querying his involvement in the case of David Douglas, and that he would respect his silence whether or not he considered it to be innocent.

If it wasn't for Jonathan Douglas he might be happy again.

The garden ceased to shimmer. *Emily. Ah, Emily. But it's as I said to Eleanor about her grief. It isn't forgotten, "got over." It's just eventually covered up by other things.*

"Not so good, any of this, for you, Maurice?" he ventured as they crossed the hall.

"Not so bad, either, Hump." Kendrick forced a smile. "And pretty good for everyone else. The Monster won't kill again, and I haven't arrested any innocents."

Or the guilty one. Although what did the word mean, so far as Jonathan Douglas was concerned?

"How will it be now, Maurice, with the police and the public?"

"I should say the general view among the police—and the public for that matter, if they go on bothering to think about it—will be that David's murder was a copycat job. There were four dead girls, after all, lying for several hours where wandering men could have seen them and the mark on them." As Jonathan had done. "David to all intents and purposes was another young girl, and the Monster publicity campaign was showing all over town. Truth to tell, I'd been afraid of just such a killing, posters of the kind we've had to display have sometimes proved inflammatory. So no one has any incentive to look beyond that." He paused in the open doorway. "You and Eleanor Douglas?"

Humphrey's joy rushed back. "It looks like it. I can't really believe it yet. I'm much too old for her. You'll be best man, of course."

"I'd be furious if you asked anyone else."

Kendrick was full of pleasure on Humphrey's behalf, but there was a sour sense of contrast with his own situation. In an attempt to clear it he drove on up the cliff road to where the houses finished and parked by the sea, turning his window all the way down.

The wind had died, and he imagined the colourless unmoving sea as a void, a lack of substance, until a gull folded its wings on the surface and he saw the thin grey rent of its wake. He tried not to be irritated that a Monster poster still hung frayed against the sea-wall. The press were spreading the idea that Charlie Hutchinson had thought he was saving young girls by putting them out of a dangerous world, citing his, Kendrick's, quote to them that the Monster had told the lucky one it was "all right."

Charlie's wife had left him, his daughter had died. If Jenny had died, what of himself? Was it "there but for the grace of God"? He didn't, he couldn't, think so, but he would have one more try with Miriam.

Kendrick sat with his eyes on the elusive horizon until he started to feel cold, then wound up his window and began the short journey to his own office at Divisional Headquarters.

About the Author

Eileen Dewhurst was born in Liverpool and educated at Huyton College, later at Oxford. As a free-lance journalist, she has published numerous articles in such periodicals as *The Times* and *Punch*, and her plays have been performed throughout England. A PRIVATE PROSECUTION is her eighth novel for the Crime Club.